Jeb's Promise
A Morgan's Run Romance

By: M. Lee Prescott

Jeb's Promise

A Morgan's Run Romance

By M. Lee Prescott

Published by Mt. Hope Press

Copyright 2016, M. Lee Prescott

This book is a work of fiction. Names, characters, places, and events are products of the author's imagination or are used fictitiously. Any resemblance to actual people (alive or deceased), locales, or events is entirely coincidental.

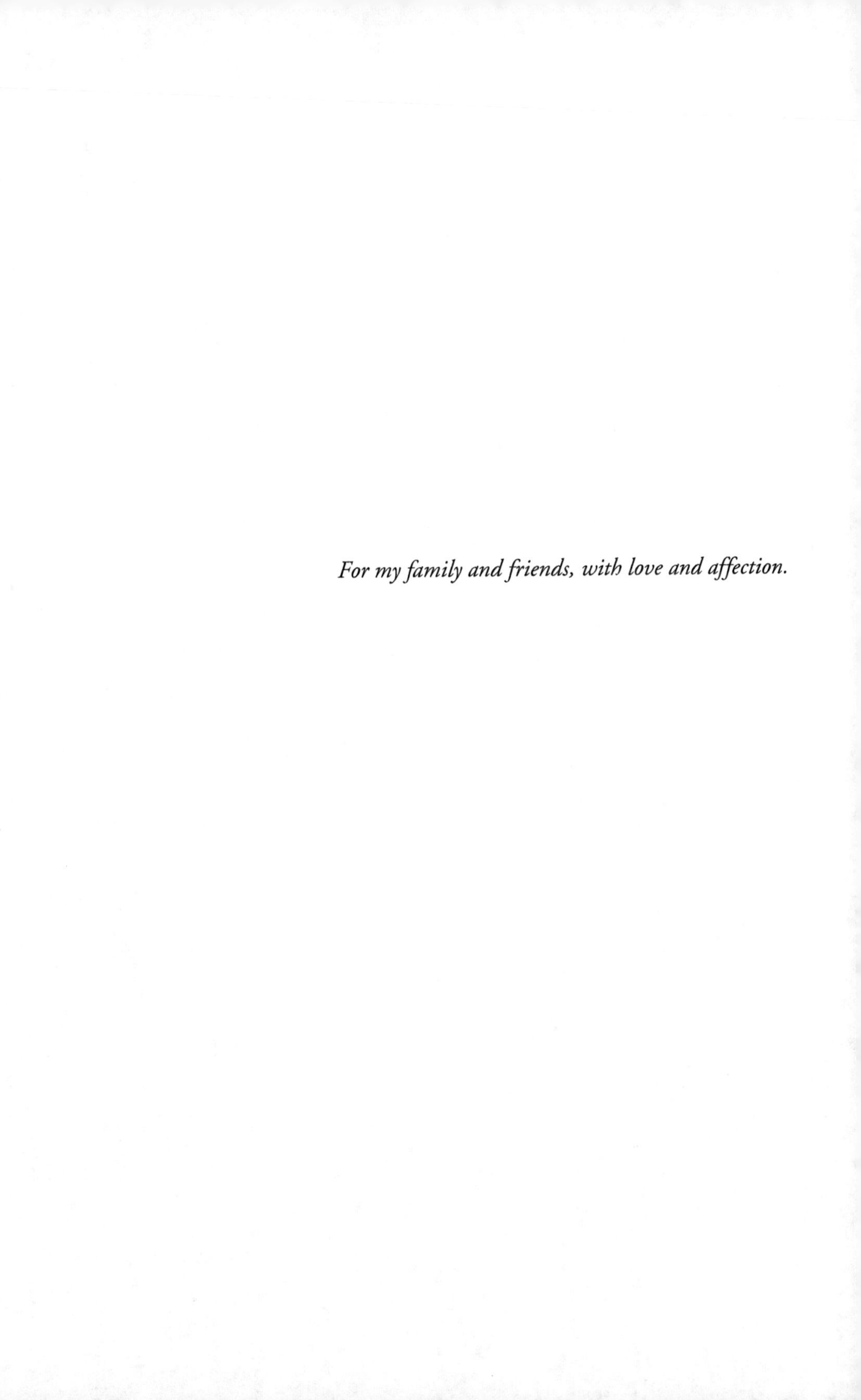

For my family and friends, with love and affection.

CHAPTER 1

"You can do this, cowboy."

Jeb spoke the words aloud as he pulled the jeep alongside the barn. An hour early for work, he wanted to get settled in on his first day back before the rest barreled in. As horses nickered, recognizing his familiar step, he thought back to a month ago and the dreadful aftermath of a work day that had promised so much.

"Your parents were great, Jebo!"

"They loved you, that's for sure. Who wouldn't? Now, if their good-for-nothing cowboy son could just go to college, everything would be hunky-dory."

"Let's have a picnic tomorrow. Who knows when we'll both get another day off at the same time?"

"Okay, Stace, if you want."

"Promise?"

"Of course."

"'Cause I don't wanta hear how you have so much work, you can't take the time."

"No chance."

"'Cause the most important thing in life is to be happy, right? Promise me we'll always be happy."

"Always."

He reached down and felt the ring in his pocket, the beautiful engagement ring he had picked out a month earlier. Tomorrow I pop the question, *he thought, just as lights blinded him and a deafening boom descended.*

"Hello, are you in charge here?"

Lost in remembering, he hadn't heard the car approach. He turned to spy a young woman hopping out of a huge white SUV. About his age, she wore jeans, new shiny boots, and what looked like a brand new Morgan's Run tee shirt in the ranch's newest color, coral. If he hadn't been off the market, she would definitely have been his type. Curvy, and fair-skinned, her shoulder-length auburn hair was held back in a loose ponytail. She held a ranch baseball cap in one hand, backpack in the other.

"Me, in charge? Not by a long shot. Can I help you?"

"I was told I could come down and go for a ride."

"Excuse me?"

"Ride. You know, on horseback?"

Ignoring her sarcasm, his eyes took in every inch of her. She might be stunning in her new cowgirl duds, but who the hell did she think she was? Boots looked like they'd just come out of the box, the jeans right behind them.

"Who gave you the idea that you could come down at sunrise and go for a ride? Are you staying on the ranch?"

She nodded. "And you are?"

"Jeb Barnes. I work here."

"Well, then, you must not have gotten the message."

"From?"

"Mr. Morgan. He called and talked to someone yesterday."

"So you're staying with the Morgans?"

"We're at the Lodge, for the wedding?"

The wedding! He'd been so wrapped up in grief and recovery that he'd totally forgotten about the eldest Morgan daughter Beth's wedding. It was sometime soon. The invitation was tacked to his fridge, but for the life of him, he couldn't remember the date.

He shook his head. "I thought the wedding was a ways off."

"It is. Five weeks, actually. My dad dragged me here on an enforced vacation."

He stared at her as if she was an alien. "Sorry. I've been away, so I'm kind of out of it."

On a different planet, more like it. Amy Foster stared at the young cowboy. A deep scar ran across his forehead, the wound fairly recent by the look of it. Other than that, he was perfect, if you liked cowboys, which she didn't. Her dad had dragged her along on this trip, and she couldn't wait to get through it and back to civilization. Still, the man standing in front of her was awfully cute. His reddish-brown hair curled under his Stetson. His tan face was sprinkled with freckles. About her height, five-eight, and broad-shouldered, he was all wiry muscle. When she met his eyes, she was surprised to see sadness reflected in their gray-blue depths.

"I think we've gotten off to a bad start," she said, extending her hand. "I'm Amy Foster. My dad and Mr. Morgan were roommates in college. We just got in last night, and I asked if I might take a ride this morning."

"Jeb Barnes." He stepped forward and shook her hand, surprised to feel sparks as their hands connected. *Maybe you came back too soon, cowboy. Surely this ain't s'posed to be happening so soon after Stacy.*

He shook himself. "Are you an experienced rider?"

"Yes. Been riding since I was five. Mostly in the ring or barn, though. Never ever been out on a trail. In fact, I was hoping someone around here might be bored enough to ride out with me."

Jeb grinned. "People rarely get bored around here."

Watch out, Amy Foster! You've sworn off men, and this guy has a smile that almost has you drooling.

As they stared at each other, a battered green truck pulled up and a tall, rugged cowboy stepped out. "Hey, buddy, welcome back!"

"Hey, Harley. Good to see you."

As Amy watched, the two men hugged and patted each other's backs. The newcomer was drop-dead gorgeous. What male around here wasn't? *He may be a poster cowboy with that sandy hair and killer smile, but my money's still on Jeb Barnes.*

After greeting his boss, Jeb remembered her and stepped aside. "Amy Foster, this is my boss, Harley Langdon. He runs the stables."

"Pleased to meet you, Ms. Foster." Harley came to shake her hand. "Mr. Morgan called about you last night."

"Yes. Would it be okay if I take a ride?"

"Not alone." He stepped back, scratched his head. "We've got a couple of lessons, but the kids can handle those. I've got…let's see. Hey, why doesn't Jeb take you?"

"But Boss, I just got back."

"A perfect way to ease back into things. You take Ms. Foster out for an hour or so. Then we can go over things. Maggie's bringing the baby by around ten to talk about the camp opening. Long as you're back by then, you've got plenty of time." He referred to Maggie Morgan, wife of the eldest Morgan son, Ben. Until the baby's birth, Maggie, assisted by Jeb, had run most of the lessons and pony camps while Harley managed the stables and led pack trips for the ranch's wealthy clientele.

"But—"

"No buts about it. Go get Tara for Ms. Foster, and you take either Rowdy or Royal. We won't need 'em this morning."

Amy watched the interplay between the two handsome cowboys and wondered why Jeb Barnes had been away. Did it have something to do with that angry scar across his forehead and his sad eyes?

"Come on in, Ms. Foster."

"Amy, please," she said, trailing behind him. She doubted Barnes had heard her as he sprinted into the barn.

CHAPTER 2

"I was thinking we'd take an easy trail that winds around Echo Lake. Not too hilly and should take us about forty-five minutes."

"Sounds good," she called to his retreating back as her gentle sorrel morgan followed his. The sun was already scorching hot, as they started off, and he had tied his flannel shirt round his waist. Rider and horse moved as one, giving Amy a chance to study the man's strong, sturdy back straining at his faded ranch tee shirt.

Ordinarily Jeb would have followed her, but she looked comfortable in the saddle, if a bit nervous. He decided he should lead until they reached the high meadow. They rode at a leisurely pace, the horses comfortable on the familiar, meandering trail. As they reached open ground and the valley stretched out in front of them, he circled Royal round so they rode side by side. "You doin' okay?"

"Absolutely! It's beautiful up here, isn't it?"

"Prettiest valley in the world."

They gazed across the fields to the mountains running north and south, each silent for a few minutes. Finally she said, "It's so green. When Dad said we were coming to Saguaro Valley, I pictured dry desert. That looks like a huge tract of farmland." She pointed to the southwest.

"All Morgan's Run. Biggest organic farm in this part of the country."

"But how do they keep it green?"

"It's the tail end of the rainy season now, so most of Arizona is green, but we're green all year here. Really unusual, at least for this part of the country. An orographic effect, they call it. There's an unusual cloud cover over the valley that keeps it moist and green even though we're surrounded by desert on either side of the mountains. Saguaro Canyon's the town, but everyone calls it Saguaro. The Valley's what they call 'undiscovered,' thanks to mega-wealthy ranchers like Ben Morgan and a handful of others."

"How'd they manage that?"

Jeb grinned and she blushed, averting her eyes. After the colossally self-absorbed Ryan had broken her heart, Amy had sworn off men, but this cute cowboy was already begging her to bend the rules.

"Mega-bucks, as I said. They bought up all the land, created their huge ranches, and had their lawyers write up docs that ensured no one could subdivide the giant land parcels."

"That's gonna make my dad furious. Minute we got here he was talking vacation property."

"Good luck with that. If he's got money, he can probably get his college buddy to help him find something. As I say, Ben Morgan and a handful of his rancher friends own the Valley."

"Have you always lived here?"

"Since after high school. Was raised in Flagstaff, but then I got the job at Morgan's Run. Been here five years. The Morgans are good bosses. Really generous."

"Do you live on the ranch?"

His face drained of color, and he shook his head. "Started out in a cabin, but I moved."

"To?"

"Apartment in town. What'dya think? Time to head back?" The edge in his voice had come out of nowhere.

"I thought you said this was a circle?"

"Yup, let's go!"

With that, Jeb gave Royal a kick and took off across the open meadow. What had she said to provoke such a dramatic change in the man? She urged Tara on and the horse followed her stable mate, soon breaking into a full gallop. Amy held on for dear life.

As they reached the trailhead, he slowed down and glanced behind him. "You okay?"

"*Now* you're asking? Could we take it a little slower, please?"

They rode in silence down a trail that skirted the stable's corrals. As they headed in, she noticed what appeared to be a new road branching off to the east. Curious, she called out, "Can we ride down there?"

Jeb shrugged and reined in Royal, circling back to enter the drive. She followed him round a bend where the road opened to fields and a complex of buildings, barns, bunkhouses, corrals, and a large pool area. They all looked brand-new, and it appeared that construction was ongoing.

"Wow, didn't notice this on our way in. What's is it?"

"Emma's Dream. It's a camp. It's the ranch's newest venture, brainchild of my boss, Maggie Morgan. She and her husband will run it, but we're all helping out. It's a camp for disabled kids. Where they can ride, play, and act like regular kids."

"How wonderful."

"Here's the boss man now." Jeb tipped his hat to a tall, dark-haired cowboy who stood nearby, conferring with several men in hard hats.

"Hey, Jeb, welcome back! Looking good!"

Yet another cowboy, gorgeous of course. Is there something in the water out here? Amy stared as the man approached, reminding herself to close her mouth.

"You must be Amy, Spark's daughter? Ben Morgan. Welcome." He reached up and extended his hand, which she took.

"This is quite a facility."

"My wife's dream. Happy to give you a tour when you have time. We open in three days. Twenty-five campers are comin' whether we're ready or not."

"That's so exciting. I'd love a tour, but I expect you've got your hands full right now."

Ben Morgan tipped his hat. "Always time for a pretty lady."

Jeb watched his boss and marveled at the easy way the Morgan men had with women. Ben Morgan could charm the pants off any woman he met, and he regularly did with the ranch's high-paying clientele. At the same time, Jeb knew it was just that—charm and Morgan hospitality. Ben was crazy in love with his wife, Maggie, and there was only one woman in his life. *One woman? Was Stacy my one woman?*

Morgan turned to Jeb. "You heading back to the office? Mags's comin' by with the baby pretty soon."

"So I hear. How is Ben the third?"

"Perfect, except at three a.m. His mother's threatening to come back to work, but Harley and I are going to try to convince her otherwise, at least for a few months."

"I'll be happy to join the chorus."

"Good man. I'll see you in a few. Nice to meet you, Ms. Foster."

"Same here."

Morgan tipped his hat again before turning back to the men.

*****

When they reached the corral, Jeb hopped down and came to assist her.

Not that she needed help, mind you! As his hands grasped her waist, she gazed down, and their eyes met. There it was, for a second, a glimpse of attraction that he felt as much as she did. Just as quickly, it was gone, and he looked down, but his touch was liquid fire. As her feet hit the ground, Amy's knees wobbled.

"Steady now," he said, catching her under the arms.

"I'm fine." She stepped back and patted Tara's nose. "Shall I come in and rub her down?"

"No, we'll do it. You head up to the Lodge so you don't miss breakfast. They're pretty amazing."

"I don't mind."

"No trouble. We've got a bunch of kids working. They'll take care of her." He whistled, and two young teenagers emerged from the barn. "Rip, Sandy, come take these guys. I've gotta meet with the bosses."

The young men walked the horses into the barn as Jeb reached into a cooler by the corral. "Water?" he asked, holding out a bottle.

"No thanks. I'll get something at the Lodge. Don't want to keep you from your meeting."

He tipped his hat. "Okay, then."

As Jeb turned away, he willed himself not to think about the woman's silky skin and soft curves, the scent of something like honeysuckle that lingered from the few seconds when he had held her tiny waist.

Amy watched him until he disappeared into the barn. Then she turned and walked to the ridiculously huge car her dad had rented. It looked like a white whale parked alongside the bunch of trucks and dusty vehicles in the side yard. As she reached the car, a woman drove up in a dark green SUV. Curious, Amy watched as the beautiful brunette stepped out, then opened the back door and pulled out an infant car seat.

"Hello," the woman said, shielding her eyes as she approached, baby seat draped over one arm.

"You must be Maggie Morgan."

"And, you must be Spark's daughter. Amy?"

"Yes, hello."

The two women shook hands.

"And this must be Benjamin the third."

Maggie laughed. "The very one."

"He's adorable. I just met your husband."

"Oh? Is he here already?"

Amy shook her head. "No, we rode down to the camp. What an amazing place."

"It will be. We're really excited."

"Your husband offered to give me a tour."

"Anytime. So you said you were riding?"

"Yes, Jeb took me out."

"Oh?" Maggie's face turned serious as she set down the car seat. Worry and concern shimmered in her lovely blue eyes.

"His first day back, I understand."

"Yes," she said quietly.

"Is he okay? I mean, I don't mean to pry."

Maggie stared at her for a few seconds before replying. "I hope so. He recently lost someone very dear to him, his girlfriend. Terrible accident. Only happened four weeks ago."

"Oh, dear, how sad. I thought the scar looked new."

"Yes, he's lucky to be alive."

As the baby began to fuss, Maggie hoisted the carrier. "Well, I'd better get inside and nurse him before it's a full-blown wail. Nice to meet you, Ms. Foster."

"Amy, please."

"I expect we'll be seeing lots of each other with all the wedding festivities."

"I look forward to it."

Amy watched Maggie Morgan head to the barn, then hopped into the white whale. As she turned the key, she thought about Jeb's smoky sad eyes and how his touch had made her go weak in the knees. *Get a grip, Amy Foster! He's a cowboy, he's here, and you will be back in Portland in five weeks.*

CHAPTER 3

"We've got it covered, Mags. Jeb, Harley and the counselors will all be there."

"Ben Morgan, are you forgetting how much this means to me?"

"No, sweetheart, but you have the baby."

Harley leaned back in his chair and grinned as he and Jeb watched the couple.

Chest aching, Jeb gazed downward. *Will I ever find someone who loves me as much as Ben Morgan loves Maggie and she, him?*

"Listen, Mother Hen," Maggie continued. "As I've explained to you every day for the past month, Dara is coming for the entire day. Dad and she will keep Ben and Emma at the house. They'll have a great time."

Maggie and Ben's almost six-year-old daughter, Emma, had been the inspiration for the camp. Paralyzed as a toddler after a drunk driver hit her mother's car,at four, Emma had had surgery enabling her to walk again. Now her mother wanted to help the thousands of children who, unlike Emma, might never walk again.

"Fine, let's move on," her husband said. "Where are we with the food?"

"All set." Maggie reached for a clipboard at the far end of the table. As she started to shift the baby from one arm to the other, Ben took his son and nestled him in the crook of his arm. She gave him a sweet glance, then read through the notes in front of her. "We have a few kids with mild food allergies, but Johnny and his staff are all set with that. No peanut allergies, no need to isolate anyone. Just a few no-dairies and a couple of no-glutens."

"First meal is dinner, right?" Harley asked. "Jeb and I'll be there for crowd control so you two can head home."

"We'll see," Maggie said, and her husband rolled his eyes. "Leonora and Carmela are bringing sandwiches, snacks and drinks for when people arrive."

"Complete with gluten-free and dairy-free choices!" Leonora Morgan exclaimed as she breezed into the office, carrying a large basket. The matriarch of the family was dressed in "cowgirl chic," as she called it: designer jeans and a Western-style shirt in soft green that matched her eyes. Even at fifty-eight, the ash-blonde beauty knew how to make an entrance.

"Mom, what are you doing down here?"

"Nice to see you, too, Bennie darling. Can't a grandmother pop in for a glimpse of her grandson? Besides, we knew you were meeting, so Carmela made lunch. I also wanted to check to see what you need from us on Saturday. Dad had one of the guys bring down the camp shirts. They arrived today. Adorable, lots of sizes and colors."

"We're great, Leonora," Maggie said, smiling up at her mother-in-law. "You've done enough already."

"Oh, pish tush! Jeb, honey, it's great to see you back. How're you doing?"

"Fine, thanks, Mrs. Morgan." Leonora had always been a bit intimidating, and today was no exception.

"Your parents well?"

"Last time I talked to them. I've been back in Saguaro for a couple of weeks now."

"That's good. Get back into the swing of things soon as you can."

"Looking good as always, Mrs. M," Harley said. "You gonna join us for lunch?"

This invitation elicited a glare from his best friend, which was not lost on Leonora.

"Heavens, no! Don't want to intrude."

Ben rolled his eyes. "Don't be ridiculous. Join us, Mom."

"No, thanks, darlin'. Your dad's waiting. We're takin' Spark into town, to Gracie's."

The minute the words were out, Leonora blanched as she watched the color drain from Jeb's face. "Oh, sweetheart, I'm sorry." Stacy Winchester, Jeb's girlfriend, had waitressed at the popular local eatery until the day before she died.

"It's okay." Jeb said, looking round to find all eyes on him, full of concern. "It's okay, really. I've eaten at Gracie's a couple of times since I got back. We—Gracie and I—had a good cry, and it's fine."

"Of course you did." Leonora bent and hugged him round the shoulders. "I'll be off, then. I'll expect you all for dinner tonight. You, too, Jeb. And Maggie, please ask Ned to join us."

"But, Mrs. Morgan, I—"

"First of all, the name's Leonora, Jeb, dear. And, second, no excuses! You're family, just like Harley, and I will not take no for an answer. Mr. Morgan told me you took Amy on a ride this morning. That was very sweet of you on your first day back. Casual dinner, on the terrace. See y'all there!"

With those words, she breezed out, leaving them shaking their heads.

Harley laughed and patted Jeb on the back. "You heard the lady, Barnes. You and I are family. Can't say no to the boss lady."

Maggie smiled and gave her assistant a sympathetic look. "It'll be fine. I survived it. You will, too. Just hang by Em, Ben and me."

"Are you referring to our son or me?" Ben asked.

She smiled at her husband, eyes full of love. "What'd you think, Mr. Morgan?"

Harley chuckled. "We've all run the Morgan gauntlet and lived to tell the tale,"Ben gave his best friend a jab to the ribs and said, "I skipped breakfast and I'm starved." He bent to kiss Maggie, then settled his son on a blanket on the floor. "Let's see what Carmela and Mother packed for us. Don't know about you guys, but I'm eating an early lunch."

CHAPTER 4

"What a spectacular night," Spark Foster exclaimed, clapping his old friend on the shoulder.

"Ordered just for you, buddy."

The men stood on the terrace, gazing out over the valley as the guests trickled in. Maggie and Ben had arrived earlier, and she was inside nursing the baby as Ben and Emma played catch with the farm dogs. Ruthie, the youngest Morgan, soon joined them, and the three began a lively game of tag. Amy watched the group, smiling at the antics of Emma's freckle-faced aunt. Her oldest brother teased, calling her Shortcake as he and Emma tried to elude her tags. Red hair flying, Ruthie chased them, clearly allowing Emma to get away. The child ran with a limping gait, laughing and screaming as her aunt drew near.

"He's incorrigible," Maggie said, stepping onto the terrace.

"What a lovely family you have."

"Yes, I'm lucky. You haven't met my dad, Ned Williams." She stepped aside as a tall, lanky cowboy came round to shake Amy's hand. He held his grandson in the other arm.

"Pleased to meet you, Ms. Foster. I hear you'll be with us for a good long stay."

"Yes, till after the wedding. And please, call me Amy. I was just admiring your family."

"Pretty cute, aren't they? And you've only got half the Morgan clan here."

"So I understand. I've never met any of the Morgans, that I remember. Dad and Ben Senior have usually gotten together at Stanford reunions or on Leonora and Ben's occasional visits to Portland."

"Well, Robbie and Kyle'll be here for the wedding, if not sooner, and you'll meet Sam this weekend," Maggie said. "Sam's the architect for the camp project, so he's coming down from Flagstaff for the opening. And here are Beth and her fiancé, Lang, now."

Amy turned to spy a tall, willowy woman, her dark brown hair falling round her slender shoulders. She held hands with a six-foot-four sandy-haired man with sky-blue eyes. Gorgeous, but not a cowboy, she thought. *There's something more citified about this one.*

The couple approached and shook hands. Lang offered to get drinks and disappeared as Beth smiled down at Amy. "So glad you'll be here for a nice long visit. It means the world to Dad."

"My dad, too. Since Mother died, he's been kind of a lost soul."

"I'm sorry about your mom. Our parents have always spoken so highly of her."

"Yes, she was an incredible person. Missed by everyone." As Amy spoke, she spied Harley Langdon and Jeb Barnes step onto the terrace to greet the elder Morgans and her father. Against her will, her treacherous jaw dropped open.

"Are you okay?" Beth said, surprised at the change in their guest.

Amy shook herself, turning back to Beth. "Yes, sorry." She knew she was bright red. It didn't take much to make her blush. She would have to steel herself against the attraction she felt for the handsome, sad-eyed cowboy.

As Harley embraced Leonora Morgan and the two began chatting, Spark Foster grasped Jeb's hand in a firm handshake. "So here's the fella who took my little girl riding this morning. I'm beholden to you, son. Gotta keep my daughter busy so she doesn't start nagging me about going home to Portland."

"My pleasure, sir," Jeb said, smiling at the bald, robust man. Almost as tall as his college buddy, Amy's dad reminded him of actor and politician Fred Thompson. "We get a lot of novices at the stables, but Amy knows how to ride."

"Sure does. Won lots of championships in her teens. Her trainer was pushing us to consider the Olympics, but Amy's stubborn. Wasn't interested and that was that. Her mom and I learned early on to never push her into things she didn't want to do."

As they talked, Jeb spied Amy staring across the terrace, and he smiled. *Championship rider, huh? What other secrets are you hiding, girl?*

Ben Senior patted his shoulder. "Good to have you back, son. I know Ben and Harley have missed you."

"Good to be back, sir."

"How are your folks?"

"They're well, thanks."

"You've been in our thoughts and prayers, son."

"Thank you."

"And there's plenty of space here on the ranch, if you'd like to move back. Don't think anyone's taken your cabin, and my wife would like nothing better than a redecorating project to get it ready for you."

Jeb smiled at the elder Morgan, the most generous person he knew. "Thanks, Mr. Morgan. I'll probably stay put for now."

"Think about it, will you, Jeb? You're like family and we—Nora and me—we like to keep family close."

"I will."

"Now, I expect you'd like to join the young folks?"

Jeb smiled. "Yes, sir. Good to meet you, Mr. Foster," he said, nodding to Spark Foster.

"I expect we'll be seeing plenty of you, young man, so forget the 'Mr. Foster' business. Everyone calls me Spark."

Ben Senior grinned. "Been tryin' to break him and that rascal Harley from the 'Mr. Morgan' thing for years!"

"Good to see you, Spark, Ben," Jeb said, grinning as he turned away. He would never get used to that!

As Lang returned with their drinks, margaritas for the ladies and beers for himself and Ned, Harley and Jeb approached. "Sorry, guys, you're on your own. Just made a bar run."

"Hey, Dillon, how're things back east?" Harley asked.

Lang Dillon's business, Rambler Sports, was located in Boston, where he had lived before getting reacquainted with Beth Morgan a year earlier. Now he worked from Saguaro, and the company had expanded to establish Rambler Sports West, which specialized in Western athletic gear along with the company's original product line. Lang ran the new division as well as keeping his hand in the Boston operation, which meant frequent trips back east. He had just returned from a week in Boston. "All's well. I'm stepping back slowly. Hopefully, I can stay put here more and more as we train people to run Boston."

"What's your company?" Amy asked.

"Rambler Sports."

"Oh, I love their gear. I belong to a hiking club in Portland, and a lot of us use your boots and packs. They're the best."

"Thanks. We're opening a western division here in Saguaro, developing a Western line, especially riding gear, a new venture for us. Thanks to the advice and input of these two cowboys, and Ben Morgan and Maggie, of course, our designers have been working overtime to develop the new lines."

As Harley and Lang chatted, the women listened. Amy stole furtive glances at Jeb, who looked uncomfortable. Finally he excused himself to grab beers for himself and Harley. After handing Harley a Dos Equis, he turned and headed down to play with Emma, Ruthie and Ben without so much as a glance at her. In fact, she realized he had not even said hello!

She watched as Jeb scooped Emma up and began chasing her father around in circles. The child clung to his neck squealing with laughter as Ruthie followed in hot pursuit.

As soon as Jeb lifted Emma, he let out a sigh of relief. The sight of Amy Foster dressed in a soft pink sweater and gray pencil skirt had literally taken his breath away. Never mind that she was a bit overdressed, the rest of them in jeans and casual shirts. She looked spectacular. Her outfit hugged her soft curves, and two-inch heels accentuated a perfect set of legs. Her auburn hair fell round her shoulders, framing her beautiful, delicate face and her soft hazel eyes. *Get a grip, cowboy! This is not supposed to be happening. Not now!*

CHAPTER 5

As the group sat down, Jeb found himself at Leonora Morgan's right, with Spark Foster, Amy's dad, at her left. Amy was at the opposite end of the table beside Ben Senior, who could charm the pants off a rattlesnake. Dinner at the big house meant mountains of food prepared by the elder Morgans' cook and housekeeper, Carmela Roderiquez, and her husband, Raoul. The latter manned the grill, and his wife did the rest. Tonight, Carmela passed platters of what she called Southwestern spiced pork, the thick slabs of tenderloin perfectly cooked and topped with a piquant salsa. Bowls of rice, quinoa and green salad were passed, and Carmela placed baskets of moist Mexican cornbread and freshly made, warm tortillas in the middle of the table. She had prepared a special plate of tacos for Emma, and the child clapped her hands when she spied them.

Amy watched Ben and Maggie's daughter, clearly adored and doted upon by everyone sitting round the table. Even Jeb seemed smitten as he asked her about her pony. Emma's dark curls and chestnut eyes mirrored her dad's, but she had her mother's beauty. *Almost takes one's breath away.*

Lost in reverie, Amy realized that her host and Maggie had been talking and now expected her to answer a question. They both stared at her, waiting. She blushed crimson. "Oh, I'm sorry. I was watching Emma. She's so adorable."

"Yes, she is," her grandfather said. "We were talking about the camp opening Saturday."

"My father-in-law tells me that you're a physical therapist."

"Yes," Amy said, still embarrassed at having missed the entire conversation. *Truth be told, I was staring at Emma and Jeb Barnes!*

"We have been trying like crazy to get a physical therapist to join us, at least part-time. We have someone coming up from Tucson two days a week, but that's not enough."

Suddenly the vacation was looking up. Amy loved her work, and after the break-up with Ryan, it was her respite and solace. "I would be happy to help out. Since graduation, most of my patients have been adults, but I worked with lots of kids in my training, and they come to Portland Rehab on and off."

Maggie's face lit up, and she looked ready to jump across the table and hug her. "Are you sure?"

"Absolutely. Let's talk more when you have time, and you can tell me your immediate needs."

"Are you free tomorrow morning?"

"Anytime."

"Oh, Amy, I cannot tell you what a relief this is. Ben, did you hear that?"

"What, babe?" her husband asked, pulling himself from a conversation with Lang and Beth.

"Amy's a physical therapist! She agreed to help out while she's here."

Leonora overheard and beamed. "Bennie, I thought you knew Amy was a PT?"

"Well, let's see. The last time I saw her, I was about seven and she was in diapers. Don't think the subject came up."

"Oh, pish tush, don't be fresh! Amy, you are the answer to our prayers! I hope it won't spoil your vacation?"

"Nonsense," her father said. "It'll make it. Amy hates to be idle, and she loves her job."

Amy laughed. "Dad's right, Mrs. Morgan. I'd love to help out."

"Good. Then it's settled. Dig in, everyone! Don't want Carmela's food to get cold. Is the fish okay?" she asked her son, who did not eat meat except for seafood.

"Perfect, Mother. Thanks, Carm."

Conversation drifted into pockets as Ruth conversed with Harley, and Ben returned to chatting with Beth and Lang. Jeb listened quietly to one, then another conversation, wondering if he had come back too soon. He thought about evenings on the deck with Stacy, beers in hand, as they held hands and watched the stars come out. The ache in his heart returned, and he almost choked. *Shake it off, buddy. Gotta get back in the saddle!*

As Jeb turned his attention to his immediate companions, he realized that they were talking about Amy.

"Poor baby," Leonora said, shaking her head as she gazed down the table.

"Bastard broke her heart. I'd string him up if I could."

"That's always the Morgan answer when one of the siblings gets hurt, but they always calm down. Does she have to see this Ryan in day-to-day life?"

"Not anymore. I got him out of her house. *Her house.* The house that I purchased for her after college. He's an attorney for a big firm in Portland. Makes a fortune. Environmental law. They met in high school. Only boyfriend Amy's ever had. We were crazy about him because he seemed to make her happy, but there was always an edge to Ryan Houseman. He's a ranked polo player, so she won't be hanging around with that crowd anymore. Just as well. They're a snotty bunch."

"Oh, dear, so hard when our children aren't happy, isn't it? Maybe the camp will be a good distraction."

"Yes, I expect it will."

Jeb watched Amy Foster as she talked with her companions. In between the animated conversations, he spied what he'd missed earlier. A glimmer of pain that played round the edges of her soft, hazel eyes, and a sadness that seemed to mirror his own.

CHAPTER 6

Jeb spent most of Thursday giving lessons and supervising the young part-timers they'd hired to help in his absence and Maggie's. Despite the busyness of the day, he found himself watching for the huge white SUV, wondering if a certain champion rider might want to go out again. As he saddled horses for the lessons, he recalled her lovely sad eyes, alabaster skin and perfect lips, waiting to be kissed.

Even as he daydreamed about Amy, he could not help but notice how much things had slipped in four weeks.

Ben Morgan had been distracted and often absent supervising the camp construction. Everyone acknowledged that Maggie really ran the show and made sure things were done right. Now, with her away, the stalls looked shabby, the corrals needed attention, and the office was in chaos. Ordinarily, Harley ran the pack trips and the office, but for the past month he had been giving most of the lessons and had actually run a one-week pony camp with local teenagers assisting. Pony camps and lessons were definitely not Harley's thing. As they worked side by side, Rip and Sandy recounted hilarious stories about their boss and "the kiddies."

*****

Amy ate breakfast with her dad, then left him to his crossword puzzle and headed out on foot. What she really wanted to do was stroll down to the stables and Catch a glimpse of a certain blue-eyed cowboy. Instead, she walked down to the big house and knocked at the back door. Leonora opened it.

"Hello, darlin'. You're up bright and early. How did you sleep? Did you have a good breakfast?"

"Delicious, thank you, and the beds at the Lodge are the most comfortable I've ever slept in."

"I spent a long time on those. They're excellent mattresses, but the real secret is the toppers. I ordered them from England. Discovered them during a trip, at one of the B and Bs where we stayed."

"Very comfy."

"I forgot—which rooms did they give you?"

"Dad's got the Red Rock Suite. Gorgeous views. I'm in the Warbler. They are lovely rooms."

Leonora smiled, patting her arm. "They're our best. Now, what can we do for you? Carmela and I are planning today's meals and also prepping for Saturday. So much to do!"

"Can I help?"

"Not this morning, darlin,' but I suspect it will be all hands on deck Saturday morning. Better rest up while you can."

Amy smiled, thinking how lovely Leonora was, her blonde hair perfectly coifed in a soft, natural style. How lucky she and Ben Senior were to have each other, still so in love after so many decades. "I'm actually meeting Maggie at her house at ten, but thought I'd take a walk before heading their way. I'm not entirely sure which road leads to Ben and Maggie's."

"Super easy. Down our drive and take a right. Follow the road along the creek and at the fork, turn right and climb the hill. Can't miss it. Only house down there. It's almost a mile from here. Sure one of us can't drive you?"

"Thanks, but now I have my walk. Two miles will be perfect. I'm still nursing a hamstring pull from a tennis game last week."

"Well, enjoy. It's a glorious day. Do you have this number and Maggie's, in case your leg gives out?"

Amy laughed and entered the numbers in her cell. "Thanks, Mrs. Morgan."

"Leonora, please. Are there any other numbers you need? The stables, perhaps?"

Instantly, she blushed. "No, thanks. I'll be off. Good luck with your planning."

As the door closed, Leonora winked at her housekeeper. "There's something brewing there. Mark my words. If Amy and Jeb aren't a couple by the time she goes home, I'll be very much surprised. Now, what shall we have for dinner tonight?"

*****

Amy started off at a brisk pace, trying without success to banish thoughts of Jeb Barnes from her mind. She had just reached the end of the drive and turned south when her cell phone rang. Without thinking, she answered, not bothering to check caller ID.

"Hello."

"Hi, sweetheart."

His voice knocked the wind out of her, and she sat hard on a large boulder at the side of the road. "Ryan?"

"How are you, Ame?"

"Why are you calling?"

"Just wanted to hear your voice."

Hang up! Don't let him drag you in! "Why?"

"I miss you, sweetheart."

Hang up, Amy! "That's a surprise. I thought I was boring and our life was boring."

"I was an idiot, Ame. Don't know what came over me. I wanted to see you, so I went by the clinic yesterday. They told me you were on vacation."

"Yes."

"Can I see you?"

"No, that's not a good idea."

"I have a mover scheduled for tomorrow to collect the rest of my stuff from the house."

"Great. Just leave your set of keys on the counter when you're finished."

"I don't need to move out."

"Yes, you do."

"I meant, maybe we should see each other and talk? See if we can patch things up."

"The house is rented."

"What? Where are you going?"

"It's really none of your business."

"Please, Amy. I'm dying here."

"Have you forgotten that *you* broke us up, not me? You said all those hateful things, then just walked out the door."

"I was a complete ass, idiot, fool, bastard, whatever."

"I can't argue with that."

"Please, Ame. I want to see you."

"No."

"Where are you?"

"Away on vacation with my dad, who would be only too happy to shoot you."

"Guess Spark is pissed, huh?"

Amy stood up as tears blurred her vision. "Listen, Ryan, I'm busy right now, and phone service is spotty out here, so I'm going to hang up."

"Please tell me where you are."

"Good-bye, Ryan."

She clicked off the phone and jammed it into her back pocket as she wiped tears from her eyes. *No more answering the phone without checking caller ID!*

Breaking into an easy jog, she made it to the Morgans' in a little over twelve minutes. By the time she crested the hill, she felt better and had pushed away thoughts of Ryan and her aching heart. When she caught her first glimpse of the house, her jaw dropped. Sitting at the top of a rise, it was one of the loveliest houses she had ever seen. Wings rambled north and south, as much a part of the landscape as the ancient, towering trees and wild fields that surrounded it. What had she heard? Ben and his brother Sam had designed and renovated the old homestead as a surprise for Maggie? *Yes, this is where he proposed. How romantic is that?*

As she stood gawking, Maggie and Emma appeared on the porch, waving.

Amy hurried up to join them. "Hello. I was just admiring your house. It's gorgeous."

"Thank you. We love it."

"Daddy built it!"

Amy smiled at the child, her curly hair tied back in a funny lopsided ponytail. "Well, he did a super job! Aren't you lucky."

"Yes, we are. Come in," Maggie said.

CHAPTER 7

Emma chatted with them for a few minutes, then went to the sun porch to play. Amy and Maggie settled at the kitchen table, mugs of coffee in hand. "Thanks for coming. I can't tell you how excited I am to have you with us. We are so grateful."

"It's I who is grateful. You've saved my vacation. I'm really excited, too."

Maggie studied her guest for a minute. "Are you okay?"

"That obvious?"

"I'm sorry. I don't mean to pry. It's just, with the valley dust, tears usually leave telltale smudges."

"My former boyfriend just called. He's a narcissist who has now decided that he's made a mistake and our life wasn't that boring after all. Translation: whoever the woman was that he was seeing either dumped him or wasn't as interesting as he thought."

"I'm sorry."

"Thanks, I'm okay."

"The valley is a good place to heal."

"That's what Dad's hoping. Even though I get eight weeks of vacation time a year, I had to pull a lot of strings and call in a lot of favors to get five weeks in a row off."

"He's a wonderful man, your dad."

"Yes. I thought we'd lose him after Mom died, but the last six months, he's started to come back and rejoin the living."

They spent several hours chatting about the camp, going over the list of campers, and determining who would need the most time with Amy. Their conversation was interrupted by the baby waking and needing to be fed. Once he fell back to sleep, Maggie set him in a portable crib in the kitchen's alcove. "It's about twelve-fifteen. Emma and I would love it if you'd stay for lunch. Just tuna and salad, nothing fancy."

"Sounds lovely, but I don't want to impose."

"We'd be delighted to have you join us. Would you like to get us drinks? There's lemonade, iced tea, water?"

"Of course. What will you have?"

"Iced tea for me, and Emma can have a small lemonade. Glasses in the cupboard, plenty of ice in the freezer drawer."

Emma stayed at the table for about five minutes, then asked to be excused to groom her pony.

They watched her clatter out. Several times the beautiful brown-haired child grabbed hold of the counter to steady her wobbly legs.

Amy said, "She's incredible."

Her mother smiled. "Yes, incredible and very brave. She's come through so much and been mostly cheerful the whole way."

"Her recovery sounds miraculous. I might be able to give her and you some exercises and stretches to strengthen her legs."

"That would be terrific. Ben and I would be so grateful. Now, how about you? Tell me what you've been up to. Have you been riding again?"

"Not yet. Maybe I'll get over to the barn tomorrow. I suppose it would be a huge imposition if I went late in the day?"

"Not necessarily. Depends who's around and whether you'd want to go out on a trail. We usually don't let people take the ranch's horses out without a guide. You're such an experienced rider that I bet once you know the trails, Harley might send you out, but frankly, even I don't like to go on the trails alone. Better to have someone with you in case something should happen."

"I would definitely want a guide. Got any ideas?"

"Well, if you make arrangements, I'd bet either Harley or Jeb would ride out with you. I'd say Ben could take you out, but he's out straight preparing for the camp opening."

"Of course he is."

"There's always my dad in a pinch. He still likes an occasional ride."

Maggie stood and retrieved a pad and pencil. "I'll put down Harley's, Jeb's, and my dad's cell numbers. Give them a call and I'm sure one of them might like a sunset ride."

"I hate to impose on your dad or Harley."

Maggie gave her a knowing look. "Then try Jeb first. I expect he's still at sixes and sevens and would like the distraction."

"How long had they been together?"

"A little over a year. They started dating around the time Ben returned to town."

"What was she like?"

"Full of fun, very warm and friendly. Cute like him. Stacy waitressed at Gracie's in town. She was going to U of A, speech therapy."

"Very sad."

Maggie nodded.

"How long had they been engaged?"

"They weren't officially engaged. Jeb had the ring with him when they had the accident. I suspect he was planning to ask her that night or soon after but was waiting for the right moment."

"Oh, my goodness, how tragic."

"Yes, we all love Jeb. He's like family. It's been devastating."

"I'm so sorry."

"Thanks. I'll bet he could use a friend now."

"He *is* pretty cute, isn't he?"

"Yes, he is." Maggie said as she studied her companion. "He's a great guy and a dear friend. He's also very fragile right now. To my knowledge, Stacy was his first really serious girlfriend. I'd hate to see him hurt. You either."

"Well, I haven't been through what he has, but don't worry. I've sworn off men after Ryan."

"Oh?"

"After nearly eight years together, he said I was boring and our life was boring. Said he needed a change, then walked out. It's pretty much an ongoing awful situation, but they say time is a healer. "

"Oh, Amy, I'm sorry. Time is a healer. I'm living proof of that."

"Dad dragged me along on this extended vacation to get my mind off Ryan, but unfortunately, he forgot about cell phones. Ryan's now begging me to come back."

"Will you?"

"Never. I'm moving out of the house. It's mine. Dad bought it for me, but I can't bear to stay in it right now. Maybe someday, if I completely redo it."

"Is he still there?"

"No, just some of his stuff."

"Well, I'm glad you're here! Maybe you and Jeb can be friends and take each other's mind off things. He's lots of fun and always up for anything."

"Thanks, Maggie. This lunch was delicious. Best tuna I've ever had."

Her companion laughed. "Secret ingredients—farm celery and local vinegar. The Dillons' winery makes it."

"I'll see you Saturday morning, if not before. Here's my card with my cell number in case you need to reach me before that."

As the baby began to stir, Maggie hugged her, then bent to pick up Ben the third. She walked Amy to the door and waved.

Maggie had pointed her to a trail that led back round the stables to the Lodge. As she started along the winding path, clouds obscured the sun, the breeze kicked up, and Amy shivered. It had been wonderful to spend time with Maggie and her children. Now that she was alone again, her thoughts returned to the conversation with Ryan. It had shaken her more than she wanted to admit. Shaken her because there was a part of her that longed to return to him, to start up where they left off, as if he hadn't said all the hateful words that had broken her heart.

CHAPTER 8

Lost in thought, she rounded a steep section of trail and heard the horse's hooves just before the creature reared up directly in front of her. Amy stumbled backward and landed on a barrel cactus, its spines piercing her thin tee shirt and jeans. She screamed in pain as she rolled off the cactus and struggled to stand.

"Hey, Royal, hey," the familiar voice cried as Jeb reined in the startled morgan. "Jesus Christ, we could've killed you!"

In so much pain she could not speak, Amy rolled to her stomach and stood up. When Jeb saw her face, he hopped off Royal and came to her side. "Geez, you really got stuck."

"Ya think?" she said through gritted teeth. "Get them out, please."

"What we should do is take you back. Much easier with ice."

"Forget the ice," she said, pulling off first her shirt, then pants and tee shirt. Before he knew it, Amy Foster stood before him in lacy bra and panties, her back and buttocks still sprinkled with spines that had pulled right through her clothes. Even with spines and red welts, she was glorious, her round, perfect breasts peeking up from their lacy halter, her soft curves and lovely legs flushed and pink.

"Are you going to help me or just stand there gawking?"

Jeb shook himself. "Sorry. Wasn't expecting that move."

"Oh, stop being such a cowboy and get the prickers out, *now!*"

"Okay, let's see. Come over here and lean against this mesquite.

She went to the tree and gripped the trunk.

"You ready?"

"Just do it!"

As he began, her legs trembled, but she never made a sound. Methodically he extracted each spine, stacking them on the rock. In some spots she bled, but for the most part, only angry red welts remained behind. He started with her back and worked his way down to the lacy panties that barely covered her round, perfect ass. Jeb felt himself harden and pushed thoughts of Amy's gorgeous bottom from his mind. *This should not be happening, no way, no how. Concentrate on the task at hand, buddy!*

"You doin' okay?" he asked.

"Fine."

"What are you doing out here, anyway?"

His left hand rested on her slender hip to steady her as he worked. His rough hands felt like liquid fire on her skin, and it was all Amy could to do stay standing. "Could we just not talk till this is over?"

"Sure, anything you say. We're gettin' there."

Silence ensued for several minutes until she finally said, "Sorry I snapped."

He laughed. "Under the circumstances, you're entitled."

"I was walking back from Maggie and Ben's. She said riders seldom used this trail."

"They don't, but we were thinking of taking kids out here next week, so I thought I'd check it out. It's flat and less rocky than most of the trails surrounding the ranch. There we go. That's the last of 'em."

Reluctantly, Jeb let go of her waist and she turned to face him. Amy wobbled and grabbed hold of his shoulders to steady herself. Without thinking, he reached out, and his hands grasped her waist, and drew her close. Their lips brushed against one another's in a chaste but definite kiss. Every fiber of his being longed to pull her to him and kiss the life out of her, but Jeb came to his senses. *Whoa, tiger, not gonna happen!* Assuring himself that she was upright, he let go.

"Now, let's take a look at your clothes. Why don't you sit on that boulder and go over your shirt, and I'll take your jeans. Look real carefully, cause they're tiny little suckers and you don't wanta sit on 'em again."

Still in her bra and panties, Amy sat sideways on the rock, avoiding pressure on her sore bottom. Jeb sat on a stump nearby, trying without complete success to ignore the gorgeous beauty five feet away. Her silky hair fell over her face as she worked, and he longed to brush it back and caress her sun-kissed cheeks. As they worked in silence, he was surprised to hear sniffles.

"Does it hurt that bad? We have some great salve at the stables. Will take the sting right out."

"It's not the cactus." She gazed over at him, finding his blue eyes full of concern. He gave her a half smile, and Amy marveled again at the handsome cowboy, who seemed so uncomplicated and genuine. *Where has he been all my life? Out here in the middle of nowhere, that's where. You're leaving in five weeks. Do not, I repeat, do not get involved!*

She shook herself and wiped her eyes, surprised to find him squatting in front of her when she looked up.

"I suck at heart-to-heart stuff, but I'm a pretty good listener. Wanta talk about it?"

"Nope."

"Okay, then. Here you go," he said, handing her the jeans. "Clean as a whistle. Want help with the shirt?"

Their eyes met for a second, and each glimpsed the naked, desperate longing in the other. Amy broke the spell, snatched the jeans and stepped away from him. "Thanks, if you don't mind double-checking this?" She handed him the shirt and walked a safe distance away to slip on her jeans, then her boots.

Jeb's eyes carefully scanned her tee shirt, inside and out. "Looks good."

He handed it to her. As Amy slipped it over her head, he watched for a second, then turned to his horse. When he turned back, she was pacing, stiff-legged, clearly uncomfortable.

"Okay, looks like you need a ride back. Come on."

"Sitting is not going to happen right now."

"No problem," he said, hopping into the saddle. "Give me your hand."

She regarded him with a puzzled expression, but then decided to trust him. *For some crazy reason, I feel safe with this cowboy, safer than I've ever felt in my life.*

Amy reached up and grabbed hold of his hand. With one swift movement, he swept her up to lie on her belly across his lap.

"Oh, no, you don't! I'm not riding to the Lodge like a sack of potatoes."

"Got a better idea? I could strap you to the side of the saddle, but not sure Royal will like it."

"Fine. Just get going."

He took it slowly, one hand on the reins, the other on Amy's slender back to steady her. She had gone limp, and after a few minutes, he wondered if she'd fallen asleep.

She had not. Wide awake, Amy reveled in his touch. The warmth of his hand on her back provided solace from the last month of hurt and heartache. *How did he do it?*

"We're back," he said finally as they rounded the western corral and headed down to the barn. "Wanta stop here for the salve?"

"No, thanks. I've suffered enough indignities for one day. I can go to the spa. I'm sure they have something there."

Jeb reined Royal in and headed up the hill and around the back of the barn. As they came into the drive, Harley was getting out of his truck. He raised both arms, giving Jeb a questioning look.

"Long story, Boss. Headin' up to the Lodge. Be back in five."

"Oh, Lord," she groaned, lifting her head to spy Harley, arms crossed, watching them pass. "I'll be the laughing stock of the ranch now, won't I?"

Jeb grinned at his boss. "No worries. Harley's the soul of discretion."

"Yeah, right, and I'm Miss America."

"Nope, you're much prettier. And, you're not the first person to sit on a cactus."

Despite her embarrassment and the pain, Amy smiled and rested her face against his leg, wishing he could hold her and take care of her forever.

When they reached the Lodge, he helped her down, his arm circling her waist as they headed for the spa doors. She allowed herself thirty seconds to rest her head against his strong shoulder, then pulled away.

"Thanks, cowboy. I can take it from here."

"You sure?" His voice was husky, and his arm still circled her tiny waist.

No, I'm not sure. "Yup, thanks." She gazed into his beautiful blue eyes for a second, giving him a shy smile. "See ya around."

Before he had time to reply, she disappeared inside, leaving Jeb feeling cold and lonely.

CHAPTER 9

The salve helped. By evening, Amy's welts had all but disappeared, so she and her dad headed into town to eat at Gracie's. They invited the elder Morgans, but they had other plans. When they arrived, the diner was full. There was only one empty booth, which they gratefully slipped into.

"How you doing, baby girl?" Spark Foster asked, regarding his daughter, eyes full of concern.

"I'm fine, Dad, really. Not even sore anymore."

"I'm not talking about your tumble into the cactus."

"I know."

"Was I wrong to drag you away from Portland?"

"No, I'm glad you did." Amy was surprised at her words, but knew they were true. She was glad to be here, to be helping with the camp and getting as far away from Ryan and her life as possible. Didn't hurt that a certain cowboy had nearly swept her off her feet, either.

"Well, that's the best news I've heard all day."

"Dad, I'm sorry I've been such a grump lately."

"Honey, you've been nothing but an angel every day of your life."

"Some angel, moping around from dawn to dusk."

"I could still have Houseman disappear, you know. I have friends."

Amy laughed. *Along with all these cowboys who'd be only too happy to form a posse and hunt Ryan down.* "Let's eat and forget about everything except Gracie's food, okay? I hear it's terrific."

"'Tis."

They were sharing a slice of Gracie's cherry pie when Jeb walked in and sat at the counter. When she spied him, Amy's heart skipped a beat, and she gasped.

"You okay, honey?" her dad asked, then turned to follow her gaze. *Ah, the charming Mr. Barnes. We'll have to keep an eye on him.*

"Fine, never better."

"On our way out, I'll have to thank your cowboy for rescuing you."

"He's not *my* cowboy."

"Uh-huh, and I'm not your dad."

"You gonna eat that last bite, or shall I?"

"All yours, honey. I'll settle up at the counter."

As he paid the check, Spark Foster chatted with the waitress, dark-haired Rosa Faria, who had just started working. Amy approached the counter and said hello to Jeb, who practically jumped off his stool.

"Hey, didn't see you."

"My dad and I are just finishing up."

"How're you feeling?"

"Much better. The salve worked wonders. In fact, I'm pretty sure I could ride in the morning. I'd love to go out, if you think there's someone who'd take me for a short ride?"

"As you can imagine, we're really busy with prep for the camp, but I could come early and take you. Is six too early?"

Amy gave him one of her gorgeous smiles. "Perfect."

"Hey, Barnes, good to see you again. I hear you saved my daughter out on the trail."

"Well, that might be overstating things, sir. If Royal and I hadn't startled Amy, she wouldn't have fallen back on that cactus in the first place."

Spark patted his shoulder. "Well, I'm grateful nonetheless, son. This gal means the world to me."

I can see why. "No problem, sir. Happy to help."

"And none of this 'sir' business. As I told you last night, everyone calls me Spark."

"Yes, sir. I mean, Spark."

At that moment, Rosa delivered Jeb's meal. She set the enormous burger with curly fries in front of him, eyes lingering on the handsome cowboy. For a second, Amy feared the woman might actually swoon.

She touched her father's arm. "Well, we'd better get going, Dad, let Jeb have his dinner."

"Course. Night, son."

"Night." Jeb gazed from father to daughter.

"See you in the morning," she said.

"Sure thing." Jeb gave them both a hundred-watt grin.

As they strolled down the sidewalk to the white whale, Spark asked, "What was that about? You two have a hot date?"

Amy laughed. "No, he agreed to take me for a quick ride in the morning, that's all."

"Sure you'll be up to it?"

"I'm sure of it," she said, taking his arm as they strolled to the jeep.

CHAPTER 10

Amy woke at five. *I'm looking forward to this ride more than I should be.* She dressed quickly but carefully, choosing a flattering tee shirt that hugged her in all the right places, the color picking up the green in her eyes. When she came downstairs, she found the Lodge's sumptuous continental breakfast already laid out. *If I don't gain twenty pounds on this trip, it'll be a miracle!* She grabbed a muffin, a poached egg and a steaming mug of their delicious coffee and sat at a table by the window, enjoying the spectacular view. As the sun rose over the valley, she gazed around the room and found herself alone with her thoughts, which mostly concerned a certain handsome cowboy she would be seeing shortly.

*****

Jeb got to the stables at five-thirty and saddled Royal and Tara. He was tempted to saddle Rowdy for Ms. Expert Rider but knew the bosses would not approve. His stomach growled as he had forgotten breakfast in his haste to get to work. He grabbed two granola bars from the office and a cup of coffee from the pot he had started, then headed out to sit in the shade of the barn to wait for her.

Amy arrived shortly before six and came through the barn, where she spied him talking softly to the two horses, already saddled and tied up waiting. He hadn't heard her, and she watched for several minutes, marveling at the gentle way he had with the beautiful creatures. There was something about a cowboy, his horse, and a Stetson.

"Good morning."

Her voice startled him, but Jeb turned and gave her one of his gorgeous smiles. "Hey, you ready?"

"Absolutely." As she approached, she watched his gray-blue eyes take in the tee shirt and knew she'd chosen well. *What are you doing, Amy Foster?*

"Sure your ass is up to this?"

"You worry about your ass. I'll take care of mine."

"Okay, Ms. Champion Rider, let's hit it. I have to be back in an hour."

He led them up the ridgeline trail that wound round the side of Blue Mountain. After they reached higher ground, the trails split. One path led east into the hills, the other west toward open meadows and the river. He took the west trail, and they were soon in a vast open meadow the ranch used for grazing. The grass was knee-high, and wild flowers dotted the landscape with riotous color.

"What'd ya say?" He said giving her a look.

"You're on."

She let Tara go, Amy's heels barely touching the morgan's flank before she broke into a full gallop. Jeb gave Royal a slap and they headed off. She had a head start, and as he urged Royal on, he watched, amazed, as the rider and horse moved in perfect synchrony. She might not have been out on a trail much, but he'd wager a million bucks she'd done plenty of steeple chasing and jumping. *What a woman!*

As they reached the far side of the meadow, she spied the river—a meandering creek, really—and reined Tara to a trot, allowing her to go to the water's edge for a drink. Jeb brought Royal up beside them and hopped off.

Jeb pointed to the rock wall on the opposite side of the creek. "Wanta take a climb? The horses can't go up the side of the ridge. It's about a ten-minute climb, and the view's amazing."

"Love to. What about Tara and Royal?"

"They're fine. They'll stay right here even if we don't tie 'em, but there's that tree."

Amy hopped down and followed him to a dead tree by the creek. "Good thing they'll stay put. One good tug and that stump'll come right out of the ground."

His blue-gray eyes danced with mischief as he took Tara's reins. "You don't know mesquite. Nothing's takin' this baby down. Come on."

He led the way to a narrow spot in the creek where they could cross by hopping from rock to rock. As she followed, Amy kept her eyes on his strong, gorgeous back and, *let's be honest, the best ass I've ever seen on a man.*

"I don't exactly have the kind of footwear for rock climbing," she said as they started up the embankment.

"What? A little old pile of rocks too much for your spankin' new boots?"

"Ha, ha, very funny! And they aren't spanking new. It's just I didn't think my regular riding boots would be suitable out here, so I didn't bring them."

"Whatever you say, Ms. Champion."

"Ha, ha!"

Halfway up, she slipped on a gravelly patch. Before she could cry out, his hand grabbed hold of hers, and he pulled her to safety beside him. "New boots?" he said, smiling as he held on to her.

"Something like that," she sputtered, unglued by his nearness. "You can let go now, cowboy." *Even though I could stay in your arms forever, lost in those sad eyes.*

"You sure?"

"Yes, I'm sure," she said, stepping back. As she did, their eyes met. *Oh, my goodness, he is handsome, with that killer smile. If I don't watch out, my knees are going to buckle.*

Jeb had never wanted to kiss a woman as much as he did at that moment. It took all his strength to turn away. *Never once in all my time with Stace did I feel like this. What a shit you are, Jeb Barnes.*

"You okay?" she asked. "You look a little green."

"Fine. It's just a bit farther."

All business now, he led the way to the top of the rise. The valley stretched before them green and verdant to the mountains beyond. Behind them were meadows and farmland as far as the eye could see. Some of the ranch buildings were visible, barns, the Lodge, and the rooftops of Ben and Maggie's and the senior Morgans' homes.

Awestruck, Amy spun around, looking in all directions. "What a view!"

"Yes, it is," he said, his eyes on her, oblivious to his surroundings.

When she noticed his gaze, Amy reached up and touched his rough chin, which he had clearly not taken the time to shave. "Something's happening between us, isn't it?" she whispered huskily. *If anything more was happening, we would both spontaneously combust!*

In answer, he drew her near, his lips finding hers in a deep, lingering kiss. She responded, their tongues teasing, delving, entwining, two parched lovers drinking deeply after a long drought. Suddenly he pulled back, breathless and beet-red.

"No, I can't…we can't. This is wrong on so many levels." Without waiting for her reply, he turned and started down the ridge.

Bewildered, Amy followed. She called for him to wait, but Jeb seemed possessed as he practically sprinted down to the horses.

When she reached him, he had already untied Tara and Royal. "Come on. We've gotta go. Lot's to do today. Can't be late."

"Jeb, wait, please." She placed a hand on his forearm, eyes pleading.

"What?"

She noticed he was still flushed and almost looked angry. "What's wrong? What did I do? What do you mean that it's wrong on so many levels? If two people are attracted to each other, why can't—"

"I just buried my fiancée, for Christ sake!"

"So you're not allowed to be happy again?"

"Not four weeks after her death."

"That's ridiculous. Not that I'm equating your terrible loss with my situation, but I had a nasty break-up recently and swore off men. Then you come along."

"Look, lady, you're on a vacation and probably lookin' for a romp in the hay. This is my life!"

"Is that what you think?"

"No. I don't know. Look, Amy, we're from different worlds. You're a college graduate, a professional, and I'm a cowboy who never went past high school. What could we possibly have in common?"

"Who knows? We just met, but don't you think it'd be worth finding out?"

"Not a great idea. Here." He thrust the reins into her hand. Then, without another word, he hopped onto Royal and took off across the meadow.

Shaking her head, Amy mounted and followed. When she reached the stables, Jeb had disappeared and one of the hands, Rip, greeted her.

"I'll take care of her, Ms. Foster. We've got lessons in an hour. Can I get you something to drink?"

"No, thanks. Where'd Jeb go?"

"Into the barn with Royal."

She marched in and found him alone, feeding Royal oats as the horse cooled down. His body language screamed *furious* and she knew it would be better to leave without talking to him, but instead she approached and stood at his side.

"Jeb, I know you've been through hell and back, but you're still a horse's ass to say the things you did when you don't know me at all."

He opened his mouth, and she put up her hand to silence him. "Don't try to explain, and don't worry, I won't bother you again. After all, ranch guests shouldn't be trying to pick up the help. My mistake!"

With those words, she turned heel and stalked out of the barn, leaving Jeb, mouth open, remembering the feel of her lips, her pale, soft cheek, the scent of honeysuckle, and the curve of her body as she gave herself to him. *She's right. I am a horse's ass.*

Chapter 11

Amy spent the afternoon on one of the Lodge's verandas, reading through the files Maggie had sent over with the needs and challenges of each camper. Clearly it would be all hands on deck in order to support the children with so many different kinds of challenges. They came mostly from the Southwest and a few from the West Coast. One girl was traveling with her father from Chicago. She was staying for two weeks while he went to California on business. While the camp would be open for eight weeks, most campers were staying for two weeks. All except one child, Toby Hooper, from Phoenix. As Amy read through the four-year-old's file, her eyes filled with tears.

Toby's mom was in rehab. There was no dad in the picture or any relative who could keep him. This was mom's last chance before social services moved to revoke her parental rights and put him up for adoption. He had been in and out of foster care his entire life. His case worker, Isabelle Winkler had heard about Emma's Dream from a conversation with Robbie Morgan. Then, when she read a write up in the *Phoenix Sun,* she had called immediately and begged the Morgans to take Toby for the summer. Maggie and Ben had welcomed him with open arms.Paralyzed from the waist down, Toby had been wheelchair-bound for over a year. The notes in his file did not explain the nature of his paralysis or what had caused it. In fact, Toby's file gave very little information beyond the basics and his particular daily needs. Amy made a note to be there to speak with his case worker when Toby arrived.

After perusing the last few files, she leaned back on the comfortable chaise and closed her eyes. *Thank goodness I'll be busy for the next few weeks. No time to think about Ryan or Jeb Barnes!*

*****

"What's lit the fire under you, boy?" Harley asked, observing his assistant scurrying from barn to corral, barking orders to the part-timers as they tried, without success, to keep up with his frenetic pace.

"Just tryin' to get things all set for tomorrow."

"Hey, hey," Harley said, taking hold of his arm as he passed by. "This is me you're talkin' to. What's up?"

"Nothing, Harley, nothing," he said, not entirely successful in hiding his feelings.

"Did you come back too soon, buddy?"

"Harley, let me get on with things. I'm fine."

The tall cowboy gazed down at his young assistant, and for a second he thought he glimpsed tears rimming his eyes. "Well, I'm here if you need me, buddy."

"Thanks," Jeb muttered, breaking away and running into the barn. Damn, damn, damn, why did it have to hurt so much? How could he betray Stacy like that? What a stupid fool he'd been to agree to the ride. Amy Foster's beautiful eyes haunted him as he worked alongside the part-timers mucking out the stalls. Touching her, loving her, even for a moment, had brought feelings he had never experienced before. Without her he felt alone and bereft, but with her, he felt like a world-class shit.

CHAPTER 12

"Here they come," Ben Morgan said as the first cars drove in Saturday morning. He stood proudly alongside his wife, arm round her shoulders, as the dream they had worked so hard to achieve became reality. The stables were closed for the day, except to the few people who boarded their horses, so Harley and Jeb stood beside the Morgans. They had hired bunkhouse counselors and assistants so there would always be at least one adult for every two children. These workers and Amy stood nearby as the first campers were helped from their cars. Amy and Jeb attempted to ignore each other, but they both stole furtive glances at one another as they greeted the campers.

Bunkhouse counselors, mostly college kids, greeted the children and helped them find their quarters. Amy assisted them all the while keeping an eye out for Toby Hooper. Most children were in wheelchairs or walked with leg braces. They ranged in age from six to ten, with the exception of Toby Hooper and the five-year-old girl from Chicago, Ginger Murphy, whose dad had called and asked if she might come, assuring them that she was "very mature for her age."

Amy was sitting on a bench, chatting with Ron Murphy and Ginger, when a car pulled up and short, dark-haired woman with intense brown eyes stepped out. "Would you excuse me, folks?" Amy said, leaving the Murphys with Ginger's bunkhouse counselors.

Maggie spied Isabelle Winkler at the same time as Amy, and they reached the car simultaneously.

"Hello, welcome," Maggie said. "You must be Ms. Winkler? I'm Maggie Morgan and this is Amy Foster, one of our physical therapists."

"Hello, yes, I'm Isabelle Winkler. Everyone calls me Izzy. Thanks so much for having Toby. He's over the top with excitement."

When they peered into the backseat, they spied a beautiful child, reddish-brown curls matted with sweat as he slept, head bent to one side.

"Wish I had eyelashes like those," Maggie said. "What a cutie."

"Yes, and you haven't even seen his eyes."

"He's tiny, isn't he?" Amy said softly.

"Malnutrition does that to a young body," Winkler said, eyes serious as she gazed from one to the other of them.

Amy looked at Maggie, then at Izzy. "Would you have time to speak with me or us for a few minutes before you head back?"

"Of course, but I don't want to leave Toby alone."

Maggie stepped forward. "Why don't you two step into the camp office?" she said, indicating the nearby building. "I'll stay here and come get you if Toby wakes."

"Are you sure?" Amy asked.

"Of course. We're in great shape. Most everyone is headed to the circle area for a picnic lunch. We can bring Toby when you're done."

When the two women had settled in the office, Amy began. "Maggie gave me Toby's file to read through, and I just wondered if there was anything I should know that was not included."

Winkler sighed. "Where to begin? I think the file explains that he has limited use of his legs. He does have leg braces with him, and if he could have PT twice a day with them, it does help keep the legs healthy, in case there may someday be hope for surgery. It's been such a challenge with his various foster home placements. The PT and his medical appointments have often fallen through the cracks."

"Is he okay with the braces?"

"Some days yes, some no. They don't push on the bad days."

"It doesn't say in the file how he was paralyzed."

"No."

"Was it an accident?"

"We're not entirely sure what happened, because Toby only started talking a few months ago. When he was injured, he couldn't tell the doctors, and his mother wasn't there when it happened. One of her boyfriends was babysitting. The doctors think Toby was either thrown or pushed down a flight of stairs, but we could never prove it. Boyfriend claims he fell."

Amy gasped, then shook her head.

"Toby's been through so much," Winkler said. "I've been his case worker since Cora Hooper brought him home from the hospital. He was born with meth in his system. His mom's an addict who uses anything she can get her hands on from meth to heroin. Not sure beyond the speech delay if Toby'll have other developmental delays. He was walking before the episode. I refuse to call it an accident because I know that bastard did it. Toby had a broken arm and wrist as well as three cracked ribs and the injury to his spine. He was in the hospital for two months and then his mom had him for a brief time before she was ordered back to rehab, then jail. He's been in four foster families since his fall. They're all caring people, but in each case, Toby's care got to be too much for them."

"How's his emotional state?"

"Remarkably, pretty good. He's scared of thunderstorms and stairs, but other than that, he's a pretty happy kid, except when someone's poking or prodding him, or making him exercise when he doesn't want to."

"Is he speaking in sentences?"

"Oh, yes. He went from nothing to full-on gab. He'll happily talk your ear off. Despite all he's been through, he's an affectionate, sweet little guy most of the time."

"Does he miss his mom?"

"Truthfully, he barely knows her. She's pretty messed up, and he's been in the care of others more than with her."

"But she still has parental rights?"

"We're working on that right now, which is one of the reasons his file's so slim. We're—"

At that moment, the office door swung open, and Jeb stepped in. He blushed crimson from ear to ear as his eyes met Amy's. "Oh, sorry. Came to get something for Ben."

Amy felt her face reddening as she sputtered, "It's fine. Come in. This is Izzy Winkler, Toby Hooper's case worker. He's the little boy sleeping in the car outside."

Jeb grinned. "Not anymore, he's not. Harley has him on his shoulders and they're touring round the camp."

Izzy laughed. "Toby's very outgoing and not at all shy." She had been watching the interplay between Amy and the handsome freckle-faced cowboy. *Something's cookin' in that kitchen*, she mused. *They seem made for each other.*

"Okay, well," Jeb said. "I'll just grab Ben's backpack and get out of your hair. Nice to meet you, Ms. Winkler." He grabbed a large canvas pack, tipped his hat and stepped out, closing the door softly.

"He's a cutie, isn't he? Lots of gorgeous cowboys out here, I'll bet."

Amy shrugged, taking the first normal breath since he had barged in. "Are there?"

Winkler studied her companion for an instant, then decided it was not her business. "As I was saying, we are collecting documentation, evidence and whatever we need to make the case for Toby. He deserves to be adopted by a family who will love him and give him a stable home. So far Cora Hooper refuses. She doesn't care two hoots about Toby, but she doesn't want to give up her assistance."

"Well, if there are other things we should know, please don't hesitate to call. Here's my card with my cell number. I'll be here for the first month, at least. The Morgans are incredible people, and they have a phenomenal staff. Toby will be loved and cared for. I guarantee it."

"That's why I begged so piteously," Winkler said, handing Amy her card. "I knew this would be perfect for Toby. I know one of the Morgan brothers, Robbie.

He works for my uncle. Last time I was in Sedona, Robbie was telling me about Emma's Dream. Then, when I saw the write-up in the paper, I thought this was the answer to our prayers."

They walked out into the sunlight, finding the courtyard empty. Everyone in the grassy field was eating lunch. As they drew closer, they spied Toby Hooper laughing and squealing with delight as he sat between Jeb and Harley, a huge slice of watermelon in his hands.

"I'd say he's settling in nicely," Amy said, smiling at Izzy Winkler.

The social worker grasped her forearm. "Thank you," she said softly. "A dream come true."

CHAPTER 13

The first day of camp was a blur for all involved. Homesick campers kept counselors and most everyone on the ranch working into the night as they learned the needs and challenges of each child. Leonora and Ben Morgan, as well as Carmela, spent most of the day at the camp, bringing cheer and lots of extra treats. Maggie barely saw her children until Ben ordered her to go home after the evening meal. Ben slept in the office that night, and between him, Harley and Jeb, they were able to assist with the boys' first-night jitters. There were twelve boys, and Ruthie, Beth and Amy would stay to help with the thirteen girls. Amy made time to check on Toby several times during the day.

Eight bunkhouses ringed the green space, each with the capacity to sleep eight campers and up to four counselors. For this first year, they had decided to stay with smaller numbers so only six of the bunkhouses were in use. Each housed four children, except for one of the two girls' bunkhouses, which had five occupants plus three counselors. Each bunkhouse was equipped with two bathrooms, both handicap-accessible. Counselors lived with the kids day and night, with others on call as needed.

Toby shared a bunkhouse with three boys—Willy, age six, Pete, seven, and Dexter, nine. Willy and Dexter were from Tucson, and Pete was from San Francisco. Dexter immediately established himself as the leader of the group and set about organizing the other three. Born with cerebral palsy, Dexter walked with crutches and braces but had brought a wheelchair as well. The other three were wheelchair-bound, with Toby the only one whose therapy included daily walking with his braces. Saying good-bye to Izzy Winkler had been hard for Toby, but Harley, Jeb, Amy, Ruthie and others kept him active and busy that first evening.

The following morning, Amy arrived at the dining hall as counselors were bringing the campers in for breakfast. She spied Toby and waved. Andy Burrill, one of his counselors, pushed his wheelchair.

"Hey, Toby!"

The child's face lit up with a huge grin. "Hey, Amy!" Maggie and Ben had decided that all staff and campers would be on a first-name basis, unless any adult felt uncomfortable with the familiarity.

"How was your first night?" she asked, smiling down at him.

"Great!"

Amy caught Andy's eye, and he gave her a look. "Why don't you find a seat, and once I walk around a bit, I'll come have breakfast with you. Is that okay?"

"Yup!" Toby gave her a beautiful smile before he and Andy headed for a table.

Amy watched as Andy placed him next to Dexter, who immediately began helping him with food and utensils. As Andy stepped back, she approached and caught his arm. "Everything okay?"

The tall, dark-haired nineteen-year-old, a public health major from the University of Arizona, nodded. "He's a great kid. Really sweet. Only problem is the nightmares."

"Oh, did he have one?"

"Try five, maybe six. Greg and I took turns trying to settle him back down as well as the others. Every time Toby started screaming, Willy and Pete woke up and started crying, asking to go home. Dexter was a big help, until even he started freaking out from lack of sleep at about five a.m."

"Oh, Andy, I'm sorry."

"Not your fault. If you've got any ideas, we'd love to hear 'em."

"Have you spoken to Maggie or Ben?"

"Not yet. Greg was gonna try and catch Ben after the guys are settled."

"I'll check with him, too, and come back to sit with Toby in a sec."

Amy's eyes scanned the room, but she couldn't see either Ben or Maggie. Harley was assisting with serving. Carmela, too. Finally she decided to eat, then resume her search. As she was about to sit down next to Toby, she saw that the place next to him held a heaping plate of food.

"Oh, do you already have company, Toby?"

"Yup, Jeb's comin'."

At that moment, Jeb appeared, coffee mug and wad of napkins in hand. He blanched when he spied her. "Oh, were you going to sit here?"

Amy's face turned red, and she forced a smile. "No—I mean, yes—but it's fine. Toby's so excited." *Get a grip, Foster! You cannot spend the next month falling apart every time you see this man!* Before her knees gave way, she turned her attention from Jeb to Toby, ruffling the curly head. "Hey, buddy, have a great breakfast and I'll see you in morning therapy, okay?"

Jeb's chest ached as he watched her walk away. Shaking himself, he sat and turned to the beaming child. "Okay, buddy, let's dig in! Blueberry pancakes are my favorite!"

As Amy made her way toward the kitchen, she bumped into Maggie, who appeared to have just arrived. "Good morning!" she said, smiling as her eyes scanned the room. "I'm sooo late. Baby cried half the night and Emma wanted me to stay with her this morning. My husband's barely speaking to me."

"Oh, dear, can I help?" Amy asked.

When Maggie's eyes came to rest on her, she paused. "No, I'm fine, but you look a little flushed. Are you okay?"

"Yes, fine, just been running around. After you get organized, can we talk for a few minutes?"

"About Toby Hooper?"

"Yes."

"Greg caught me outside. After breakfast, let's try to grab some time in the office before you start the therapy sessions. Would that work?"

"Not much time. First child's in fifteen minutes. Want to try over lunch?"

"Of course. Let's find each other then. I'm sure we'll figure out a solution. Oh, doesn't he look happy with Jeb? He's been so good with him. Harley, too."

"Yes," said Amy wistfully.

Maggie watched her gaze. "How are things with you two?"

"They aren't."

"Oh, I'm sorry."

"It's okay. As you told me, he's fragile, and I'm not much better. Not meant to be, I guess."

Maggie squeezed her arm. "You never know. You've got the next month to find out. Take it slow and see what happens."

Amy laughed. "As if I have a choice."

"Aren't I lucky?" Ben Morgan asked, arm circling his wife's shoulders. "Two beautiful women in the same space so early in the morning."

Amy smiled and said hello as she watched Maggie stiffen. "I'll leave you two to get organized. Good luck and I'll see you at lunch, Maggie."

She headed off to the buffet, grabbed a muffin and a peach and headed over to the main building where the therapy rooms were located. The state-of-the-art equipment gleamed in the exercise room, a large, colorful space decorated with children in mind. Bright murals on three walls depicted desert and farm landscapes, with all manner of local plants and animals. The Morgans had contacted an artist from Tucson who had donated her time and used valley teenagers to help with the installation. Off the main exercise space were four smaller rooms for massage and other types of individual therapy. Karen Edwards, a massage therapist from town, would be here four days a week and the part-time physical therapist from Tucson two days.

Amy waved to Karen, who was setting up her table in the first of the smaller rooms. "Morning!"

"Hi. You must be Amy?" A tall, broad-shouldered redhead emerged from the smaller room. She was dressed in a bright green camp tee shirt, beige capris, and Birkenstock sandals, her hair tied back in a red bandana. Rosie the Riveter came to mind.

"Yes, hi."

"Maggie's been over the moon that you're here. Don't know what she'll do when you leave. I'm Karen, by the way."

"Have you gotten a schedule for your morning?"

"I know I have three kids, but the first one doesn't come till ten."

"I wonder if you'd be willing to spend a few minutes massaging my first little guy, Toby Hooper, the four-year-old with the spinal injury."

"I heard about him. How's he doing?"

"So far, so good. He's coming in for exercise with his braces, which I understand he hates most of the time. I thought maybe a little massage before we get started might make it easier on him."

"Of course. Happy to help. This is quite a place, isn't it?"

"Sure is. Would you like half my muffin and peach?"

The redhead chuckled. "Thanks, but I had a huge breakfast when I arrived. Johnny's a good friend." She referred to Valley chef Johnny Stockdale. Semiretired now, his Late Place in Phoenix had been a popular destination for foodies. After closing the popular late night eatery, Johnny purchased a condo in town with a pool, tennis courts and gorgeous views of the Valley, and declared himself retired. After six months, he was going stir crazy. He did a few select catering jobs but hadn't found the right project until Leonora had asked for his advice as they sought a cook for Emma's Dream. Stockdale, who adored children, had jumped at the chance. While he refused compensation for himself, he had assembled what he called a "crackerjack team," who were well-paid and well-trained.

"They were lucky to get him, I guess," Amy said.

"Lucky doesn't begin to cover it," Karen said. "Johnny's food is out of this world, even if he's cooking for kids."

"Muffin's great," Amy said, waving a half-eaten corn muffin.

"Those come from Bakery on Main. Johnny's not a baker."

Amy smiled at the tall therapist, guessing her to be in her late twenties. "Have you lived Saguaro long?"

"Since college. Had summer jobs at Gracie's for six years. Then, after my training, I came back for good. I own a small condo right next to Johnny's. That's how we met. I'll be working here for the summer and I'm already at the Lodge's spa three days. I also have a small place in town with a bunch of regular clients. I suspect they won't be speaking to me by September as my open appointment times are very limited during the camp season."

"So you probably knew Stacy Winchester, the young woman who was killed last month?"

"Yup, a real sweetie. Half the cowboys in the valley were in love with her. She certainly brought 'em in to Gracie's. Horrible tragedy."

"Yes."

"How's Jeb Barnes holdin' up, anyway? I understand he's back."

"Yes. I don't know him well, but I'd guess it's a slow process."

Edwards studied her companion, aware of the sudden change in her demeanor. *Hmm…that was quick.* The new PT arrived in Saguaro four days ago and she's already got something going with the cute, grieving cowboy? "Well, well, speak of the devil," she said, waving as the door opened behind Amy.

Amy turned to spy Toby with Jeb pushing his wheelchair. She wasn't sure if Karen was referring to man or child, but she decided to focus her attention on the little boy. "Hey, Toby! We're all set for you. This is Karen. She's gonna rub your legs a bit before you and I get started. Would that be okay?"

Suddenly shy, Toby grabbed hold of Jeb's arm and buried his face in his side.

Jeb squatted beside the chair. "Hey, buddy, what's wrong? You're gonna have a great time. I gotta go get your saddle so it'll be ready later, okay?"

Amy watched Toby gaze up at him, eyes adoring. *He's already in love,* she thought. *It's impossible not to fall in love with Jeb Barnes.*

Toby nodded, and without a word, he held out his arms. Jeb lifted him gently and followed Karen into the side room. The masseuse took her cues from him and let him get comfortable, Jeb chatting nonstop as they got him settled. A few minutes later, he said, "Okay, buddy. After you're through with Karen and Amy, Greg or Andy'll come back for you and bring you to the barn. I've got just the right saddle for you."

Toby nodded, and Jeb stepped out and partially closed the door, nodding to Amy as he headed for the exit.

"Jeb, wait, do you have a minute?" she asked. *This has gone on long enough.*

"Just. We've got a load of excited riders waiting." He refused to meet her eyes.

"They're not riding this morning, are they?"

"No, but Lang's comin' down to fit them all, see if we need anything. Might take the older ones out this afternoon."

He gazed up and met her lovely hazel eyes. Her thin camp tee shirt hugged her round, perfect breasts and khaki shorts revealed her glorious legs. If he stayed much longer, his treacherous body would betray how much he wanted her. *Get a grip, Barnes!*

"It'll only take a sec." She followed him out of the room, and they walked down the hall to the empty office.

When the door had closed behind them, she said, "I just thought we should clear the air."

"We're good."

"No, we're not. You can barely look at me. You've been avoiding me like the plague, and it's really uncomfortable."

For a second, his eyes softened, but just as quickly turned steely. "Look, I'm not sure what you're talking about. I hardly know you and, in case you hadn't noticed, we've been a little busy around here the past few days."

Amy threw up her hands in defeat. "Okay, I'm not going to argue with you. I like you, Jeb, I do. I'm not afraid to admit it. I also know you're grieving and have no interest in a relationship. I cannot imagine what you're going through. I'm so sorry for your terrible loss, and I certainly won't intrude or press you, but if we're going to work together, couldn't we at least agree to be friends?"

She extended her hand, and he took it, the touch sending fire through each of them. For a second, Amy imagined he might lean forward and take her in his arms, but instead he said, "Friends," then withdrew his hand.

The handshake unnerved her, but she managed to reply, "Good. I'm glad we can be friends. So much to do around here."

"Okay, then," he said, stepping back. *Get out of here, Barnes, or you'll have your hands and mouth all over her before you can count to ten.*

Watching him inch toward the door, she did not miss the brief second of longing in his eyes. Just as quickly it disappeared, sadness taking its place. "How was Toby at breakfast?" she asked.

"Great. He eats like a horse. He's really smart for a four-year-old."

"I suspect he has had to be. Only way he's survived."

"That rough, huh?" he asked, pausing, hand on the doorknob.

"Horrible."

"Poor little guy."

"Yes. Did Andy or Greg talk to you about last night?"

He shook his head. "Was there a problem?"

"Toby apparently had nightmares. Woke up screaming all through the night. No one in Javelina Bunkhouse got much sleep. I'm going to talk with Maggie at noon. Maybe his case worker will have some suggestions. Either way, he should probably have a nap after lunch. If you see Greg or Andy, tell them I said so and see if someone can sit with him."

"Will do." His body had relaxed, expression less haunted.

"Jeb?"

"Yup?"

"I'm glad we talked."

On guard again, he swung the door open. "Okay, see you around."

Well, that's about all I'm gonna get, she thought.

Chapter 14

Toby looked terrified as Karen carried him in. Amy's heart ached as she watched the thin, sweet child cowering in Karen's arm. "Hey, sweetie. No worries. We'll take it slow today, okay?"

"Don't like those," he said, pointing to the tiny leg braces Amy had taken from the pack strapped to his wheelchair.

"Let's just try 'em, okay?"

Tears rimmed his dark eyes, and he nodded. She reached forward and brushed dark curls from his forehead. "That's my brave boy."

Amy gently took hold of Toby's spindly legs and manipulated them, assessing his strength and range of movement. Finally satisfied, she strapped on the braces and adjusted them. Throughout, Toby sat still, jaw clenched.

"Okay, my friend, ready?"

He nodded, allowing himself to be lifted. As soon as his feet touched the ground, he flinched and said, "Ow," and began wriggling out of her grasp, grabbing for the chair.

Amy grasped his waist and carried him a few feet from the chair. It was like lifting a baby bird. He weighed less than thirty pounds. "I've got you, sweetie. Let's try one step, okay?"

He tried to let his legs go limp, but the braces held them in place. Finally he dug his fingers into her arm and straightened up, taking one painful step, then another before collapsing into her lap. Setting him back in his chair, Amy resolved to call Izzy as soon as possible to ask for any medical records related to his injury.

*****

Andy arrived to collect Toby, and Amy's morning was swallowed up with other campers as she assessed their needs, made copious notes, and began initial therapy. Eight of the children could walk, some with crutches or braces. Others limped or had halting gaits due to birth deformities or injuries. Several had challenges with their upper bodies or conditions such as MS or spina bifida. Ginger, the five-year-old girl from Chicago, had a club foot, which made her gait awkward, but not impossible. She was a lively, happy child, the last one Amy saw before breaking for lunch.

"Okay, Ginger, you hungry," she said as they finished their fifth game of tag.

"One more," the child said, eyes pleading.

"We have lots of time, sweetheart. I have an appointment now, but I'll walk you over to the dining hall, okay?"

As she and Ginger walked slowly, hand in hand, across the grassy area that separated the dining hall from the main building, the child chattered on about her plans for the afternoon, which included riding a pony and playing more tag. When they started up the ramp to the dining room, Amy spied Jeb with Toby and smiled. *He'd better be careful,* she thought, watching the two. *This is day one. How will they ever say good-bye at the end of the summer?*

As Jeb settled Toby down, Dexter on one side and Andy on the other, he watched Amy talking with Ginger and her bunkhouse group. Could she be any prettier? What a gentle way she had with the mischievous girl at her side. He ruffled Toby's curls. "Okay, buddy, have a good lunch, and I'll catch you later."

"I want to sit with you!"

"Sorry, buddy. I gotta go to work. I'll catch you later, after naptime, okay? Have fun with Dexter and Andy."

Not waiting for the child's reply, he stepped back and bumped into Maggie. "Oh, Jeb, hi. Where are you off to in such a hurry?"

"Hey, Mags. Thought I'd grab a sandwich and head over to the stables. We've got a lesson that we forgot to cancel, and I want to check up on the guys."

"Why don't you grab your sandwich and join us in the office? Ben, Amy, Harley, and I are meeting. You've gotten to know Toby Hooper a little. I'd like to have your input."

"Okay, sure," he said as she flew off to catch Amy.

When the group was assembled, Maggie began. "As you all know, this is about Toby Hooper. I've had a long talk with his counselors, Greg and Andy, and I've also talked to his case worker, Izzy Winkler. He suffers from night terrors, pretty severe ones. In other words, last night was not unusual."

"Last night?" Harley said, the only one who had not heard about the nightmares.

"Basically, everyone in Javelina Bunkhouse was up all night, and they're a tired crew today," Maggie said.

"So, what did Izzy say?" Amy asked.

"The nightmares are pretty normal for Toby. His most recent foster parents usually took him into their bed every night."

"Poor little guy," Harley said. "He's a scrapper."

"Yes, and he's been through hell and back," Maggie said. "Amy talked to Izzy, so she knows some of it."

Ben gazed over at his wife. "We may have taken on more than we can handle here, guys."

"What does that mean?" Maggie asked, giving him a sharp look.

"You know what I mean, Mags. We're not equipped for this. We only have the social worker two days a week, and we can't very well subject the rest of the kids to this every night. They were all cryin' to go home, according to Greg, and can you blame 'em?"

"Whoa, whoa," Harley said. "We don't think he'll settle in?"

"No," Maggie said. "According to Izzy, Toby's had night terrors most of his life."

Jeb tossed his sandwich wrapper in the trash and cleared his throat. "I'll take him," he said quietly.

"Excuse me?" Maggie asked, turning to stare at her assistant.

"He can stay with me."

"Where?"

"Your dad asked if I wanted the cabin back. We could stay there."

Amy watched the interplay between boss and employee, marveling at the closeness they had and at Jeb's generosity, even as warning bells sounded. "That's incredibly kind, Jeb, but do you think it's a good idea?" she said. "It's a huge responsibility. We know so little about Toby, and what we know is disturbing. Also, he'd be separated from the other children."

"As he clearly needs to be," Jeb said, eyes flashing fire.

"Okay, folks, let's back up. As Amy says, this is a huge responsibility for Jeb to take on," Ben said.

"Toby's already attached to Jeb," Amy said, refusing to look at the gray-blue eyes, which she suspected were still glaring at her. "With this arrangement, think how he'll be by the end of the summer."

"You'll be long gone by then, so what the hell do you care?"

Amy shook her head as the other three gazed at Jeb, wondering what had provoked such a strong reaction in the easygoing cowboy. Finally Maggie said, "Okay, everyone. Let me mull things over. Maybe we could shuffle bunkhouses and have Andy or Greg stay with Toby alone. Unfortunately, the two empty ones are still under construction. They don't have beds or anything, but I suppose we could find a couple?"

"That's bullshit," Jeb said, jumping up. "I've got a lesson in five. The offer stands. I can move out here this afternoon if you change your minds. You know as well as I do that it's the best solution."

Without waiting for a reply, he stalked out and slammed the door.

"Oh, dear." Maggie sighed as the four shook their heads, staring at the closed door. "Maybe he did come back too soon."

"Or maybe he has a good idea?" Harley said. "I get what Amy's saying about the attachment part. There'll be hell to pay at the end of the summer, but if we keep him, he's clearly going to glom onto whoever stays with him. He's four years old, for Christ's sake. He's gonna latch onto anyone who's nice to him, poor little fella. And we should let him."

"Amy?" Maggie said, turning to her.

"I don't know what to say. I would hate to send him back. Maybe we could ask Izzy what she thinks."

"We could always rotate who stays with him," Ben said, gazing back and forth at the others.

"Okay, let me try to reach Izzy again. Then I'd like to talk privately with Jeb. If nothing else, Ben and I can take him home with us. The house is wheelchair-accessible, and we have plenty of room."

"Speaking of home," her husband said. "I thought you said you were heading home for the afternoon?"

Maggie rolled her eyes. "Thank you, Mother Hen. After I make the call and talk with Jeb, we'll see." As Ben opened his mouth, she raised her hand.

Harley poked his friend. "Okay, partner, we're late for some easy riders."

After the men departed, Maggie gave Amy a long look. "Are you okay?"

"Yes."

"He's not usually a hothead. In fact, Jeb Barnes is one of the most easygoing people I know."

"Grief does funny things to people."

"Grief and longing. He's at war with himself, Amy, not you."

Amy gave her a wan smile. "Good luck with Izzy and Jeb. I've got two appointments this afternoon, and I've barely seen my dad for two days. After the last therapy sessions, I'm going to check in on Toby. Then I was going to head up to the Lodge."

"Good. The counselors have a full afternoon of activities planned, including the kids' first dip in the pool. I've got extra people coming from the ranch to help. Ruthie, Beth, and Lang and the stable guys."

"If you need me, I'll stay."

"No, we've got lots of help. It'll look like Coney Island."

Amy smiled. "We'll start the water therapy Monday. A few really need it. Ginger's practically busting a gasket to get in there, and I think it'll be great for Toby."

"I know it's been torture for them to go by that beautiful, sparkling new pool and not be able to jump in."

"Are you sure you don't want me to stay for pool time?"

"Absolutely not. I'm bringing Emma back down, and my dad and Ben's parents will be here, along with lots of help. We should have an adult for almost each child. Take a break. This is your vacation."

"Yeah, right," she said, not entirely successful in keeping the sarcasm from her tone.

"He'll come around. Give him a few days," Maggie said, patting her hand.

"We agreed to be friends this morning, but that didn't last long."

"He's a man. What can I say?" Maggie asked.

CHAPTER 15

Maggie reached Izzy Winkler on her lunch break, and the social worker endorsed the plan for Jeb to bunk with Toby, saying, "I know he'll become attached, but honestly, that's a healthy thing for Toby right now. We'll deal with the fallout in September, and maybe his custody status will be resolved by then. In the meantime, love, attention, and attachment are just what he needs. I approve anything that keeps him with you guys for the summer."

They rang off, and Maggie gathered her things. She missed her children terribly, especially the baby, with whom she had spent almost every minute since his birth. She hopped into one of the ranch trucks and drove the short distance to the stables, where she found Jeb saying good-bye to one of their regular clients, Helen Morrison, who boarded her Arabian with them. Maggie waved as Helen headed for her car.

"How'd it go?" she asked, smiling at her assistant.

"Fine. I'm not Harley, and you know she's madly in love with him."

Maggie laughed. "Who isn't?"

"We took a short trail ride, and I learned something. Rowdy and her Bella do not get along."

"Or, maybe they get along too well?" Maggie said, grinning. "Care to buy this lady a drink?"

"What'll you have?"

"Iced tea, if you have it."

Jeb reached into the cooler they kept stocked in the backyard by the corral and brought out two teas. They sat on a bench in the shade, watching the college kids come and go.

"Wanta talk about it?" she asked.

"No."

"It's gonna hurt for a while, partner. That doesn't mean you can't keep living."

"I feel like such a shit."

"Why?"

"Stacy's been gone a month, and I'm already ogling someone else."

"Ogling? Is that what you're doing?"

He hung his head. "I miss her, Mags. She was like me. We fit, you know?"

"I know," she said, placing a hand on his shoulder.

Before he knew it, Jeb was crying. He leaned against her, and she turned to hug him. "That's right, let it all out."

Out of the corner of her eye, she spied their college kids and waved them into the barn to give Jeb some privacy.

As his sobs subsided, she patted his back. "Want me to run in for some tissues?"

"No," he said, smiling as he wiped his eyes and face. "Cowboys don't use tissues."

"Better?"

"Some."

"You still wanting to move back and bunk in with Toby?"

He nodded. "It'll do me good to get out of the apartment. Too many memories."

"Toby's social worker okayed it. Thinks it'll be great for him. He's going to get attached so prepare yourself. It'll be a wrench for all of us at the end of the summer, especially you."

"I want to do it."

"I'll talk with the Morgans and see if your old place is habitable. The farm might have turned it into storage."

"I actually saw Raoul on our ride. I asked him, and he thinks it's pretty clean. I'll head over there in a bit, then get back for pool time. While Toby's doing the evening activities, I'll run home and grab some things."

"There were two twin beds in the bedroom, right?" He nodded. "I'll ask Carmela about sheets and towels. Maybe she could pop over and give it a quick dusting."

"Okay."

"Thanks, partner."

As she moved to stand, he grasped her arm. "I only told you half the story, Mags."

"About?"

"About all this. I loved Stac. We had a good life, a fun life. We were best buddies."

"I know. She was a terrific person."

"Yes, and she deserved someone better."

"That's ridiculous!"

"No, it isn't. I loved her, yes, but it wasn't like this. What I feel when I look at Amy... I get within twenty yards of her and my palms start sweating and I can't breathe. I feel like such a shit, Mags. I feel like I was living a lie."

"It's called being human."

"Maybe I'm feeling this way cause I'm missing Stace?"

"Maybe. I mean, I know you're missing Stacy terribly and that's one part, but then there's Amy. She's a wonderful person, and I'm glad you've resolved to be friends. I'll bet she needs a friend right now, too."

"Yeah, right. She's probably dying to be friends after my temper tantrum."

"Do you know how many temper tantrums Ben Morgan and I have had since we met?"

"Yeah, but you love each other."

"Yes, we do," she said, patting his arm. *And so do you.* "Give it time, partner. Get to know her and have some fun. You've earned it."

"Thanks, Mags."

"See you at the pool."

"You're coming back?"

"Yup, Dara's watching the baby, and Dad and I are bringing Emma. She's so excited to meet everyone."

"Great, see you then," he said as his boss headed into the barn.

Have some fun, he thought. *That's a new idea.*

CHAPTER 16

Amy found her father on a wicker sofa on the Lodge's veranda reading a book. One of three verandas that wrapped around the rambling Lodge, this one overlooked the Valley, magnificent views in every direction.

"Good book?" she said softly, not wanting to startle him.

Spark's eyes lit up. "Hey, honey. How's my girl?"

"Truthfully, I've been better, but I'm glad to see you. Did you have lunch?"

"Just finished. Ben and Leonora came up." He patted his stomach. "I'll be forty pounds heavier by the time we go back to Portland. Want me to order you something? You're lookin' a little pale."

Amy shook her head and he patted the cushion beside him. "Sit, baby girl. What's wrong? Tough morning at camp?"

"No, the camp's fine. Kids are all adorable and so excited. A few homesick ones and our youngest little guy is having nightmares, but overall the opening of Emma's Dream couldn't be a bigger success."

"I'm glad. Little gal who inspired it is certainly a sweetheart. She's been around a lot. Her grandparents are crazy about her. Hope I'm still around to see grandchildren."

"Well, don't hold your breath with me. Maybe you'd better start nagging Buck."

"Speaking of your brother, he called. He's doing an installation in San Diego and is thinking of driving over. I think he said in time for the wedding."

Just what I need. Another nosey Foster asking me how I am. "That'd be great."

In truth, Amy missed her older brother, who lived and worked in Laguna Beach. A highly successful artist, Buck painted and did mostly residential stained glass commissions.

"Now sit down and tell your old man what's troublin' you, honey."

"Love, Dad. It's always love, isn't it?"

"Aw, honey, come here."

Amy sat beside him and allowed the tears to come.

*****

Jeb pulled up to the cabin just as Carmela was loading bags, buckets and a vacuum cleaner into one of the ranch trucks. "Hey, Carmela, you're fast."

"Ms. Morgan called and I wasn't busy. Hope it's okay for you."

"I'm sure it's great."

"Let me know if you need anything. The beds are made, and I put in a little food."

"That's great, thanks. Toby, the little guy, will have all his meals at the camp. This is just for sleeping."

"Good to have you back," she said, smiling as she hopped into the truck.

Jeb waved, then headed into the tiny house that had been his home for almost three years before he and Stacy moved in together. Adjacent to the farm, it and the four nearby cabins sat on a ridge affording the same spectacular valley views as did most high ground on Morgan's Run. Carmela and her husband, Raoul, lived in the biggest cabin, some of the other ranch workers in another, and two were vacant and currently used for storage.

Ghosts, he thought, walking through the tiny living room to the bedroom, which Carmela had spruced up with new bedspreads and a vase of flowers. She had opened the windows, and a gentle breeze ruffled new curtains. In the kitchen, he found the refrigerator stocked and a bowl of fresh fruit on the table. Not for the first time, he marveled at the generosity of his employers. *Will Toby feel as safe here as I do?* he mused, gazing out the kitchen window. *Guess we'll find out tonight.*

He walked out to his truck and grabbed the duffle with his bathing suit and towel. It also had a change of clothes. *Might as well settle in*, he thought. Once changed, he sat in one of the porch rockers, watching sheep grazing in a nearby field. He took a deep breath and sighed. *Home.* With Stacy gone, the apartment in town felt cold and empty, no longer the space where they had shared such good times. This felt like home, and Jeb wondered if he shouldn't move back permanently as Ben Senior had suggested. *One day at a time, buddy. One day at a time.*

Jeb leaned back and closed his eyes. When he woke, he was startled to see the time. He had slept for over an hour. Grabbing the towel, he hopped into the truck and headed over to camp. When he arrived, kids were already in the pool, each with an adult buddy. The children were laughing, shouting and squealing with delight in the gleaming new pool. He spied Ginger with Beth Morgan, while Ruthie helped a tall, dark-haired girl from her wheelchair to the pool steps.

"Hey, Jeb!"

Jeb turned to see Toby waving, with Andy, his counselor, pushing the wheelchair. "Hey, buddy!" He hurried over and relieved Andy, who went back for Pete, as Greg helped Dexter and Willy toward the pool. One of the farmhands paired up with Willy, and Greg assisted Dexter, although the nine-year-old was already protesting that he did not need help.

"Ready, buddy?" he asked, gazing down at Toby, who suddenly looked terrified. While he nodded at Jeb, his eyes told another story.

"We don't have to go in. We can watch tonight, wait'll you're ready."

Toby reached up his arms, and Jeb bent down, lifting him from the chair. "Never gone in a pool. Can't swim," he whispered.

"I tell you what. We'll sit here at the edge and we can dangle our feet. Would that be okay?"

Toby nodded, fingers clinging to Jeb's tee shirt.

They sat side by side at the pool's edge, Jeb holding tight to Toby's waist as they watched the others. The pool had been specially designed for handicapped children. At its deepest, it was four feet. Railings were everywhere, and there was a ramp for water chairs at one end. Two of the campers were in water chairs, splashing and laughing. "Those are cool," Jeb said to Ben as he cruised by, holding a pudgy little boy.

"Dillon got 'em for us. They're not his company's, but he had some connection. We've got six of them."

Jeb looked across the pool and spied Maggie holding Emma, her in-laws chatting beside them. As he watched, Maggie handed Emma to Ben Senior and reached up to take another camper, a tow-haired boy who appeared to be six or seven. She took him over to introduce to her daughter. So intent was he in watching his beautiful, amazing boss that he didn't see Amy and her dad until Spark spoke behind him.

"Wowee, what a pool!"

"Amazing, isn't it?" she said, her voice like the call of a siren.

When Jeb turned, his jaw dropped. Beside Spark, who was dressed in baggy swim trunks, Amy stood in a floral one-piece suit that, while modest, flattered every inch of her beautiful figure, revealing slender legs and the swell of her round, soft breasts. Fortunately, he was in baggy trunks, too, he thought as he felt himself grow hard.

"Hey, Mr. Barnes," Spark said, gazing down. "Who's this fine young fella?"

"Hello, sir. This is Toby Hooper. Toby, this is Amy's dad, Mr. Foster."

Jeb glanced at Amy, relieved to see her focused on Toby, her kind, gentle eyes smiling at him.

"Spark, son, remember? Everyone's goin' by first names here at camp so I certainly don't want to sound like an old fogey. So, no 'sirs' and no 'Mr. Fosters,' okay?"

"Hi, Toby," she said, sitting on the other side of him. "How's the water?"

"Good," he said shyly, leaning closer to Jeb.

Spark leaned down and patted his daughter's shoulder. "Honey, I'm gonna join the oldies, see if I'm needed, okay?"

"Okay," she said, suddenly feeling awkward. She smiled at Toby, then gazed out at the pool full of splashing swimmers. "Do you think anyone needs me to buddy up?"

"Looks like they're set. Lots of hands."

"Do you want to swim? I could sit with Toby."

"That's okay," he said, meeting her eyes for the first time. "I'm happy here with my buddy. Right?"

The child nodded. Amy noticed he held Jeb's forearm in a death grip and wondered if he had ever been in a pool or near the water.

As if reading her mind, Jeb said, "Toby's first time in a pool. We're takin' it slow."

"Good idea," she said, sharing a smile with Jeb.

"I'm surprised to see you here."

"Couldn't stay away. Pretty dull at the Lodge compared to this."

"How was your afternoon?"

"Quiet. I took a nap."

"Me, too," Toby said, grinning up at her.

Jeb knew from Andy that Toby had not yet been informed about their plan to have him move to the cabin. Maggie had decided Jeb should broach the subject. Amy's presence felt soothing, and he decided this was as good a time as any.

"Hey, buddy, how'd you like to share a cool cabin with me?"

Toby's jaw dropped. "I'm in the bunkhouse. Javelina Bunkhouse."

"Yup, and you'll still be with Dexter, Pete, and Willy most of the time, but we were thinking that with you wakin' up sometimes with bad dreams, everyone'd get more sleep this way."

"Don't want to."

Now Toby looked terrified. Jeb met Amy's eyes.

"I tell you what," she said. "After swimming, why don't you, Jeb, and I ride over to the cabin and check it out? Then we can talk some more. How does that sound?"

"Okay," he said softly, not looking at all enthusiastic about the idea.

*****

An hour later, they pulled up alongside the cabin, and Jeb lifted Toby from Amy's arms. They had dressed him, and Andy had slipped a duffle with some of his clothes and things into Jeb's truck. Amy and Jeb were still in their bathing suits. She had slipped a delicate lacy cover-up over hers, and he wore a damp tee shirt. They had decided not to bring his chair, as they were only stopping in before getting him back to the dining hall. As they stepped into the tiny cabin, she wondered if leaving the chair behind had been a mistake.

"What do ya think, buddy?" Jeb asked.

Toby shrugged, but when they took him into the bedroom, he perked up a little. "Cool. I've never had nice beds like this."

"They look pretty comfy," Jeb said, setting him down on one and sitting beside him.

Amy sat on the other, observing the two opposite her. Both looked like thet were on their first sleepover away from home. "Oh, they are comfy," she said, reaching out to pat the bedspread with both arms. "Wish I could stay here. Much nicer than the Lodge!"

Wish you could, too, Jeb thought, watching her lovely eyes dancing with warmth as she tried to reassure the frightened child. He longed to invite her to sit beside him, to feel her soft skin as they held hands.

They sat chatting for a few minutes until Jeb announced that it was time to get back to dinner. When they arrived back at camp, Amy said good-bye and joined her father as Jeb dropped Toby with Andy, who had his wheelchair waiting. "I'll be back soon, buddy," he said, ruffling Toby's curls and heading back to the truck. *This is gonna be a long night*, he thought, *and probably a long summer.*

CHAPTER 17

The first week of camp went by in a blur. The campers were happy, the staff busy, and the weather perfect for riding, swimming, and their many outdoor activities, including campfires and sing-alongs under the stars. Amy spent her mornings in the therapy room and most afternoons helping with activities, especially pool time. She tried to get back to the Lodge by dinner to be with her dad. When she saw Jeb, he looked like the walking dead from lack of sleep. Several times, she offered to spend the night at the cabin in his place, but so far he had refused.

After a rocky first night, Toby and Jeb settled in at the cabin. Every morning they rose bright and early to get Toby back in time for breakfast with his bunkhouse crew. They did not return until it was time for bed. Toby napped for several hours every afternoon in the bunkhouse and had clothes and supplies in both places. His nightmares continued, sometimes just one or two, other nights as many as a dozen. When Toby screamed, Jeb would reach over and pat his back. Sometimes that was enough, sometimes not. After watching his assistant sleepwalk through a work day, Harley ordered Jeb to go home to his apartment, and he stayed the night with Toby.

As Jeb closed his eyes in his own bed, their bed, he decided he would hold on to the apartment, at least for the summer. *Having an occasional good night's sleep sounds good to me,* he thought as he drifted off.

*****

Thursday morning, Amy and Toby had just completed an exercise session when Pam Joslin, the part-time social worker, came in. Pam's days were Monday, Tuesday, and Thursday. In her early thirties, she had chocolate curls cut in short bob, a turned-up nose and a compact, athletic figure. She wore shorts, a camp tee shirt, and flip-flops.

Amy waved to Joslin. "Hey, Pam, good morning!"

"Morning, you two. How's it going?"

"Great!" Toby said. "Can we paint today?"

Pam smiled, holding up a large canvas bag. "You betcha! I brought all my stuff."

"Wanta come with us, Amy?"

"I'd love to, sweetie, but I've got Sadie coming in, see?"

They turned to spy one of the woman counselors holding the door for a pretty eight-year-old, her blonde hair in two long braids, her thin legs in braces. She handled her crutches like a pro, but Amy knew that every step was painful for the brave little girl with MS.

Toby pushed out of Amy's lap and slid into his wheelchair. "Hi, Sadie!" he called as he maneuvered his chair across the room.

"He's a happy camper today," Pam said.

"Yes, he is. Had a pretty good night's sleep. Harley says he only woke once."

"I thought Jeb Barnes was staying with him."

"He is, but Harley ordered him to take a night off. Toby's crazy about both of them, so he didn't care."

"How's he doing with the braces?"

"Not much change, but he tried so hard this morning."

"You know that Lang Dillon's sister Rose works at the Heavers Clinic?"

"Where Emma Morgan had her spinal surgery? Yes, I heard that. There's been talk of having him looked at, but there are so many issues with Toby right now, they don't want to interrupt his opportunity to be a kid for a few weeks. He's never had that."

"No, he hasn't. Here's his handsome cabin mate now."

Amy followed Pam's gaze and saw Jeb step through the door. He smiled at her, then turned his full attention to the two children, grinning. "Hey, buddy! Hey, Sadie! What's up?"

Pam watched Amy's cheeks redden, her eyes watching his every move. *Hmm,* she thought. *Yet another woman to fall under Jeb Barnes's spell.* "He's certainly a charmer, isn't he?" she said.

Suddenly aware that Pam had spoken, Amy said, "Huh? Oh, yes."

"Now that Stacy's gone, every young woman in the Valley has her sights on him. They're just waiting a respectable time before pouncing."

"Oh? I mean, can we talk about Toby for a sec?" *Much safer than Jeb Barnes, whose smile turns my whole body to Jell-O!* "Have you got any suggestions for us? We've been having him nap every afternoon for at least an hour, usually two. That wouldn't affect the nightmares, would it?"

"I doubt it. He's four. Lots of four-year-olds still nap and need naps. The nightmares are most likely from events he doesn't even remember. Things that happened to him before he could talk."

"Poor little guy."

"Yes. I checked with Izzy last night. That hideous boyfriend of his mom's has been arrested for child molestation and pornography. Hopefully they can make the charges stick this time. The latest raid on his 'business' was pretty awful, I guess."

"Oh, Pam, will Toby ever recover from all that, do you think?"

"Time will tell. He desperately needs a stable, loving family, so I hope they succeed in severing his ties to Cora Hooper. They don't think he was molested by the boyfriend, but apparently this guy has quite a temper."

"Well, we'd better get cracking or we'll get backed up."

Pam crossed the room to the trio. When she reached them, Jeb nodded, excused himself, and headed toward Amy. "Good morning," he said, eyes meeting hers.

"Hi. You look better today."

He nodded shyly. "I have Harley to thank for that. Just wanted to let you know I'll be at the stables all day. In case Toby's looking for me, here's my cell number. I already told Andy and Greg." He handed her a small slip of paper.

Flustered by his touch, Amy said, "Thanks. He'll be fine. Seems to have slept pretty well last night."

"Yeah? That's good. Harley must have the magic touch."

As he turned and walked away, Amy wondered about Harley's touch. *Terrific as he is, Jeb Barnes is fragile and unsteady right now. Harley Langdon, on the other hand, appears steady as the Rock of Gibraltar. Much as he loves Jeb, maybe Toby feels safer with Harley.* She decided to run that thought by Pam and Maggie later.

CHAPTER 18

Thursday evening found Spark Foster dining with his dear friends at the big house, enjoying an informal meal of Carmela's enchiladas and salads. Joining them were Ben, Maggie, and their two children. Amy, Ruthie, Beth, and Lang were helping out at camp.

"How'd the farm trip go today?" Ben Senior asked his eldest.

"It was super!" Emma said, her mouth full of cornbread.

Her father smiled at her. "Someone enjoyed being the tour director. It couldn't have been better. Beth and Ruthie had the kids all over the place, feeding the goats, picking vegetables and fruits, and taking hay rides up and down the valley."

"That's quite an operation," Spark said. "Your daughters and Rodriquez really know what they're doing."

"Raoul's a good man," Leonora said. "He's been with us for, what? Carmela, how many years have you and Raoul worked on the ranch?"

The housekeeper smiled. "Next year will be my fiftieth. Raoul came a few years later."

As Carmela disappeared into the kitchen, Ben Senior said, "Before I met my Nora, I had a huge crush on Carmela."

"Who didn't?" his son said.

Leonora threw up her hands. "Oh, no, not this again. Spark, all my men have been in love with Carmela their entire lives."

"I can see why," Spark said, smiling wistfully.

"What'dya think, old buddy?" Ben Senior said, noticing his friend's expression. "What kind of trouble can you and I get into this weekend? Nora has a Cowbelles event, the kids are all camp-crazy, and Maggie's taking a break so I can't even babysit."

"I'm up for anything once I get my baby straightened out."

Maggie turned to him, eyes full of concern. "Is she okay? I thought she seemed a little distracted at pool time."

"We just heard from the property manager back home. Her renters want to move in next week, and she hasn't cleared out her things. She told them to throw everything away, but she doesn't mean it. She still hurting and doesn't want to bother with anything associated with that horse's you-know-what ex-boyfriend."

"What can we do to help, Spark?" Leonora asked.

"She's gotta go back, now, even though she claims she's not interested."

"This weekend?" Maggie asked.

"Yup. Someone's gotta do it. I rented a truck and am just waiting to book her flights. I don't want her to go alone. I was thinking I'd fly up with her. I can pack a box, but I'm 'fraid I'm not much help with the heavy lifting."

"You need muscle," his old friend said. "Young muscle."

"Why don't we send Jeb?" Leonora asked. "Good for him to get away. I'm sure Harley can spare him for the weekend, right, Maggie? Harley or Ruthie can bunk in with the child, or he can stay here."

Maggie gave her husband a look before saying, "I don't know, Leonora. It might be—"

"Nonsense. He and Amy are good buddies. Having him along will cheer her up, won't it, Spark?"

Spark thought back to his conversation with Amy earlier in the week. *Could be fine, could be disaster.* He liked Jeb Barnes and, more importantly, so did his daughter. *Maybe throwing them together isn't the worst thing in the world?* "Well, if Barnes is willing, I s'pose it'd be okay."

"*Willing* does not enter into it. Will one of you tell Jeb tonight?" she asked, looking from Ben to Maggie.

Maggie nodded. "I'll tell him after campfire."

"Good. I'll book the flights for late tomorrow," Spark said. "On second thought, I'll call and have the company jet come down."

"That's settled, then," Leonora said. "Let's have coffee inside, shall we?"

Maggie and Ben excused themselves and headed over to camp with the kids. As they strolled toward the campfire circle, Ben held the baby, and Emma skipped along beside her mother.

He leaned over and kissed the top of his wife's head. "Good luck with Jeb."

"I'll need it," she said, lacing her fingers through her husband's, thinking for the millionth time how lucky they were.

*****

"What're you, nuts, Mags? I can't leave for two days. We're so far behind at the stables, and that'll mean Harley'll have to be at the camp, plus stay with Toby at night."

"Ruthie can take a night. We'll manage."

"This is not a good idea," he said, blue eyes pleading with his boss. They stood at the edge of the clearing, the children's laughter and singing behind them.

She reached out and patted his arm. "Maybe not, but the elder Morgans volunteered you, so you're going."

"Why didn't you stop it?"

"Have you ever tried to stop Leonora Morgan from doing anything?"

"Maggie, come on!"

"I'm sorry, partner. It caught me off guard and I didn't know what to say. Then, something told me that it might be good for you, and maybe for Amy?"

"This is bullshit."

Maggie raised her hands in defeat. "Okay, okay, I'll call Leonora and say you can't go."

"After all they've done for me?"

"They'll understand."

"Yeah, right."

"That's the spirit!"

"How are we getting there?"

"Spark sent for his corporate jet."

Jeb shook his head. "This just keeps getting better and better."

"Night, partner," she called, but he had already stalked off.

*****

"No, no, no! I told you, Daddy, they can chuck everything on the sidewalk, throw it all away."

"What about the things from your mother?"

"I already packed them up, remember? They're in your basement."

"Not the furniture from Aunt Rosie or your grandfather. Those pieces are not going to Goodwill."

Amy thought about the antique cherry rocker, the Shaker tables, the beautiful china cupboard that her great-grandfather had made. Her father was right, of course. She could not throw them out. "But I can't leave now. They need me."

"It's all arranged. They've got you covered. The jet'll be here, refueled and ready, by three tomorrow, and I've got a truck waiting for you at the airport."

"Even if I were to go, I'd need help. I'm not sure who's around on such short notice to help me move."

"Got you covered there, too."

"Oh?"

"Mr. Barnes is coming with you."

"Excuse me?"

"All set. The Morgans arranged it."

"What are you, crazy? Didn't we talk about this last weekend?"

"Yes, and you told me you had agreed to be friends. What better person to take along than a new friend? No associations with the recent past. You need muscle, and that strong cowboy'll have everything in the truck before you can blink an eye."

"Has he agreed to this nonsense?"

"Yup."

"I don't believe you!"

"Maggie Morgan was gonna ask him tonight."

So that's what was up, she thought, remembering the two stepping away from the campfire. Jeb had not returned to the sing-along, except to whisk Toby away. Probably too horrified to face her!

"So his bosses have ordered him to help me?"

"Now, now, honey, it's not like that. He's happy to go."

"I'm sure."

"'Sides, you've both been workin' hard. Good to get away."

"Not for this!"

"Amy," he said, voice stern. "I don't ask much of you, darling. Do I?"

Oh, boy, here it comes, she thought. "No," she said softly.

"Well, I'm asking you to do this. Go up, pack up your things, close that chapter for good. Then, when we go back next month, you can make a fresh start."

"Fine, okay, I'll go! Night, Dad. See you in the morning." She kissed the top of his head and left his room before he could utter another word.

She's mad as a hornet, Spark thought. *That's good. Stay mad, darlin'. Maybe it'll keep the heartache at bay.*

CHAPTER 19

"Feel like I'm on the set of *Pretty Woman*," Jeb said, sitting opposite her in the small, beautifully appointed Foster Enterprises jet, trying not to let his libido run wild. If he kept his tone light and jocular, maybe he could pull off the next forty-eight hours without ravishing her. A petite brunette had brought them drinks, and they were halfway to Portland. The brunette was pretty, and definitely his type, but he couldn't take his eyes off his companion. She looked especially lovely today in a blue open-collared shirt and short beige skirt that showed off practically every inch of her legs. She had tossed her sandals aside as soon as they sat down and now had her legs tucked up underneath her.

"I'm surprised a cowboy like you has seen *Pretty Woman*."

"It's my sisters' favorite movie. They've watched it a gazillion times."

"This is my dad's life, not mine."

"Yeah, well, you look pretty comfy in that fancy leather seat."

"I've only been on the plane a few times. Dad rarely uses it for pleasure or personal use."

"Could've fooled me."

"Can we please have a truce? I'd rather not listen to your 'poor little rich girl' sarcasm. Let's just the packing done and get back, okay?"

"Yup."

She closed her eyes, shutting out the pain his words caused.

After several minutes of silence, he said, "Sorry, Amy," but she appeared to be asleep.

*****

"You must have a load of stuff," he said, glancing up at the large truck waiting for them at the airstrip.

"Not really, but Dad ordered it."

"Want me to drive?"

"That'd be wonderful," she said, smiling at him gratefully. *Concentrate on practical stuff and getting through the move,* she told herself. *If I avoid his beautiful sad eyes and do not touch him, I might just make it!*

Jeb came round to help her up, but Amy took a flying leap and was safe inside the cab before he reached the door. *Okay, super woman,* he thought, shutting the door behind her.

"What's the game plan?" he asked as she directed him out of the airport.

"I thought we'd head over to the house, survey the situation, then pick up my car and grab some dinner. You've never been to Portland, so I thought we could find a place down by the waterfront. I have a couple of favorites. Maybe we can pack some boxes when we get back?"

"Sounds good."

"And dinner's on me, Jeb. No arguments. Actually, it's on my dad, since I have his credit card."

"But—"

"No buts. You can be gallant sometime when we get back to Saguaro, if we're still speaking to each other."

"I bow to the queen."

"Ha, ha. Take a left up there."

*****

"Oh, my God, this place is amazing," he said, popping a bite of spicy clam and sausage into his mouth.

"This is my favorite restaurant in Portland," she said, savoring a bite of her salmon. "Everything's great."

Amy's house was in the Nob Hill section of Northwest Portland, but she had brought him to the Pearl District, to her favorite bistro.

"Can't wait for dessert," he sighed.

"Thank you, Jeb," she said softly, meeting his eyes.

"For?"

"For agreeing to come, to help me."

"Hey, when the bosses say jump, I say how high." He was horrified to see her face fall, the hazel eyes downcast. "Sorry, that didn't come out right. Happy to help. That's what I should've said."

"You don't need to pretend."

"Amy, listen. I'm a jerk. I say things without thinking. I've never been out of Arizona. I'm happy to be here, really." He met her eyes and for an instant lingered, lost in their depths.

"Okay, well…thanks," she said, deciding a change of subject was in order. "How do you think Toby's doing?"

"Great, good. He's a strong little guy. Wish the nightmares would go away. He seems to do better with Harley. Maybe he feels safer with him?"

"Harley's formidable, that's for sure. No one messes with him, do they?"

Jeb laughed. "Not if they want to live."

"But Toby loves you," she said, quietly.

"Not sure about that, but we're buddies."

"He does, Jeb. I watch you two together. He never takes his eyes off you."

Jeb felt a lump in his throat. "Hanging around with him has been as good for me as it is for him. The stable work ramps up in the next few weeks as we get ready for a pack trip, so I'll probably have less time. He seems to be settling in, though."

"Who's leading the trip?"

"Harley. It's only four people. A movie star and his family, Jackson Corey."

"Ooh, he's a hunk." *Although not nearly as gorgeous as you.*

"Is he? Anyway, they come every year, and they're good riders. Harley's taking one of the college kids 'cause Ben can't go."

"Do you ever go?"

"I have, a couple of times, but that's Harley's and Ben's territory. Technically, I work for Maggie, and she and I run the day-to-day at the stables, lessons, and pony camps."

"So that's all on you right now?"

He shrugged. "We all chip in. A well-oiled machine and blah, blah. They keep tryin' to get Robbie Morgan, Ben's brother, to come home and work the pack trips. That's pretty much what he does in Sedona."

"They're quite a crew, those Morgans, aren't they?"

He grinned, and Amy sighed, glad she was sitting or her knees might have buckled.

"Every one of them can charm the pants off any woman who comes within fifty feet."

"Is that so? I haven't seen them since I was a baby so I don't remember them. I'll look forward to observing them in action at the wedding."

"Good luck with that!"

"You'll be there, won't you?"

"Yup."

"Will your family be there?"

"My parents, yes. The Morgans were kind enough to include them since they've only met a few times."

"What do your parents do?"

"Dad's a professor at the U of Northern Arizona. Mom teaches second grade."

"What about your siblings? Is it just thebtwo sisters?"

"Yup, Catie and Les. They're in their thirties, both successful. Catie's a pediatrician, Les an attorney. Catie has the three kids who are the center of my parents' life, especially since the runt of the family has not turned out as they had hoped."

"Oh?"

"My dad wanted me to go to U of A He's a history professor and was pushing liberal arts, but I was good at math and wanted engineering. In the end, we fought so much, I chucked the whole thing and moved to Saguaro."

"Do you ever think about going back? To school, I mean?"

"Sometimes, but then I'd have to give up my black sheep identity."

"Is that so bad?"

Jeb shrugged, smiling at the waitress as she cleared his plate. The woman nearly swooned. "Maybe not. We've been doin' better lately. They were great after Stacy died. Couldn't have gotten through it without them."

Amy watched him down the rest of his beer, his hand shaking. "It must have been terrible."

"It was." He looked up and met her eyes, comforted by the warmth of her gaze. "But life goes on, doesn't it?"

"Yes," she said quietly as their desserts were placed in front of them.

*****

After a call to Ruthie to check on Toby, they spent several hours in the kitchen, then her study, packing boxes. Finally she declared, "Enough. I'm taking a hot shower and going to bed. The guest room's all made up, and there are clean towels in that bathroom. You okay?"

"Yup."

"Let's plan to go out to breakfast. Then I have to make a stop at the clinic. After that, we'll only have a few hours' work. The movers come at four."

"And?"

"We'll follow them to Goodwill, then Dad's. I'm storing everything in his barn."

"Sounds good," he said, leaning against the kitchen counter. He took a sip of water, and drops trickled down his chin. He wiped them away and found her staring at him. "You okay?"

"Absolutely," she said. "Good night." She hurried away on wobbly legs. *Oh, my God—another minute and I'd have jumped him!*

A scared rabbit, he thought, watching her disappear, wanting nothing more than to take her in his arms and kiss her fear away.

CHAPTER 20

They ate a huge breakfast at a small outdoor café, then Jeb bought newspapers. After a tour of the clinic, he told Amy he would wait by the truck for her. As he sat on a park bench in the shade of an enormous cottonwood tree, he felt like a man of leisure for the first time in his life. *When have I ever taken time to read a newspaper? Never, that's when,* he thought, leaning back, sipping his coffee.

Amy found Sharon White, her boss, on the phone. Sharon waved her in and hung up quickly. The tall, substantial blonde, with piercing gray eyes and angular features, hopped up and came to hug her. "Hey, girl. So glad to have you back."

"Just for a few minutes, I'm 'fraid. How's it going?"

"Busy, but we're holding on. Your patients miss you, and so do I. How's life in the wild West?"

"Wild, and busy. I'm volunteering at a summer camp for handicapped kids. It's been wonderful, challenging, exhausting, and fun."

"Oh? Would I know it?"

Amy shook her head. "Not unless you got a flyer. It's brand new. Emma's Dream. An amazing facility. I suspect once the word gets out, their waiting list will be a mile long. I'll bring back some materials for next summer."

"So? What're you doing here?"

"Had to move out of my house for the renters. Just stopping to pick up mail and a couple of my books on exercises for kids."

"I bet you're great with 'em."

"I don't know about that, but I do love it, Shar. It's making me rethink next steps."

White grimaced and covered her ears. "Don't tell me you're not coming back."

Amy laughed. "Don't worry. You can't get rid of me that easily. Good to see you, Boss."

"Same here. Got time for coffee?"

"Sorry, just got to grab things and get going. I've got a cowboy with me, helping me pack up. He's waiting on the street."

"Cowboy? That sounds promising."

"And you haven't even seen him?"

Sharon hopped up and ran to the window. Her view of the street and bench where Jeb sat was obscured by the tree. "Darn that cottonwood! Shall I come down and give him the once-over?"

"Please don't! I'll tell him you say hi."

Sharon White studied her colleague. She had watched Amy's heartache thanks to her narcissistic boyfriend. The woman standing before her was no longer, broken, and certainly not moping. There was color in her cheeks and a light in her eyes. Sharon smiled as she rose to hug her good-bye. "Well, next time you come, I want to be introduced. Promise?"

Amy started to say there wouldn't be a next time, but stopped and said "You got it" instead.

As she rifled through files and slipped the books she needed into a canvas bag, Amy wondered if she would be back. Of course she would return and not leave Sharon in the lurch, but would it only be temporary? Were her passion and heart already racing in other directions?

She was quiet on the ride back to the house. They began packing with little conversation, all business for the final push. They had grabbed sandwiches, chips, and drinks from a café and paused midday to eat. Around two, they were closing the last boxes when the door opened and a stranger walked in. Tall and slender, in jeans and a blue oxford shirt, his dark, straight hair fell across his forehead, over his brown eyes.

A glance at Amy's face and Jeb had no doubt of the stranger's identity.

Ryan crossed the room in three strides. "Hey, babe."

As he moved to hug her, Amy stepped back behind a stack of boxes. "Ryan, what are you doing here?"

"Heard you were in town. Thought I'd stop by."

"Who told you?"

"Come on, babe, you know Janice at the café has me on speed dial."

"Well, she shouldn't have called you, and you shouldn't be here. Please leave."

Houseman glanced around, eyes moving from Jeb to his surroundings. "You've been busy. Aren't you going to introduce me to your friend?"

"Jeb Barnes, this is Ryan Houseman, who is just leaving."

"Pleased to meet you," Ryan said, extending his hand to Jeb.

Jeb nodded, shook his hand, then said, "We're kind of busy, so maybe you'd better head out."

"Oh, you think so, do you, pal? This is *my* house, so if anyone should head out, it's you. I want to talk to Amy."

Jeb looked at Amy, who was now trembling and appeared to be trying hard to stem tears. Calmly he walked to her side. "Look, Houseman, I'm not your pal, this is not your house, and Amy has asked you to leave. So turn your snooty ass around and get the hell out."

"And who's going to make me?"

Ryan stepped forward, clearly ready for a fight. Before he could raise a fist, Jeb had his collar and practically lifted him off the floor, propelling him forward. In one swift motion, he threw him out the door onto the front stoop. Houseman collapsed in a heap, a look of surprise on his handsome face. "Why, you…"

"Don't even think about it," Jeb said. "You get up and I'll knock you flat. Now, I'm going to close this door, and we'd better not see or hear from you again, *comprende?*"

"Go to hell," Ryan said, rubbing one knee.

"You first. Good-bye, Mr. Houseman. I hope I never see you again."

Jeb closed the door and ran the deadbolt across. When he turned back, he found Amy crumpled in a heap in the corner of the room, sobbing. "Hey, hey, sweetheart," he said, squatting beside her, taking her into his arms. "He's not worth it. Guy's an asshole and not nearly good enough for you."

He held her until her sobs lessened and ceased. When she looked up, her puffy eyes and red cheeks nearly broke his heart. Without thinking, Jeb gently lifted her chin and kissed her, softly at first, then deeper, his tongue seeking hers as he parted her lips. Amy responded, turning to press herself against his warm, strong chest, the comfort of his touch enveloping her.

Jeb's hands slipped under her tee shirt and inched from her belly to her breasts, caressing, teasing, stroking through her thin, lacy bra, groaning as he felt her nipples harden with his touch. "Oh, Amy," he said, voice a husky whisper. "Tell me to stop or I can't promise what'll happen."

"Don't stop, please, Jeb," she whispered, her hand moving down to stroke his erection. "Please don't ever stop."

"Oh, geez, Amy."

He wondered if he could hold on. Her touch was literally driving him crazy. He removed her shirt and bra in one movement, his tee shirt quickly following. As she worked the buttons of his jeans, he took hold of hers and slipped them away, along with her panties.

"Darlin', you are so beautiful," he whispered, his lips trailing from her long, slender neck to her perfect breasts, licking, sucking, teasing with his tongue until she arched her back, begging him to take her. His fingers, then lips and tongue found her sweet, wet depths and Amy cried out in climax.

"Okay, darling, what's next?" Jeb whispered, voice husky. "You tell me. More?"

Amy reached down and took his head in her hands. "I want you inside me, Jeb. Deep, deep inside me. Now!"

He grinned and grabbed his jeans, extracting the condom he kept in his wallet and slipping it on as he parted her legs. "Your wish is my command, oh queen."

He grasped her buttocks, lifted her and thrust deep. *Oh, sweet Jesus,* he thought. *Not sure how long I can hold on!*

Amy matched him thrust for thrust as they moved as one, heedless of the hard, dusty floor, their rumpled clothes, or the boxes that surrounded them. All thought obliterated, they moved toward a thundering climax, each calling out,

"Amy!"

"Jeb!"

"Amy!"

"Jeb!"

Afterward, they lay entwined, the heat and fire of their lovemaking glowing around them. Slick, hot sweat trickled between their sated bodies as he softly kissed her eyelids, nose, and mouth.

"That was incredible, Amy. Thank you."

She smiled, hand caressing his strong chin. "My pleasure, cowboy," she whispered. *More pleasure than I ever thought possible!*

Jeb started to speak when they heard a knock at the door. She grabbed her watch lying on the floor beside them and read four o'clock. "Oh, shit, it's the moving guys!"

They broke apart, the agony not lost on either as they rifled around, grabbing clothes. "Hold on. We'll be right there!" she called.

Jeb grinned as he pulled on his jeans. "Think they'll guess what we were doing?"

"You're bad," she said, swatting his arm. "But, truth be told, I don't care!"

"Me, neither," he said, drawing her into his arms. "You're one amazing woman, Amy Foster." He kissed her softly.

"You, too, cowboy. Can we take up where we left off later?"

"Count me in," he said, the grin on his face wide enough to put the Cheshire Cat to shame.

CHAPTER 21

After loading the truck, their first stop was Goodwill. Then they swung back toward Nob Hill and drove into a neighborhood of very large homes and mansions. At the end of a shady boulevard, she turned in to a driveway and pulled up beside an enormous Victorian, all turrets, towers, and porches, its colors like the grand old painted ladies of San Francisco, in this case grays and blues with accents of red and green. Near the house was a four-car garage and beside it, a large old barn.

Jeb whistled, gazing around at the beautiful property.

"She was my mom's pride and joy," Amy said. "Come on, let's unload, and I'll give you a tour if you like."

It didn't take long for everything to be stored in the barn. The back anteroom appeared to have been cleared and swept in preparation. There were new drop cloths on the floor and more in a pile in case Amy wanted to cover furniture. She shook her head. "My dad must've called Ralph and had him get this ready. He's our handyman and caretaker. He and his wife live in the apartment above the garage, but they're supposed to be in Wyoming visiting their kids. I hope he didn't drag him back on my account."

"That's the last of it, miss," the taller of the two burly movers said as he and his partner set down the couch.

Spark had already paid them, but Amy gave each a tip and thanked them.

The three-story house was hot and musty, the AC turned off with the caretakers away. They wandered through each floor, with Amy pointing out meaningful places or things.

"Is this where you grew up?"

She nodded. "Moved here when I was three. Crazy, huh? A nine-bedroom house for my parents and my brother and me."

"It's amazing."

"My mom collected antiques. Before she got sick, she and her sister, Mabs, were always traveling around looking for finds. She wasn't above picking something up on the side of the road and refinishing, either. That chair was a roadside find, and so was that corner cupboard. When Mom dragged it home, it was painted puke yellow, but she stripped it and found tiger maple. Who would paint over that?"

"So, she did the work herself?"

Amy nodded. "That's how we got the barn. Dad got sick of her using sanders and Strypeeze in the garage, so he found the barn at a farm about sixty miles from here and had it disassembled and reassembled here. When she died, he had Ralph take away all traces of her workshop—tools, workbenches, everything. His way of grieving, I guess."

"They sound like they were happy."

"They were, very. Like Leonora and Ben Morgan, they were high school sweethearts. Ben can talk about his crush on Carmela, but I'll bet like Dad, he's never had eyes for another woman. Dad never dated anyone else but our mom." Amy gazed over and watched Jeb's eyes cloud with sadness. She smiled and reached out to touch his hand. "What do you say? Want to head back, shower, and go out to dinner? Believe or not, even after eating all day, I'm hungry again."

"Me, too," he said, warmth returning to his blue eyes.

As she locked the door, Amy had to admit to a slight disappointment. After their earlier lovemaking, she had assumed he would grab her as soon as they stepped into the empty house—but then, her parents' mansion home was enough to intimidate the most intrepid soul, extinguishing one's ardor with one glance at its cavernous rooms and sumptuous furnishings.

Still shaken from Ryan's visit, Amy was dreading stepping back into the house they had shared. Jeb drove the rattling truck, listening and responding to her directions, although it appeared he knew the way without her.

All business as they stepped into the living room, she turned to him. "Okay, you have towels still, right? I'll pop down and shower. Then we can get ready to go out."

Jeb reached out and took her hand. "Want some company?"

She gave him a smile he hoped was his alone. A warm, loving smile with a hint of flirtation in her expression. "What do you think, cowboy?"

They left a trail of clothes along the hallway. By the time they reached the shower, Jeb held her in his arms, cradling her naked body, her legs wrapped round his waist. Breathless, Amy slipped her arm around to the faucet., "Is this safe, do you think?" she said. It was her last rational thought.

Jeb's lips were everywhere, capturing her lips, nibbling at her ear, trailing hot kisses down her neck, his tongue circling her nipples, teasing till she cried out.

"You like?"

"What do you think?" Her arms circled his neck, hands running through his thick, tousled curls. "If you're not inside me in thirty seconds, I'm going to lose my mind."

"Well, now, we wouldn't want that, would we?" He pulled back long enough to meet her eyes, his face lit up with a peace and happiness she had not seen before. As he shed his jeans, he had grabbed one of the condoms he had purchased when they were out.

"Let me," she said, surprised at her own boldness. Finding his lips, she kissed him deeply as she slid her wet legs down to stand in front of him.

A surprised smile played across his face as Jeb handed her the foil-wrapped packet. "Your wish is my command, m'lady."

"I'm going to get you back for all that queen stuff, you know," she said, giving him a wicked smile. She took the condom, but instead of opening it, she ran her hands over his slick body until they reached his penis.

"Trying to kill me, huh?" he managed as she slid her hands round to his ass and knelt on the soft rubber mat on the shower floor, taking him in, her soft, full lips and tongue working their magic. "Oh, my God, Amy!" he cried, struggling to hold back.

With a smile, she released him, slipped the condom on, stood, reaching up, her slender arms round his shoulders. "What'dya say, cowboy?" she said, the words barely out before Jeb lifted her and thrust deeply, moving to the shower's inner wall, his strong hands cradling her ass, as Amy cried out.

"Oh!"

Their climax was swift and simultaneous, blotting all reason as their bodies moved in perfect harmony. When the last tremulous waves subsided, he gazed down, still holding her legs. "You okay?" he asked, his blue eyes soft and peaceful.

"More than okay," she whispered, smiling up at him, kissing him gently.

They stayed pressed against the shower wall for several moments, neither wanting to break apart. Finally she said, "Portland's been in a drought all summer. Maybe we'd better wash up and hop out?"

Reluctantly, he set her down and withdrew, his body aching for her warm depths the second Amy's feet hit the ground. They washed each other gently and carefully before stepping out and grabbing thick towels Amy had kept out from the move. They had left sheets and a mattress on the floor of his room and hers, but Jeb predicted they would not be needing his. Suddenly shy, he approached her and drew her into his arms. "Amy, I've never done anything like this."

It was on the tip of her tongue to ask what he meant. Amy gazed up, her heart aching at the sincerity in the blue-gray eyes. "Me neither. It was…it was… I can't find the right words. *Amazing* doesn't even begin to describe it."

He kissed the tip of her nose. "Nope, it doesn't."

Without a word, he lifted her and laid her on the mattress. "Be right back," he said, dashing out of the room.

As she watched the gorgeous ass disappear, Amy knew damn well where he was going. Sure enough, when he reappeared ten seconds later, she saw he had something in his hand. "What'cha got there, cowboy?"

Jeb blushed. "Thought we might need these later?" he said, opening his hand to reveal a long strip of condoms.

"What about right now?"

"That's what I was hoping you'd say. I'll just set these here." Jeb knelt on the mattress, gently spreading her legs. He leaned forward and captured her mouth, kissing her deeply. "There's nothing I want more than to make love to you, Amy Foster. Would that be okay?"

Her lovely hazel eyes widened as Amy nodded, then gave herself over to ecstasy she never imagined. Jeb's mouth everywhere as he moved down to her wetness. His fingers then tongue explored, caressed and thrust until he brought her to a blinding climax.

"Okay, darlin'?" he asked as he reached for a condom and slipped it on.

Unable to speak, she nodded again, her body on fire with longing. "Please, please," she said, guiding him as she wrapped her legs round him and arched up to take him inside. This time, they moved slowly, gently, in no hurry, exploring each sensation as their passion reached a crescendo.

"Oh, Jeb, oh, Jeb!"

"I'm here, sweetheart."

"Don't stop, don't stop."

"Never!"

After, they lay entwined, their bodies slick and suffused with heat. They shared a tender kiss before dozing off. When she woke, it was dark, and Amy studied his handsome sleeping face, the long lashes, strong chin, spattering of freckles across the bridge of his nose. *What have I done?* she thought, running her finger along his jawline before turning away. *Talk about jumping from the frying pan into the fire!* If leaving Ryan had been tough, how would she ever say good-bye to this amazing man who made her feel like she never had before? *What will I do when his libido takes a hike and he remembers he's in mourning?*

"Hey, you okay? You look as though you've just lost your best friend."

Kind eyes gazed at her, and Amy wondered how long he'd been awake. "Fine, never better." She kissed him softly. "What do you think? Some dinner?"

"Won't get an argument outta me."

He groaned as their bodies moved apart. As they dressed, Jeb wondered at Amy's haunted look, but decided that now was not the time to ask. *Until you're sure what in the hell you're doing, you'd damn well better be careful. All I know is that much as I loved her, Stacy never made me feel like Amy does. Not even close.*

CHAPTER 22

They walked from Amy's to a nearby bistro, where they shared mussels, a huge salad, and an excellent sauvignon blanc. As they sipped the crisp, cold wine, they shared hopes and dreams for the future, and Amy confessed hers had been turned upside down in her short time working with the campers at Emma's Dream.

"You know, I walked into work this morning and felt nothing. No excitement at being back, no joy or enthusiasm. I mean, I like my boss and she's been super to me, but thinking about going back was kind of depressing."

"So kids don't come to your clinic?"

"Not many. It's primarily a sports rehab clinic. We treat mostly athletes—adult athletes—and a small elderly clientele."

"So? What'll you do?"

She shrugged. "How about you? Do you see yourself working at Morgan's Run forever?"

He laughed. "Honestly? I love my work, but who knows? It's not exactly a career, is it?"

"What about going back to school?"

It was his turn to shrug. He gazed across the crowded dining room. "Now you sound like my parents."

"Sorry."

"No, it's okay. They have my best interests at heart. It's just…I don't want to go back till I know what I want to do. Engineering isn't it anymore, but neither is liberal arts. I guess time will tell. Mr. Morgan, Ben Senior, has told me many times that he'd help with tuition and make sure I had the time off I needed. As I've said, the Morgans are incredibly generous."

"Yes, they are. Dad and I are struggling with what to get Beth and Lang for a wedding present. Any ideas?"

He chuckled, leaning back, sipping his wine. Amy watched him. *You have no clue how sexy you are, Jeb Barnes.*

"I'm not the one to ask. I haven't a clue what I'll get 'em, but Maggie promised to give me some ideas."

They ambled home arm and arm, slightly tipsy, and fell into bed, making tender love before falling to sleep in each other's arms. When Jeb woke at dawn, Amy was still sleeping. The sun's rays fell across her lovely face, peaceful in slumber, and he recognized in that moment that he loved her. Stacy had been his buddy and he had loved her dearly, but this was different. Amy was a whole different species. A woman who had captured his heart and soul in ways he had never imagined possible. *Maybe I am dreaming,* he thought, watching her sleep. *Maybe I'll wake up and this will all be a strange, wonderful dream?*

Unsettled, he rose and dressed quickly, then walked to the café three blocks away. When he returned with muffins and coffee, she was up and dressed, all business, going from room to room, tidying up, stacking mattresses, closing the few remaining boxes. "Hey, good morning," she said, passing by with load destined for the truck.

"Got breakfast."

"Perfect. Let me drop these and I'll come sit."

When she returned, he had laid things on the one remaining table in the living room. Amy grabbed a folding chair and brought it closer, avoiding his eyes.

"Hey, Amy, what's wrong?" He tried to take her hand, but she pulled away and reached for a muffin.

"Nothing. We've got a lot to do and not much time. I told the pilot we'd be at the airfield at noon."

He came to sit beside her. "It's just…after last night, you seem different."

"Stressed is all. We can talk later, okay?"

After two bites of muffin, she grabbed her coffee and stood. "I'll keep going. Everything goes in the truck. We'll unload at Dad's, leave my car, and drop the truck at the airport."

Before he could speak, she disappeared. They worked for several hours without a word unless it related to packing and organization. When everything was loaded, Jeb hopped into the truck and followed her to her dad's. After several trips to the barn, and the truck was empty save for their small bags. Amy pulled her car into one of the garage stalls, closed the door, and hopped up beside him in the cab. "Okay, all set. We should make it with plenty of time."

Jeb sat staring straight ahead, making no move to start the truck.

"Jeb? I said we're all set. Let's go."

"I'm not moving till you tell me what's wrong."

"Nothing, I told you."

He sat, continuing to stare at Spark Foster's mansion.

"Jeb, I said, let's go!"

"Not until you tell me what I did."

"Nothing. You did nothing. You're an incredible guy."

"Then why won't you talk to me?"

"Because, because." She gazed down, wringing her hands as tears began to fall. "I'm a train wreck. I don't think I can do this."

"What about yesterday?"

"Yesterday was amazing."

"Then what's the problem? And by the way—we're both train wrecks, not just you."

"I thought, when I woke up this morning, I thought you'd…I thought you'd gone. I lost it completely. I can't do this. I can't—"

"Hey, hey," he said, leaning over, attempting to draw her into his arms.

"No, Jeb, no. Can you guarantee you won't walk out?"

"Amy."

"No, don't answer that. I know the answer. You can't. And I can't become involved, can't fall for someone. Not now. Maybe someday, but not today. Now, please drive or we're going to be late."

More than anything, Jeb wanted to reach over, pull her close, and say he would never leave her, but she was right. He couldn't. He turned the key and pulled the truck out of the drive for the short, silent trip to the airfield. The flight back to Tucson was equally silent. It was late afternoon when Jeb dropped her at the Lodge.

She hopped out, grabbed her bag, then turned to him. "Thank you for all your help."

"My pleasure. See you at the dining hall tonight?"

"Maybe. We'll see. I have a headache. May just eat a quiet dinner here and go to bed. See you tomorrow for sure. Night."

Not waiting for his reply, she turned and walked away, leaving Jeb numb and feeling more lonely than he had ever been.

CHAPTER 23

As he walked into the dining hall, Toby spied him and shouted, "Jeb, Jeb, over here!"

Jeb grinned, heading over to the far table where Toby sat with his counselors and bunkmates. "Hey, buddy. Hey, guys. How's it going? Miss me?"

"Yup!" Toby smiled through a mouthful of mashed potatoes.

"What'cha been up to?"

The group all began talking at once, regaling him with stories about riding, swimming, chair hiking, and even a picnic at the big house. Toby leaned toward him, whispering, "They got a mansion up there, you know."

"I know. Pretty amazing, huh?"

Harley strolled in and slung his leg over a chair at the end of the table. "'Bout time you got back, Barnes! How was the trip?"

"Fine," Jeb said, averting his gaze.

Yeah, right, Harley thought, watching his assistant turn green. *And I'm the Easter Bunny.* "You all set to bunk in with my buddy tonight?"

"Sure am. Gear's in the truck."

"Not that I don't like life with the coolest dude around," Harley said, winking at Toby "But, I gotta go out of town tonight. Be back Tuesday."

"No prob. We're all set," Jeb said, wondering about the sudden change in his boss's schedule. "Lemme grab some dinner, and I'll be back to eat with you guys."

Harley hopped up and followed him. "You okay?"

"Fine. Hey, Ruthie."

"Hey, Jeb. Welcome back. Where's Amy?"

Jeb noticed that Ruthie had positioned herself so as to give Harley the proverbial cold shoulder. "Eating with her dad, I think."

"Not unless she caught up with him two hours ago. My parents and Spark are having dinner at the Dillons' tonight. Spark wanted a tour of the winery."

Not eager to continue the conversation about Amy with his boss's eagle eye studying him, he turned to him. "Where're you off to, Harley?"

"Where he always is!" Ruthie said, turning heel and stomping off.

"What was that about?" Jeb asked.

Harley grinned. "She thinks I'm off to see a woman."

"Are you?"

"In a manner of speaking, but not the way she thinks."

"Then why don't you tell her?"

"Better this way," Harley said, patting his shoulder. "Gotta go. By the way, our man Toby's been sleeping better. Only one or two nightmares. He's so tired at the end of the day. That might be helping."

"Have a good trip, wherever you're going."

Another wolfish grin and Harley turned away, glancing at Ruthie helping to clear plates before he disappeared.

When did love get so damn complicated? Jeb thought, grabbing a tray and heading for the buffet.

*****

After discovering her father was out for the evening, Amy sat in her room, staring at the wall. Her strong, visceral reaction to finding Jeb gone that morning had scared her. Her fragile heart had splintered into pieces, the slow, painful healing ripped apart. *I will not get involved! I can't. I won't let anyone hurt me like that again!*

Finally, she stood, deciding she needed to get out. She refused to go to camp and bump into Jeb. *In the morning I'll be stronger.* She would drive into town.

She had developed a fondness for Gracie's fish and her Saguaro Salad. When she arrived, she spied Maggie and Emma in a back booth, the baby in a high chair beside his mother. Maggie waved and Emma turned, giving Amy a big smile.

"Hi, ladies, and Ben the third," she said. "Having a night out?"

Maggie laughed. "Something like that. Haven't seen much of my babies since camp opened, and their dad's on duty tonight. Join us. We just ordered. We can call Rosa back."

"I don't want to intrude on your precious time together."

"Nonsense. We'd be delighted, wouldn't we, Em?"

"Please, Amy," Emma said, tugging on her sleeve.

"Well, if you're sure?"

"Absolutely," Maggie said, smiling. "You can tell us all about your trip."

Amy blanched for an instant, then covered her distress with a forced laugh. "Scoot over, lady," she said to Emma.

Watching her, Maggie decided it was best to steer the conversation to other topics. As they enjoyed a delicious dinner, they chatted about the weekend activities at camp, Emma's riding progress, and the upcoming week.

"We missed you," Maggie said as they paid the check. "Toby'll be glad to see you. I don't know what we're going to do when you go home to Portland."

"I'm really grateful for this opportunity, Maggie. It's made me rethink my future completely. I love my colleagues at the Clinic, but I really love working with the kids, and think I may pursue other placements when I go home."

"You're really good with them. Emma's been doing the exercises you gave her, too, haven't you, Sweet Pea?"

"Yup! Mommy, can we get ice cream, please?"

Maggie smiled first at Amy, then down at her daughter's eager face. "Well, since you ate such a good dinner, I guess so. Care to come along to the Daily Scoop, Amy?"

"Hmm, I do love ice cream."

"Voted best in Arizona this year," Maggie said.

"It's super good!" Emma said, jumping up and down. "Come, Amy, please!"

"Well, super good and best in Arizona? How can I pass that up?"

They ordered small cones, which were gigantic, and strolled across to sit on benches in the park. After the ice cream disappeared, Amy and Emma headed over to the swings and slides while Maggie nursed the baby. As the two played, Maggie watched, marveling at her daughter's progress and at the gentle way Amy had with her. She was relieved to see Amy smiling, her mood lightened since she'd first come into Gracie's.

Finally, they walked back to their cars, and Amy helped strap Emma's seat belt. Once the children were in, the two women embraced.

"Thank you, Maggie. I needed this."

"It was fun. Hope you're okay?"

"Getting there, thanks. Good night."

As Amy headed toward her car, Maggie phoned her husband, letting him know they were headed his way. Earlier, he had asked her to stop by so he could kiss the kids good night.

*****

Ben Morgan was waiting at the camp gates when Maggie drove in. He waved and she pulled over. "How's it going?" she asked as he leaned over to kiss her.

"Great, but I miss you guys."

"Hi, Daddy! We ate at Gracie's and had ice cream! Amy came and played with me, too."

"Well, aren't you the lucky duck?" he said, reaching in to ruffle her curls. "Wish I'd been there."

He gave Emma a kiss, then went round to kiss the baby before heading back to his wife. "So, you bumped into Amy?"

Maggie nodded.

"I was surprised not to see her here tonight."

"She seemed a little off."

"So did he. Looked frayed around the edges and had almost nothing to say about the weekend. Harley thinks there's trouble in Paradise, but he should talk. He and my sister are barely speaking."

"And it's all his doing for being so secretive about where he's going. He's driving her crazy. Do you know what he's up to?"

"I'm giving them all a wide berth, my love. So glad I'm out of the dating scene." He leaned down and kissed her deeply. "I'll try to get home in a few hours."

Breathless, Maggie reached out and stroked his chin. "Okay, okay, Mr. Evasive. I'll wheedle it out of Harley eventually."

"Good luck with that."

"I'm worried about Jeb."

"He's fine, Mags. Now take our kids home so I can get back to work." He looked back at Emma. "See you later, alligator."

"After while, crocodile."

"Have fun with the kids," she said. "See you in a bit."

As Maggie drove off, Ben Morgan turned away. *I'm the luckiest man alive*, he thought, heading back to help with evening activities. *Didn't have the heart to tell Mags that Jeb looks like death warmed over, but he's a big boy. He'll survive. Whatever happened in Portland, I don't want to know about it!*

CHAPTER 24

Maggie kissed Ben, who was staying home with the kids for a few hours. "Thanks," she said, arms round his neck. "I won't be long. Just want to check in at the barn, then camp."

"No problemo," he said, winking at his daughter. "Emma and I are going to take Sunny out, that is, if our son is happy in the carrier."

Maggie laughed. "Good luck with that. He's been feeling his oats lately, and I'm thinking the front carrier's too restrictive. I was going to ask Lang about backpacks. I know Rambler Sports makes them."

"And I'm sure your future brother-in-law will give you such a deal."

Maggie swatted him. "I'm not looking for a deal, just advice."

"Okay, if you say so, gorgeous wife of mine."

"Be back soon."

"Then what? You staying here the rest of the day?"

"Most of it. Dad's coming at one, just for a little while so I can give a few lessons, but otherwise I'm here. We three'll be at pool time later. I was thinking we might all have dinner at camp?"

"Works for me." He patted her bottom affectionately as she grabbed her bag, kissed both kids, and headed out.

She found Jeb sitting in the shade behind the barn, eating an egg sandwich and sipping coffee. "Morning, partner," she said. "Okay if I join you?"

"Hey, Mags. Sure. Just taking a few minutes."

"How was Toby's night?"

"Pretty good. A couple of nightmares, not bad. He went right back to sleep. I think he feels safer with Harley, though."

"I doubt that. He's settling in, that's all. That's what the therapist told us Friday. New situations throw him off."

"Poor little guy. Have you heard anything about his status—with the mom, I mean?"

"Not yet. She's apparently coming to Parents' Day next weekend."

"Is that a good idea?"

"Don't know, but it's her right. She's allowed supervised visitations."

"You know, my parents drive me crazy sometimes, but I can't imagine life without them. Can't imagine growing up like Toby."

"I know. He deserves a loving home, and I am praying Izzy finds a way to make that possible. How are you doing?"

Jeb stared over at his boss, knowing she'd probably heard something from her husband. Despite the fact that he'd always carried a secret torch for Maggie, she was really more like a big sister. "Fine."

"How was Portland?"

"Have you talked to Amy?"

"She had dinner with the kids and me last night, but we didn't discuss details. She said 'fine' too, but she didn't seem fine, and neither do you."

"The Fosters are filthy rich, that's for sure. You should see Spark's house."

"And?"

"And, we packed everything up, had a brief visit from her asshole boyfriend, had a couple of meals, and came home. End of story."

"How was that, with the boyfriend?"

"Really upset Amy, but he didn't stay long. He's a preppy prick. You know the type. Thinks he's God's gift to the world."

"What about the rest of the time? Did you have some fun?"

"You're not gonna give up, are you?"

Maggie smiled. "Probably not."

"Some of the time was awesome, Mags. I felt…I mean, it was…without going into details…I'll just say there were incredible highs and then some lows. She's an amazing person and we really connected. Unfortunately, we ended on a low and were barely speaking when we got back."

"Oh?"

"Do you mind if we drop this now, Boss? I know you mean well and you're worried, but I'm fine, really. Maybe when the dust settles we'll have time to figure out what happened. She still really gun-shy, and so am I."

"Of course," she said, patting his shoulder. "Just wanted you to know I'm here, partner."

"Thanks, Mags."

"I'm heading over to camp now, unless you need me here? Ben's staying home for the morning, so I have some time."

"All set. Gonna get the kids started and work with them for a while. Harley told me you're coming over for lessons. You sure? I could do 'em."

"We've got five scheduled, plus the camp riders. You need me with Harley away. See you around one-fifteen, okay?"

As his boss drove off, Jeb pulled out his cell phone, intending to call Amy and ask to meet for lunch or dinner, but then he reconsidered. Maybe they needed time.

*****

As Maggie drove by the big house, Beth Morgan was just leaving. The sisters-in-law had barely seen each other since the camp opened. They each pulled over and hopped out.

"Hey, stranger," Maggie said, hugging her.

"How's it going?"

"Busy. Haven't seen you since the farm visit, and that was a blur."

Beth laughed. "Really fun, though. We'll be more prepared for the next crew."

"I can't believe we'll be saying good-bye to most of these guys this Saturday and welcoming a whole new batch."

"Is little Toby the only one staying on?"

"No, there are a couple more, but they're older. He'll have a whole new bunkhouse crew, but he's pretty easygoing except at night."

"Wish I could get over more than I have, but it's our busiest time, and Ruthie is in heaven over there."

"Don't apologize. We have tons of help. I know the farm's crazy busy *and* you're planning a wedding. How's it going, anyway?"

Beth gave her a rueful smile. "You know Leonora. I barely get a word in edgewise. She and Carmela have it all under control, and Martha Dillon and her crew are doing the rehearsal dinner at the winery. As long as Lang and I show up, we should be all set."

Maggie laughed. "Speaking from experience, surrender is your only option. I'm terrible at that stuff and you know, once Ben and I gave her the go ahead, it was fun. Not having to stress about a million details was such a gift. We actually got to enjoy our wedding."

"It was a beautiful wedding."

"Yours will be too," Maggie said, squeezing her hand. "Ruthie, Emma, and I are looking forward to hosting the shower! So much fun! How's your dress coming along?"

"Predictably, Mother's having a fit that it's coming from Gabriela's," Beth said, referring to a local dress shop. "But I love it. Had the last fitting Saturday. It's hanging in my closet right now."

"It's a gorgeous dress. Can't wait to see you walk down the aisle. Lang will be stunned."

"I hope not! He still has to speak to say our vows."

"Speaking of Lang, where's he today?"

"At the moment, I think he's at the winery, but he told me he was coming over to help at camp during the riding. Do you need him? He almost always answers his cell."

"No, just wondering if Rambler Sports carries baby backpacks."

"I want to say I've seen them in one of the catalogues. You know they have that line of Rambler Kids."

"Oh, dear—kids—I'm running late. Gotta get over to camp. So good to see you, Beth. You look so happy."

"I am. Lang's terrific and very good to me. I'm very lucky."

"You both are. Let's find a time for a girls' meal soon, okay?"

"I'd love that. Thanks, Maggie."

"And let me know if there are wedding details I can help with, promise?"

"Will do," Beth said, hopping into her truck. *If we're half as happy as you and my big brother, we'll be fortunate indeed*, she thought, watching her lovely sister-in-law drive away.

Chapter 25

The second week of camp flew by as they prepared for Parents' Day and saying good-bye to most of the children. While the first session had begun on a Saturday, they would welcome the new campers Sunday, allowing them time to straighten, clean, and prepare after the first group's departure. They had a special lunch and closing activities planned, including a riding demonstration for parents. This meant all hands on deck Saturday.

Toby's night terrors had decreased, and he had slept straight through the night twice. He knew his mother was coming to visit and seemed happy about it, but as the weekend approached, he grew agitated and out of sorts. Pam Joslin, the social worker, could get nothing out of him, but suggested that someone stay nearby on Saturday during the mom's visit.

Amy and Jeb, while cordial, interacted as little as possible until Thursday, when he caught her at the end of pool time. He had come from the stables after a full afternoon of lessons, mostly with campers preparing for Saturday's exhibition. After making sure all campers were with counselors, she had gathered her things, wrapped a towel round her waist, and was headed to the car. Spark had gone off with Ben Senior to look at land, so she had the white whale. As she grabbed hold of the door handle, he called, "Hey, Amy, wait up a minute."

She turned to see the man she adored approaching, his handsome, tanned face smeared with trail dust. "Hi."

As he neared the car, he removed his hat. With his hair matted to his head, the angry scar on his forehead was more prominent than usual. "Sorry, I'm pretty filthy, but I wanted to ask you something."

"Oh?"

"I wondered if you were busy tonight. As you know, the kids are watching a movie, so there are plenty of helpers till bedtime. Harley's stayin' with Toby tonight, so I'm free. I mean, Amy, I feel bad about what happened last weekend and thought it might be good to clear the air? I just thought maybe you'd like to have dinner."

Amy knew her dad was going to the Morgans' club for dinner. They had asked her, and she'd declined in favor of a quiet dinner at the Lodge. She opened her mouth to say no, but instead heard herself say, "Okay, that would be fine."

His eyes widened in surprise. "Really?" He had been certain she would turn him down.

"Really."

"Great, well, okay. I'll head home and shower. Pick you up at six-thirty?"

"Okay, I'll be ready. Nothing fancy, right?"

"I was thinking Gracie's, or we could try the Bulldog. They have a new cook, and their menu's expanded. Have you been there?"

"No, not yet."

"It's a saloon. Mostly a tourist hangout. Used to be just wings and nachos, but the owner's trying to lure us locals in."

"Sounds perfect to this tourist."

"That's not what I meant. I just meant—"

Her eyes lit up, and she gave him one of her beautiful smiles. "I'm kidding, Jeb. See you in an hour."

*****

When he pulled up to the Lodge, she was waiting on a stone bench in the shade of the front archway. As she waved and stepped into the evening light, she literally took his breath away. She wore a pale green sleeveless dress. Its bodice hugged her perfect breasts and the skirt hem, well above her knees, showed off her lovely legs. "You look amazing." He held the door open as she hopped into the truck, the scent of wild honeysuckle surrounding him.

"You don't look bad yourself," she said. His spicy aftershave was almost intoxicating. Oh, how she had missed his nearness, his touch, his warmth! Here was her cowboy, clean jeans, blue collared shirt, and that smile that made her weak at the knees.

As they walked into the Bulldog a short time later, every male in the place turned to watch the beautiful stranger stroll by. Jeb was relieved to see no one he knew except the bartender and owner, Russ Keeler. He nodded to the burly man as he led Amy to a quiet booth. A few minutes later, Keeler appeared. "Hey, Barnes. What can I get you and your lovely lady?"

"Amy Foster, this is Russ Keeler. He owns the Bulldog."

"My waitress is out doing an errand. We're out of sub rolls, so she's made an emergency run to the market. If we get busy, I might have to call on you two to help out."

"Happy to help," Jeb said, grinning. "What do you want to drink, Amy?"

"Beer? What've you got on tap?"

"What haven't we? You like a dark beer, light, ale, lager?"

She laughed. "I wouldn't know one from the other, but I'd say darker, but not stout."

"We have a great local brew from the microbrewery in Prescott. It's called Desert Amber. One of my favorites."

"That sounds perfect."

"Make that two," Jeb said, taking the menus from Keeler and passing one to her.

"Nice man," she said as Keeler disappeared.

"Russ is great. Lost his wife two years ago. I've appreciated talkin' to him this past month."

"That must have been helpful," she said quietly, gazing down to consult her menu.

When Russ returned with their beers, they both ordered the Bulldog Burger, which their host proclaimed to be "best thing on the menu," then disappeared. The bar was getting crowded, and his waitress was still nowhere in sight.

"So, how's your week gone?" she asked, sipping the delicious dark beer.

"Good. Busy. As you know, Toby's been sleeping better, so I'm not goin' around like the walking dead. Ruthie offered to stay with him last night, but I said no, 'cause he's been a little tense with his mom coming. I actually think he's calmer with Harley, which is why he's stayin' tonight. One of us is going to make sure we're nearby by Saturday while she's here."

"I'll try too, but I agree, I think he feels safer with you big, strong guys. Speaking of Harley, it's been such a weird week. What's up with him and Ruthie? She practically snaps his head off every time they're around each other."

Jeb raised his hands in mock surrender. "Don't ask me. They have a weird dance goin' on. Have had for years. She's had a crush on him since she was about ten, and he's a mystery man. No one knows what he does when he goes away, and she's convinced it's to see other women."

"Why doesn't she or someone ask him?"

"My boss is a master of evasion. If anyone knows the story, it's Ben Morgan. They've been friends forever. But if Ben knows, he's not sayin'. I don't even think he's confided in Maggie."

"That's odd, don't you think?" she said, relieved that they were talking about someone else's love life instead of their own.

He grinned, taking a sip of beer, the foam lingering on his lips for a second. "Hey, I'm just a cowboy. What do I know?"

They talked about camp, Toby, and other safe topics as they enjoyed their huge Bulldog Burgers and curly sweet potato fries. For a little person, Amy could sure eat, he mused, watching her savor the last of her burger.

"That was the most amazing burger I've ever eaten," she said, wiping sauce from her chin.

"Better tell Russ. Wanta head out, take a walk round town, get ice cream or something?"

"Much as I love Daily Scoop's Mountain Mash, I couldn't eat another bite, but a walk would be great. Preferably a long one to walk off this dinner."

Waving away Amy's offers to split the check, Jeb headed to the bar to settle up with Russ. As she waited in the entryway, she marveled at the beautiful black-and-white photos of rodeo cowboys astride gorgeous horses, the animals' backs arched as their riders hung on for dear life. As she gazed from photo to photo, she spied a familiar face. "I've seen this man," she said to Jeb as he came up behind her.

"Sure have. It's Ned Williams, Maggie's dad. Best wrangler this valley's ever produced. Retired now, but all the young guys round here idolized him. Still do. You know this guy, too," Jeb said, pointing to a photo of a young Harley Langdon.

"Harley! Does he still ride in rodeos?"

"Not around here, but who can say what he does when he goes on his mystery trips? Ready?"

They strolled down the street to the edge of town. "There's a pretty flat trail that circles round and comes back near the Bulldog," Jeb said. "Think your footwear can handle it?"

"Thankfully I wore these, not heels," she said, swinging one leg out in front of her to show off her sandals.

They started down the path packed with hard red clay, ambling along in companionable silence. Jeb had so much to say, but didn't want to break the spell. It felt good to walk side-by-side, occasionally touching shoulders or the backs of their hands. Just being near her felt peaceful and warm. He was afraid speaking might spook her.

About halfway around the circle, she paused and reached to take his hand. "Jeb, I'm really sorry about last Sunday. I shouldn't have reacted like that."

"I wasn't sure what I'd done."

"You did nothing. You were great to me all weekend. You're a loving, kind man who treated me like a queen."

"I'm sorry about the queen joke."

"Don't be. I like it."

"Well, I'm glad we're talking. I haven't been the most easy person the past month."

"You've been amazing. It's me. When I woke up and you were gone, it was like Ryan telling me I was worthless and boring all over again."

"The guy's an asshole. You couldn't be boring or worthless if you tried. Amy, look at me. You know that, don't you?"

She gazed into his blue eyes. "Some of the time."

His rough hands moved to cup her chin. "Well, believe it all the time, sweetheart."

"You sound like my dad."

"That's because it's the truth, Amy. You are the most incredible woman I've ever met, and that includes Stacy." He kissed her softly.

"You don't have to say that," she said, tears snaking down her pale cheeks.

"But, it's true. I want you to know that I will always be your friend, and you can call me anytime. I'm just not sure I can give more right now, and you deserve more, so much more. Part of what's ripping me up is guilt for falling so hard for you when Stacy's only been gone a little over a month. It seems wrong, and I feel like a world-class shit."

"Well, you're not. So let's make a pact not to beat ourselves up anymore, okay?" She extended her hand.

He took it gently. "Deal."

Holding hands, they continued down the path as the setting sun turned the sky crimson. When they reached the car, she turned to him. "I'm glad we did this."

"Me, too," he said, kissing her forehead, afraid to go further. More than anything, he longed to draw her close to kiss her deeply and make love to her, showing her how he felt, but he let her go, opened the door, and she slipped in.

CHAPTER 26

The night before Parents' Day, Toby woke every half hour, screaming, so he and Jeb were both exhausted Saturday morning. Convinced he knew the reason for the child's nocturnal distress, Jeb resolved that he would not leave Toby's side until Cora Hooper left camp.

Even at dawn, the sun was scorching, the heat oppressive. After cleaning stalls and checking on the horses, Jeb joined the rest of them at camp. Carmela was staying with the baby, and Emma came to camp for the day with her parents. She and Sunny would be riding in the exhibition, along with most of the campers.

Parents and caregivers began arriving midmorning. They had been invited for lunch, and it appeared that most had taken them up on the invitation. Johnny and his crew had been working since the middle of the night to prepare for the day's meals. After this busy day, they looked forward to a night off as the three remaining campers, Toby and two older boys, would eat with the Morgans. The counselors also had the night off, and Rip, one of the college kids helping at the stables, was staying with the older boys. Either Jeb or Ruthie would be in the cabin with Toby.

The departing campers packed after breakfast, and all the luggage was stacked outside each bunkhouse. The morning's activities included games and exercises organized by Amy, Karen, the massage therapist, and social worker Pam Joslin. Early arrivals loaded their children's belongings in vehicles, then came to watch. It was during the last half hour of games when Amy first saw Cora Hooper.

As the children competed in a modified version of egg and spoon races, a couple approached the gathering. The woman's eyes scanned the children's faces, and when she spied Toby, she waved, endeavoring to catch his attention. When he spied his mother, he dropped his egg on the soft earthen floor of the camp circle and his face paled. Even from a distance, Amy could see he was trembling. Jeb was nowhere to be seen, so she whispered to Karen, asking her to take over. As she headed toward Toby, Amy pulled out her cell and texted Jeb. She reached Toby's chair at the same moment as his mother and her companion.

"Hi, baby," the woman said, stooping to hug him.

Toby returned her embrace but cowered when the man stepped closer. "There's my main man," he said, but Amy noticed he did not try to come closer or hug the child.

Where the hell is Jeb? "Hello, you must be Ms. Hooper."

"That's right."

Cora Hooper's complexion was gray, her eyes, rheumy, and her shoulder-length blond hair hung limp and dirty. Her shirt and baggy capri pants hung on her thin frame. When she opened her mouth to speak, Amy saw that half her teeth were missing. *Meth mouth.* Probably in her twenties, Cora Hooper looked sixty. *She was once quite beautiful,* Amy thought, glimpsing vestiges of Toby's delicate features in the lines of her face. Her companion was short and solidly built, tattoos covering his arms and neck. His head was shaved, and he wore a sleeveless gray wife beater, faded jeans, and work boots.

"I'm Amy Foster, one of the part-time physical therapists. I've been working with your son."

She extended her hand to Cora, who ignored it, then to the man, who gave her a firm handshake. "Butch Reynolds. Thanks for taking care of the little guy."

Amy felt Toby's fingers digging into her left forearm. "We're just finishing up the games, if you two would like to take a seat over there and watch?"

At first, she thought Cora might argue, but she allowed Butch to lead her to two empty chairs along the edge of the group. As they moved away, Amy turned to Toby, whose eyes were filled with tears. She stooped beside his chair, blocking his mother and Butch's view.

"Hey, sweetie, what's wrong?"

"Don't let them take me, Amy! I wanta stay with you! Please!"

"Don't worry, sweetheart. You're not going anywhere. You're here for the whole summer, remember?"

"But after, I don't wanta go. Please don't make me."

At that moment, she spied Jeb and waved. He quickly crossed the distance between them. One look at Toby told him the whole story.

"Hey, buddy, sorry I missed your games. Everything okay?"

Toby nodded bravely, and Amy's heart broke for the frightened child. "Just gotta talk to Jeb for one sec, okay, sweetie? Be right back."

She led him a short distance away, still staying between Toby and his mother. "They're over there, near the water jugs."

"I saw them. Don't worry, I won't leave his side until they leave. Sorry I didn't get here earlier. We just finished bringing the horses over."

"Jeb, he's scared to death."

"I saw."

"I want to call Izzy. If that's the guy who threw him down the stairs, he shouldn't be here."

"Go. I've got this. Don't worry, there are plenty of people to back me up. I'll take him to lunch after this."

Gratefully, Amy squeezed Jeb's arm, patted Toby's shoulder, and headed for the office. She found Izzy Winkler's cell number, punched it in, relieved to hear the social worker's voice. "Hey, Amy, what's up?"

"It's Parents' Day, and Cora Hooper's here."

"Oh, Lord, how'd that happen? She called last week and I told her Toby was at camp, but didn't tell her where. The office staff must've spilled the beans. It's her right, so I guess we have to let her. She gets two hours of supervised visitation a week. Try not to leave them alone, okay? Wish I could get up there, but I've got two major crises today."

"Izzy, Cora's not the only issue. There's a man with her, Butch Reynolds, and he—"

"Oh, my God, call the police, now. He's not supposed to come near Toby. There's a restraining order. Want me to call them?"

"No, we can handle it, Izzy. We've got a camp full of strong cowboys. They won't let him near Toby."

"Amy, I would strongly urge you to call the police. Butch rarely goes anywhere without a gun."

"Okay, thanks, Izzy. I'd better hang up."

"Please call when they leave and he's safe, okay?"

"Will do."

Amy hung up, stepped out into the sunlight, and headed toward the corrals, where she was relieved to find Ben Morgan. She quickly told him what was happening and he nodded, calling to Harley. "I saw them come in. This is the kids' day so I don't want to spoil it with the police all over the place. We'll search the car, then shake him down, quietly. If he's carrying, we'll disarm him and keep him away from Toby. If things get worse, I have Sheriff Boone on my speed dial."

Harley and Ben searched the car, where they found two guns, several bags of cocaine, and a large hunting knife. They took all the weapons and the drugs to the office, locked them in the safe, then sauntered up to stand behind Reynolds and Hooper. When the games ended and the children and counselors headed for the dining hall, Ben Morgan stepped forward. "Ms. Hooper, Mr. Reynolds, Ben Morgan, one of the camp directors."

Cora Hooper grunted, keeping her mouth shut, but Reynolds came forward to shake his hand. As he did, Harley reached round and pulled a pistol from the back of his jeans. Before the man could move, he had patted down his legs, then stepped back.

"What the hell?"

Ben stepped between Harley and Reynolds. "We don't allow guns on the ranch, much less here at a camp for children. We'll hold on to this and the two you had in your car, plus the drugs."

"You fuckin' searched our car?"

Raoul and two of his men now stood at Ben's side, ready to pounce should Reynolds so much as flinch.

"Who the hell are they, the posse?"

"No, but you so much as sneeze and Sheriff Boone and his posse will be here to cart you away. This is the kids' day, or I'd have already called them since you've violated your restraining order."

"He's with me," she croaked, waving a finger at Ben and Harley. "Who the hell do you think you are?"

Ignoring her, Ben turned to Reynolds. "Now this is the way it's gonna go. You're gonna go sit in your car until Ms. Hooper is ready to leave. You move from the car, I call the cops, *comprende*?"

"It's fuckin' two hundred degrees out. I'll roast."

"There are some nice shady spots near the barn. I suggest you park there and wait. If you so much as move an inch, my guys'll alert me and I'll call Sheriff Boone. Now get going. Ms. Hooper, you're free to sit with Toby at lunch."

"If Butch can't come, I'm outta here."

"Suit yourself," Ben said as Harley came to stand beside him.

"No, Corie, go sit with Toby. We wanta make him feel easy, so when he comes home he'll be ready." He gave her the eye, and she nodded.

"Okay, but then I'm gone, and we want our stuff back."

"This way to lunch, Ms. Hooper," Harley said, gesturing to his right. "I'll help you find Toby while Ben and Raoul escort Butch here to his car."

"Assholes," she muttered, but she allowed herself to be led to the dining hall.

CHAPTER 27

Cora Hooper barely touched her lunch, and neither did her son. Toby clung to Jeb and refused to look at his mother throughout the meal. Occasionally, she made an attempt to engage him in conversation, but if he answered at all, it was with a nod or shake of his head. Finally, she gave up and gazed around the room, a morose look on her face. During dessert, Maggie came by with Emma to say hello to parents and campers.

"You must be Toby's mom," she said, smiling warmly. "I see the resemblance. So great that you could join us."

Hooper nodded. "Thanks. Nice camp you got here."

"Toby is one of our first campers, so he and his friends are helping us to make this the best camp ever, huh, Toby?"

The child gave her a shy smile while clinging to Jeb, who gave his boss a look.

"This is my daughter, Emma," Maggie said. "We named the camp for her."

"Lucky girl."

"Yes, she is. She was in a wheelchair until a little over a year ago. An operation changed her life and ours."

"Are you ready to ride, Toby?" Emma asked. "I'm goin' out now to get Sunny ready."

"Yup," he said, giving her a wide grin.

"Wait'll you see him. He's great," Emma said, smiling at Cora Hooper.

"I'll bet. Lookin' forward to it."

As the group trickled out of the dining hall and headed for the corrals, a voice called to Jeb. He turned to see his parents coming toward them. "Hey, Mom, Dad. Didn't expect you so early."

His mother smiled, first at him, then at Toby. "We wanted to see all these amazing riders."

"Mom, Dad, this is Toby Hooper and his mom, Cora."

"Pleased to meet you," Jake Barnes said, stepping forward to shake her hand, which his son was amazed to see Cora took.

"Better hurry if you want to get good seats," Jeb said.

"Would you like to come and sit with us?" his mom asked Cora. The three headed off to find chairs.

"That was kind of your mom," Maggie said, coming to stand with him.

"Is Em ready?"

"Wait'll you see her. Here they come. Have you ever seen a prouder papa or grandfather?" Maggie asked, watching her husband and his father walk on either side of Emma, riding her pony, Sunny. Both rider and horse were festooned with bows, ribbons, and flowers in hair, mane, and tail.

"Pretty cute," he said. "Better get back to Toby."

The trio stopped into the center of the ring, and Ben Senior pulled a portable microphone from his sport jacket pocket. "Welcome, everyone, to the first Emma's Dream closing ceremonies and riding exhibition. My wife Leonora Morgan and I are so proud of the hard work of my son Ben, his amazing wife, Maggie, and the entire crew. They've pulled together to make the last two weeks so much goldarn fun. There's our beautiful Maggie standin' over there, and my Leonora beside her."

The two women waved. Maggie blushed crimson, and Leonora gave a regal nod like the queen she was.

"We all got together and decided that the fittin' person to start off this riding show was my extraordinary granddaughter, Emma Morgan. Two years ago, Emma was in a wheelchair after a car accident. Surgery gave us a miracle, and our precious girl can walk, but it's been a long, tough journey. So, ladies and gentlemen of all ages, we give you Emma Morgan, for whom this amazing camp is named."

Emma leaned forward, and her grandfather gave her a hug and kiss. She then sat up straight and took hold of the reins. As their daughter and Sunny circled the ring, Ben came to his wife's side. Amy, who stood nearby, could see tears in both parents' eyes.

When Emma and Sunny completed three circles, first trotting, then cantering, and finally a short, full gallop, she reined the pony and waved to the crowd. The applause lasted until Emma and Sunny had disappeared round the side of the barn and the next rider, a ten-year-old from Scottsdale on Tara, trotted into the ring.

The riders had rehearsed slightly different routines, but essentially, each demonstration mirrored the one before it. As Toby waited for his turn, Jeb could see his anxiety rising. When it was time for him to fit Raine with Toby's saddle, he glanced over to spy the child's eyes wild with fright.

"No, no, don't want to!"

"Hey, buddy, what's wrong? You're gonna be great."

Toby took hold of the arms of his wheelchair and refused to be lifted. His brown curls were matted with sweat and his eyes ringed with tears. "Not going."

Jeb gave up trying to lift him and stooped in front of the wheelchair. "I tell you what. What if we ride together?"

Toby shook his head.

"Okay, buddy, you don't have to ride, " he said, smoothing back the damp curls, his heart aching for the frightened child. "We can just skip it, and I'll tell 'em to bring in the next rider. What do you say?"

The dark chestnut eyes stared up at Jeb in surprise. "But I practiced?"

"So, we'll do it the next time, in two weeks."

"But what about Raine?"

"Have you changed your mind, buddy? I could walk beside you."

"Okay." He reached up his arms, and Jeb gently lifted him onto Raine's back. "Ready, buddy?"

Toby nodded shyly, and they headed into the ring. As his name was announced, he gazed down at Jeb and gave him a huge grin.

Amy watched them from the sidelines, the handsome cowboy and the tiny, frail child, both of whom had stolen her heart so completely. As they circled the ring, she noticed that not once did Toby glance into the crowd to find his mother. *Just as well*, she thought. When she looked over at Cora Hooper, the woman appeared bored, as if she might fall asleep at any moment. *What will we do if Izzy Winkler doesn't come up with something? How can we ever turn Toby over to that?*

As if on cue, Izzy appeared at the edge of the crowd, waving to Toby as he and Jeb left the circle. She then caught Amy's eye, and the two met near the office building. "Izzy, what a surprise," Amy said.

"I had to come. Too worried."

"What about your crises?"

"My colleagues are covering for a couple of hours. To hear that Butch Reynolds was within a mile of Toby was enough to launch me into orbit. Where is he?"

"He's been disarmed and is confined to his car until it's time for him to drive Cora home."

"That's right, she doesn't drive. Are they sure about the weapons?"

"Trust me, cowboys know their weapons. They searched the car and Reynolds himself. Found several guns and knives and coke. Once all the campers have departed, someone'll run them in to the sheriff."

"And someone's staying by Toby's side."

"Yes, Jeb hasn't left him for a second."

"How'd his ride go?"

"A little stage fright at the beginning, but he pulled it together. He was pretty shaken up when he first spied his mom and her boyfriend."

"I'm so sorry I didn't warn you about him, but we'd heard they'd broken up. Not good for her or Toby that they're seeing each other again. Maybe she just needed the ride."

"Ms. Hooper looked a little bored by the whole thing. I wonder why she even bothered."

"Because she's bound and determined to get Toby back, or rather the almost two thousand dollars of assistance she receives every month for him. It's more than most because he's handicapped. It's meant for food, clothing, and special activities, but the child starves most of the time, and we're convinced it all goes for drugs and alcohol."

"Oh, Izzy, he can't go back there. You should have seen his face."

"We're working overtime on it. If I have anything to say about it, he'll never live with Cora Hooper again. By the way, before she slinks off, I think we should all meet with her."

"Who?"

"Certainly you, Jeb, and Maggie, as camp director. Other caregivers and Ben Morgan are welcome, but we don't want to overwhelm her completely."

"Of course. I'll tell the others. Once the riding ends and we get departing campers connected with their families, we can meet in the office."

"Great. I'll go break the news to my friend, Cora. She'll be overjoyed to see me, I'm sure."

CHAPTER 28

As the last campers drove away with their families, the three remaining headed off with their counselors for a quiet time before dinner at the big house with the Morgans. After wishing everyone goodbye, Jeb, Amy, Pam Joslin, Izzy, and Cora Hooper gathered in the camp office. Declaring that Jeb and Amy were suitable proxies for her, Maggie had begged out of the meeting. When all were seated, Izzy began.

"Did you get a chance to say good-bye to Toby, Cora?" Izzy asked. The woman nodded but remained silent.

Izzy continued. "Did you enjoy the riding?"

"Fine. Can we get on with this? Butch has been waiting in a hot car all this time, and we've gotta get back." Slumped in her chair, cheeks pale and hollow, Cora Hooper looked as if she were bracing for a root canal. Amy noticed her hand shaking and wondered if it was withdrawal or a chronic condition.

"Toby did a great job," Jeb said, receiving a grunt in reply.

"Well," Izzy said. "I believe you've met everyone, so I'll just jump right in. We think Toby's had a great two weeks. I'll let everyone tell you their perspective and then give you time to ask questions."

Amy spoke about the progress they were making with the physical therapy, and Pam Joslin and Jeb discussed the nightmares. Jeb ended his description by saying, "We'd seen less of 'em this week until last night, when he was real bad.

Izzy asked us to be honest, so I'll just say that we wondered, or I wondered, if he was upset at the prospect of seeing you."

Hooper's dull eyes flashed fire. "What the hell for? I'm his mama!"

"Who has neglected and abused him in past, Cora," Izzy said. "We're not trying to gang up on you here, but we're all concerned about Toby's health and safety."

"And you don't think I am? What the fuck? Did you raise him? Stay up all frickin' night while he screamed? Change his diapers?"

"No, but we also were not responsible for bringing Butch Reynolds into Toby's life," Izzy said. "Now, today, I receive a call telling me that you arrived here with Butch. You know damn well that he's never supposed to come within five hundred yards of Toby. Are you a couple again?"

"That's none of your damn business."

"It most certainly is, and it will be very much my business at the summer's end when we have to place Toby in his next foster home."

"Fuck, no. You ain't gonna place him in no foster home. He's comin' home with me. My lawyer tells me I've got rights."

"Not unless you're clean and far away from Butch Reynolds."

"What happened to Toby was an accident. Butch'd never hurt him. No one never proved nothin' about that. Now, I gotta go."

"Cora, wait, won't you consider freeing Toby for adoption? You've heard what everyone's said."

"Fuck no!" Hooper rose, swaying before she righted herself. "And come September, lady, I'm gettin' my boy back and there ain't nothin' you or any of you high and mighties can do about it."

Before anyone could say a word, Cora pulled open the door and stormed out.

"Well, that went well," Jeb said, looking round the room. Amy sat to his left, and he glimpsed tears in her eyes. "Hey," he said softly. "She's not getting him, trust me." He squeezed her hand and stood up. "I gotta run and make sure the posse's in place to escort Reynolds out of Dodge."

When he emerged from the building, Jeb spied Cora Hooper headed toward the grove where Reynolds had parked the car in the shade. Harley and Ben were nearby, waiting. When Hooper approached, Reynolds hopped out of the beat-up sedan and confronted them. "Okay, gimme my pieces and we're outta this hell hole."

"No can do," Harley said, strolling slowly toward the car.

"What'dya mean? I thought you said—"

"All of your belongings that we confiscated will be delivered to Sheriff Boone in Saguaro tonight," Ben Morgan said quietly as he moved to his best friend's side. "They should be there within the hour, so if you stop by the station, you can pick 'em up."

"You have no fuckin' right. This is fuckin' unbelievable!"

"Keep your voice down, Mr. Reynolds," Ben said. "There are still kids around, including Toby."

"And what? You think he hasn't heard those words before?"

"Come on, Butch, let's get outta this dump. Not gonna get anywheres with them."

"Fuck you. Fuck all of you," he said, getting back into the car and slamming the door.

After several minutes of Reynolds leaning on the starter, the engine turned over and he hit the gas, driving forward as the old sedan bumped and banged over the uneven terrain.

"Be lucky if he doesn't drop his engine," Harley said, grinning from ear to ear.

"What's the chance he'll stop in for a visit with Sheriff Boone?" Jeb asked.

"Slim to none," the others said in unison.

"I'll take 'em," Harley said. "Gotta head that way anyway. Sorry I can't make dinner."

"You can't avoid her forever, ole buddy," Ben said, referring to his youngest sister, who still wasn't speaking to Harley.

"Yeah, but I don't have to ruin your folks' dinner party with scowls and kicks under the table. See ya." He tipped his hat and headed for the office, where they'd locked up Reynolds's weapons.

"How'd the meeting with the mother go?" Ben asked Jeb as they watched Harley's retreat.

"Not great. You think they'd ever let her have him back?"

"Sure hope not," his boss said. "See you and your folks at dinner, right?"

CHAPTER 29

As Jeb and his parents walked through the Lodge's main hall, on the way to the big house for dinner, he spied Amy and Spark and waved.

"Well, hello, son. These must be your folks," Spark said, stepping forward, hand extended.

"Yes, sir—I mean, Spark. This is my mom, Lily Wilson, and my dad, Jake Barnes. Mom, Dad, this is Spark Foster, Amy's dad."

As their parents shook hands, Amy and Jeb stepped back and exchanged glances. "Did you already drop Toby at the Morgans'?"

"Ruthie has her. Says she's taking charge all night."

"So, a night off for you?"

"We'll see. Yes, if Toby agrees."

"You know what Pam keeps telling us. Don't get too attached."

"How the hell can I help it? I'm crazy about him, and over my dead body will he go near those scumbags again, ever. I'll kidnap him if I have to!"

Amy placed a hand on his arm. "Izzy'll come through, Jeb."

"I hope so."

What are you two conspiring about so heatedly?" Lily Wilson gazed from her son to Amy.

"Nothing, Ma. Let's go."

A beautiful night, the air warm with a gentle breeze, they decided to walk the short distance from the Lodge to the big house. Jeb led them to the path that wound through scrub and meadows, ending up in the Morgans' backyard, near the wide open terrace. Amy and Spark walked a short distance behind, allowing the Barnes family some privacy. Spark's booming voice carried over the fields as he related details about the land Ben Senior had offered to see him. "Want you to see it, darlin', soon as you can break free for a few hours. It's gonna be perfect."

Lily caught up with her husband and son and whispered, "That didn't look like nothing back there. Is everything alright, Jeb?"

"It's work stuff, Ma. We're trying to figure out what's gonna happen to Toby, that's all."

His father patted his shoulder. "Good luck with that, son. Mother's in pretty rough shape. I haven't seen too many cases of meth mouth, but she looks like a heavy user."

"Oh, honey," Lily said. "Please don't get too involved! What's going to happen when he leaves at the end of the summer, with you spending every night with him and all?"

"We alternate. Ruthie Morgan's going to stay with him tonight, and Harley spends at least two nights each week. I can handle it. Don't worry."

Lily gave her husband a look and he put up his hand, begging for silence.

"Here we are," Spark called, as they stepped into the open backyard. "Prettiest spot in the Valley, and wait till you see the views! Even the Lodge can't compare."

"You haven't seen Ben and Maggie's place, Dad," Amy said. "Don't tell Leonora, but I think they've got them beat."

"That reminds me. I wanta get up there and see that spread. I hear Sam Morgan does incredible work."

"Don't forget Lang and Beth's house," Jeb called over his shoulder. "Haven't seen it since it was just studs, but it's supposed to be amazing."

"Okay, then, we'll add that to our house tour itinerary. I'll ask the kids tonight!"

Ben Senior met them halfway up the lawn. "Welcome, welcome, everyone. Come on up. Raoul's got margaritas and plenty of wine and beer or whatever you'd like." He turned to Jeb's parents. "How's the Lodge treating you?"

"It's lovely," Lily said. "So kind and generous of you to have us."

"Our pleasure. Your son's like family, and so are you. Can't believe we haven't done this sooner. Come on up and we'll locate my bride."

Looking a bit overawed, Lily and Jake followed their host to the terrace, where the long table was set for sixteen. Colorful linens and Leonora's collection of bright Mexican pottery were on full display, with flowers and gleaming silverware completing the perfect table décor.

"I feel like I'm on a *Architectural Digest* photo shoot," Lily whispered to her husband.

"This is how the other half lives," he said, winking. "Want a margarita?"

"Please, and make it a double!"

Soon the terrace was filled with Morgans. Beth and Ruthie were helping their mother and Carmela, Ben was at the bar with Raoul, and Maggie was standing with her dad, Ned Williams, as he jiggled the baby on his shoulder. Father and daughter strolled over to say hello, and Maggie whispered, "A bit overwhelming, isn't it?"

Lily gave her a wan smile, and Jake shook hands with Ned.

"He's a cute little fellow. He's really grown, hasn't he?"

"Like a weed," Ned said.

"Dad and I have been through 'the Morgan gauntlet,' as Harley calls it, and lived to tell the tale. My advice—go with the flow. Ben Senior is a sweetheart. Leonora's what we call 'a force of nature,' but underneath, she's sweet, too."

"How do you think Jeb's doing?" Lily asked, meeting her gaze.

"Actually, pretty well. He's had lots of distractions with camp, and he and the crew have been holding the stables together, too. It's been a crazy few weeks."

"He seems very friendly with the Foster girl."

"Lily, don't pry," her husband said, a warning in his eyes.

Maggie nodded. "They are friends, and from my observations, it's been good for both of them."

"We just worry, that's all," Lily said, as Leonora Morgan bore down upon them.

"Hello, Barneses! So good to see you again. Welcome! Sorry, I've been slaving away in the kitchen!" Dressed in blue "cowboy chic," their hostess gave them all air kisses and hugs. She sported a fringed pale blue top over white jeans, and white strappy sandals with two-inch heels. Her blond hair was swept back and held by glittery silver combs.

Ben Senior stood beside Spark, watching his wife's entrance. "Isn't she a beauty?" he said, eyes full of love.

"Sensational," his friend said. "They don't make 'em like Nora and my Patsy anymore, do they?"

CHAPTER 30

Shortly after Lang Dillon arrived, Leonora announced that dinner was ready. Platters of garlic-mustard beef skewers and grilled oysters with mango pico de gallo and red chili horseradish began the meal, followed by a refreshing jicama salad with lime-ancho dressing. The main meal was grilled pork tenderloin à la Rodriguez with guava glaze and orange habanero. Accompanying the farm-raised pork were bowls of rice and quinoa salads, and grilled corn on the cob with garlic butter, fresh lime, and queso fresco. Carmela also prepared a platter of coriander-crusted scallops for the vegetarians.

"Oh, Lordy," Spark said, savoring a bite of pork. "What the heck am I gonna do when we go back to Portland? This is the best meal I've ever eaten!"

"All Carmela," Leonora said, waving her hand as the cook disappeared into the kitchen.

"And Raoul's grilling prowess," Beth Morgan said.

"Yes, of course!" her mother replied, raising her glass to Carmela's husband, who manned the enormous grill at the edge of the terrace. "And Lang, dear, this wine is divine. I'm so sorry your parents couldn't join us."

"They are, too," Beth's handsome fiancé replied, smiling at his future mother-in-law.

"How's your dad feeling?" Maggie asked.

Jaybo Dillon, Lang's father, a lifelong alcoholic, had suffered his second heart attack the previous year and had never regained his full strength or vitality.

"Stronger every day. We've been interviewing people to manage the winery for the past three weeks, and he's been actively involved. Doesn't like it and keeps saying he can do it, but I think he's secretly pleased."

"And pleased to have you back, too, son," Ben Senior said. "I sure was happy when Ben came home. Now we just gotta work on those other three." He referred to Morgan brothers Kyle, Sam, and Robbie, who were in Montana, Flagstaff, and Sedona, respectively.

"How're the wedding plans coming?" Ben asked. "I know Maggie and Em are looking forward to the shower at our house. Me, too."

"Great," Lang replied, gazing at his fiancée. Beth was the quietest Morgan sibling and usually listened during their raucous family dinners. Tonight was no exception. "What'dya say, babe?" he asked, his eyes full of love for his tall, willowy fiancée.

Beth grinned and threw up her hands. "Don't ask me. Mother and Carmela are the wedding experts around here. Mother? How's it going?"

"Couldn't be better! As you can see, we've got the back meadow groomed smooth as a golf course green and the tents are spectacular, a new design for the company. Caterers have coordinated the menu with Carmela, and we have all the food and drink ordered. Flowers are coming from the farm, at my daughters' request. That's the only iffy aspect, but we have backup."

Beth eyed her. "Mother!"

"Oh, pish tush, just kidding, Bethie. We're hoping for a beautiful summer evening."

"Got it on order," Ben Senior said.

Amy and Jeb sat side by side, listening to the conversation. Occasionally his hand reached under the table, grazing hers, sending shivers through her. Their interaction was not lost on either of his parents, particularly his mother, who watched him like a hawk. Toby sat with Emma, the two older campers, and

Ruthie on the lawn, where a quilt was spread for their picnic. He was laughing and looked so happy it almost broke Amy's heart. What would they do if Cora Hooper somehow managed to get custody?

After dessert of grilled pineapple with butter-rum glaze and vanilla mascarpone, and homemade ice cream for the children, the kids disappeared. Ruthie was meeting Rip at the bunkhouse as he was bunking with the two older boys. Then she and Toby would head over to the cabin. She had a huge bag of children's books and games she had unearthed in the attic that she was eager to share them with him.

Lang and Beth departed for a drive into town, and Maggie and Ben said good night and took the kids home. Ned Williams said his good nights at the same time.

As the Morgan seniors, Spark and Jeb's parents relaxed with their coffee, Amy and Jeb sat on the terrace wall, gazing out at the valley. "Pretty night," he said, taking her hand.

"Yes," she said softly.

"I've missed you, Amy."

"Me, too."

"Wanta walk the folks back, then take a walk?"

"Think that's a good idea?"

"Yup."

"Okay."

"I'll walk my folks up to their room and meet you by my truck, okay? I don't know what you're doing, but I'm not mentioning it to my parents. Too complicated."

"Gotcha," she said softly, wondering if this was a mistake, but not caring.

Lily Wilson watched her son reach over and take Amy's hand. This was more than friendship.

Soon after, Spark said, "Well, folks, this old man's gotta head home to bed."

"Can one of us run you back to the Lodge?" his friend asked. "Nora, Raoul, or I would be happy to take you."

"I don't know about the rest, but I need the walk," Spark said. "And maybe a flashlight?"

When the group reached the Lodge, Amy and Spark said good night and headed upstairs to their rooms, where she changed out of her skirt and into jeans, a tee shirt, and light jacket. Jeb walked his parents up. At their door, he said, "See you midmorning? I've got work at the stables, but I'll come take you to lunch before you head home."

"That'd be great, son," his father said, hugging him.

"Night, sweetheart," Lily said. She wanted to say much more, but decided to wait until lunch.

CHAPTER 31

When Amy reached the truck, he was leaning against the cab, gazing out into the night. "Hey, cowboy," she said softly. His handsome face, bathed in the light of a full moon, turned to her, and Amy's heart skipped a beat, her knees quivering.

"Hey yourself. Don't think we even need this," he said, shoving a small flashlight into his back pocket. "But, just in case."

"Where shall we walk?" she asked, suddenly feeling shy and nervous.

"There's a nice, open path just behind the spa. Let's use that. It's about a mile out to a meditation platform."

"Sounds perfect. Glad I put on my running shoes."

"Those the new ones Dillon gave all of us from Rambler Sports West?"

"Yup."

"You're glowing in the dark, you know."

She laughed. "Perfect. Lead on!"

They skirted the building, neither saying a word until they passed the pool area beyond the spa. "This way," he said, gently taking hold of her elbow.

"Your mom doesn't like me much, does she?"

"What're you talkin' about? She loves you. It's just…she's being protective. That's mom."

"Was she close to Stacy?"

"No. They'd just met each other the day…the day of the accident. Happened on the way back from their house."

"I'm sorry. I didn't mean to pry."

"It's okay," he said, taking her hand. "It's getting easier to talk about her."

Amy squeezed his hand and they walked in silence for a long while, the moonlit path wide open before them. Occasionally, an animal scurried across their path, but otherwise the night was still. As they rounded a bend, the outlines of a low structure came into view.

"The meditation platform, I assume? I wish I'd known this was here. I'd have come out sooner."

"Yup, this is it and also the end of the path. Do you meditate?"

"Every morning."

"For how long?"

"Usually twenty minutes, sometimes longer, sometimes shorter."

"Is it helpful?"

"For me, yes. I learned it in college—transcendental meditation."

"What's that, exactly?"

"That's when they help you to develop a mantra, a sound or word that you repeat in your head. I sometimes use my old mantra, but mostly I practice a kind of mindfulness now, where I bring my attention to my breath, or sounds, or something around me. Anything to stay focused in the present. It sounds easier than it is. If I get thirty seconds of pure awareness during a meditation, I'm lucky."

"Would you teach me?"

"Of course."

"Now?"

"Okay, I'll let you choose. Do you want to try a sound awareness or breath?"

"I guess maybe sound?"

"Okay, why don't we sit. You don't have to be cross-legged, just comfortable. I like to have my back against something, so let's go over to those benches."

When they were sitting side by side, she asked, "Ready?"

"Yup."

She gently let go of his hand and rested hers in her lap. "Let your body find a comfortable position, your spine straight, feet on the ground. If you feel tension anywhere—your neck, jaw, mouth, chest, legs, arms—just let it go and relax. Let your eyes close, or leave them gently open."

She paused, silent for thirty seconds, then continued. "Bring your full attention to the sounds around you, as you breathe in and out. Be aware of your belly, then chest filling with air, then emptying as you breathe out slowly. When you take in a full breath, pause, only till it's comfortable, then breathe out slowly until all the breath has left your body. Pause again before you take your next inhalation.

"Keep going like this, breathing in and pausing and breathing out and pausing. Don't force the pauses. Just rest and pause until comfortable and continue breathing. As you breathe, notice sounds around us. If your mind wanders, bring it back to the sounds. I'll stop speaking now and let us have a few minutes of silence to breathe in and out, listening."

With eyes closed, they sat side by side in the stillness. Jeb endeavored to follow her instructions, but his mind raced. The stillness was broken first by an owl's call, then the cry of a coyote. He longed to draw her into his arms and make love to her, but instead brought his attention back to the stillness and to her soft breathing next to him.

As if reading his mind, she said, "If your mind wanders, bring your attention back to listening without judgment."

Again, he focused on listening and heard a soft rustling near the platform, then stillness. For several seconds, Jeb experienced a kind of peace without thought until Amy's nearness drew him back. Once again, he brought his attention back to her instructions.

Amy, too, found attending to anything but her lover's warm, strong presence difficult. She endeavored to concentrate on the sounds of the night, but finally decided that she would bring her awareness to the sensation of sitting beside him, their shoulders barely touching. As she did, a kind of quiet came over her, and she felt more at ease than she had in many months. After several minutes more, she said softly, "Let's take one or two more breaths, then open our eyes and come back to our surroundings."

When he opened his eyes, he found her turned to him, smiling shyly. "What did you think?"

In answer, he gently caressed her jaw and leaned forward, kissing her deeply.

Amy returned the kiss, closing her eyes, allowing every sensation to wash over her, as her tongue found his. The kiss grew deeper and Jeb's hand moved down to cup her breast, and she leaned forward, sighing.

"That was incredible. You are incredible," he said, voice husky as he leaned back and kissed her forehead. "If I don't stop now, I won't be able to, Amy."

"I don't want you to stop, but maybe we should?"

"Your call, darlin'. I'm at the mercy of testosterone, and it's in overdrive right now."

In answer, she stood and, to his amazement, slipped out of her shoes, then let her jeans and panties fall to the ground and stepped out of them. She then shrugged out of her jacket and pulled her tee shirt over her head, her bra following it. "My call? Jeb Barnes, please make love to me. No strings, no expectations."

"I was wrong," he said, hands on her tiny waist, drawing her nearer, his penis straining at his jeans until he thought the buttons might burst. "*Incredible* doesn't even begin to describe you, Amy Foster."

Within seconds, she straddled him, barely giving him time to slip the condom on before sliding closer and drawing him in. Her kisses trailed down his neck, her hands massaging the hard chest that rippled with muscle.

"Jesus, Amy," he whispered, thrusting deep, drawing her to him as they began the rhythmic dance they did so well.

He watched with awe as her naked body arched in the moonlit, their every movement in sync, as their eyes held each other's. *Not sure how long you can hold on, Barnes, but she's sure worth it!* Then she smiled, a beautiful dewy smile that sent him over the edge. They climaxed together, aware of nothing else except each other, their bodies, their breaths, their hearts as one.

After, as she leaned her head against his shoulder, he nibbled at her breast, then trailed kisses up her slender neck to her lips. "That was what *I* call present moment awareness," he said, capturing her mouth in a deep, lingering kiss.

Amy sighed and allowed herself to rest in his arms, all thought set aside in the peace of his embrace. A cool breeze played over her back and she shivered, drawing closer, nestling against him.

"You cold, sweetheart?"

"A little, but it feels good."

"You're shivering."

"I don't care."

"Well, I do. Should we?"

"Please just hold me a little longer."

When she finally moved away from their warm connection, Jeb felt as a piece of himself had been ripped away. Amy began rummaging around for her clothes, and they dressed quickly. By the time she slipped on her jacket, goosebumps covered her arms. He drew her close and rubbed her arms up and down. "Hey, you're freezing. Come here."

They walked back arm in arm, his warmth helping a little, but when they reached the Lodge, he saw that she still trembled. After a soft kiss, he said, "Inside you go and into a hot bath. Or if the spa's still open, head down to the sauna."

"I'll be fine," she said, drawing back. "Thank you for tonight, Jeb."

"My pleasure," he said, grinning. He wanted to say more, but held back. He wanted to say, *I love you, Amy Foster, more than any woman I've ever known,* but instead, he kissed her nose and let her go.

CHAPTER 32

"Barnes is a really nice young fella. Every time I see him, I like him better!" Spark said, a twinkle in his eye as he gazed at his daughter. Seated on the Lodge terrace, they were enjoying a leisurely breakfast from the Lodge Sunday buffet.

"Yes, he's a great guy," she said, smiling at him.

"I expect we'll be seeing a lot of him, even after the wedding?"

"I don't know how, with him here and us in Portland."

"Hmm, better get our vacation house built quick, then."

"You haven't bought the land yet, have you? I thought we were going out to take a look."

"Not yet, but it's mine if I want it. What's your day like? Have you got time to take a ride out there?"

"Well, the new campers start arriving at noon. We could go now."

"I was thinking I'd like to ride out on horseback."

"Dad, you haven't been on a horse in what, twenty years?"

"Not so. Your mama and I went ridin' on our last visit out here. That was only six years ago."

"How far is it?"

"'Bout a mile from the Morgan's Run stables. I have the trail map. What'dya say? Give this old man a thrill?"

"Okay, but we'd better head over quickly. Have you checked with someone at the stables?"

"Young Ben, last night. He told the others in case he's not there."

"Hmm…"

"Now, back to young Barnes—"

"Oh, no, you don't. I've gotta head up and change." Amy grabbed a piece of toast, kissed her father's cheek, and practically sprinted off the terrace. *I am definitely not ready to talk about young Barnes!*

*****

Jeb arrived at dawn to complete stable chores in time to go to lunch with his parents. He felt guilty leaving them shorthanded for the arrival of the new campers, but Maggie assured him they'd be fine. He'd just started mucking out stalls when Ruthie arrived, her older brother right behind her.

"Morning," Jeb called, waving. "Toby sleep okay?"

"Like a lamb," she said, leaning against the side of the stall. "He's such a cute kid. Only one nightmare, and he went right back to sleep. I tired him out with all our game playing and reading. Just dropped him at the dining hall. Andy and Greg are both back and on duty."

"That's great."

"Morning, all," Ben Morgan said, arm circling his sister's shoulders.

"You're up early," she said, poking him.

"Getting ready for the new group. Twenty-four for the next two weeks."

"Sorry I can't be there when they arrive," Jeb said.

"No problemo. We've got lots of help. Harley's back and—"

"Lot of good he'll be, ogling at all the pretty moms," Ruthie said, turning up her freckled nose.

"Isn't it time to give the man a break?" her brother asked.

"No!"

"Your being so pissy makes for a tense workplace, doesn't it, Jeb?"

Jeb threw up his hand, holding his pitchfork with the other. "Don't bring me into this, guys."

Ruthie glared at her brother. "He can have a girlfriend in every town from here to Yuma for all I care!"

"That's the problem, Shortcake. You do care."

"Don't call me that! I just wish he'd be open about it, that's all. Instead of flirting with every woman in the Valley."

"Including you?" Ben smiled at his sister, her face red as a beet with indignation.

"Yes, if you must know! Then I see all the missed calls from his girlfriend on his phone. It's insulting."

"What the hell were you doin' reading his phone messages?"

"Hey, guys, I think I'll duck out," Jeb said, uncomfortable in the midst of the brother-sister spat.

"No, you stay! I'm leaving! And, I wasn't snooping on his phone," she said, turning away. "Casanova left it in the cabin, and it kept buzzing last week when I stayed with Toby!"

"Oh?"

"As if you don't know?" she said, stomping off toward the drive. "You're probably thick as thieves with the lovely Willow, whoever she is!"

"Now, Ruthie, hold on," Ben said, following her out.

Jeb went back to his mucking.

*****

"These are the best fish tacos I've ever eaten," Jake Barnes declared, leaning back, taking a sip of iced tea.

"Gracie's food is incredible," his son said, taking a bite of his burger topped with mushrooms, onions, and local artisan cheese.

Rosa Faria stopped by to refill their waters and teas, then disappeared.

"This has been fun, sweetie," Lily Wilson said, staring at her son. "When do you think you'll get up our way again?"

"Who knows, Mom? With Toby, the camp, and the stables hoppin', it'll be tricky till fall."

"Maybe after the wedding, when the Fosters depart, you'll have more time?"

Here we go, he thought. "Probably not."

"Nice people, your Amy and her dad," Jake said, giving his wife a warning look, which she ignored.

"Yup."

"Be careful, sweetheart. It's so soon after Stacy. Give yourself time to grieve," she said, reaching across the table, trying to take his hand, which Jeb withdrew out of reach.

"Leave him be, Lily. Amy's a lovely person."

"I just worry. That's all."

"Well, don't, Mom, please."

They finished lunch in silence and strolled to his parents' car.

"Love you, Mom," he said, hugging her.

"Take care of yourself, sweetheart. And please don't rush things."

Jeb turned away, coming round to hug his dad. As his mother hopped into the car, Jake Barnes led him a few feet away. "Ignore your mom, son. We both want you to be happy. Mom's just a worry wart."

"I know, Dad. And, believe me, I'm still figuring things out. Sometimes I feel guilty. Others, I don't know."

"Listen, son, there's a lot I don't know, but I do know one thing. Even though I only met the girl that one night, Stacy Winchester would want you to be happy. If Amy's who you want, don't turn your back on her."

"Thanks, Dad. Love you." They hugged again. "I'll try to get up to Flagstaff soon."

Jeb stood watching as his parents drove away, then turned back and headed for his truck.

*****

"It's beautiful, Daddy," Amy said as they sat on Tara and Raine at the top of a rise about a mile from the stables.

"Ben's agreed to sell me forty acres if I allow grazing and farming rights in perpetuity. What'dya think?"

"Not up to me."

"But this agreement prevents any further development. So if you or Buck ever wanted to build, it would not be on this parcel."

"Well, I can't speak for Buck, but please don't worry on my account. As long as you have a guest room, I'm happy."

"But you don't think, after the past few weeks, you might consider relocating?"

"No. Not right away, at least," she said, pulling her sunglasses down to give him a look. "Besides, if I did, I could always rent in town, or there are those condos by the river."

"Junk."

"Very expensive junk."

"My point exactly."

"Well, anyway, my vote is—go for it, if this is what you want."

"Good, then it's settled. The other parcels are further north. Maybe I'll buy one of those, just in case."

Amy laughed. "Whatever you say, Dad!"

"What else have I got to spend my millions on?"

"When will you start the house?"

"Soon as I talk to Sam Morgan. He'll be here a few days before the wedding. Already phoned him and set up a time. Still haven't gotten over to see Ben and Maggie's place or the house Lang and Beth are building. Maybe we can do that together?"

"Now, we've gotta head back. I promised I'd be at camp by noon."

*****

When Amy drove up, the first group of campers was headed to their bunkhouses with their doting parents and counselors. Amy waved to Maggie, who stood with clipboard, awaiting the next carload.

"Good morning!" Maggie said, waving the clipboard.

"How's it going?"

"So far, so good."

"Sorry I'm late. Dad wanted me to ride out to see the land he's buying from the Morgans."

"Up by the north pastures, right?"

"Yes, it's gorgeous."

"So happy you'll be joining the Valley community! Will be such fun to have you here regularly. Are you okay, Amy? You look tired."

"Yes. No. I'm fine. It's just I'm so tired of hearing from Ryan Houseman."

"He's still pestering you?"

"Night and day. He has an ego the size of that mountain over there, and he just will not give up. Dad says I should go into town and buy a new cell phone, or call and have my number changed, but that's such a pain."

"I'm so sorry," Maggie said, placing a gentle hand on her arm. "Is there anything Ben or I could do? You know cowboys. They're only too happy to ride to a lady's rescue."

Amy laughed. "No, please, no rescuing! Ryan's my problem."

Maggie was just about to ask what Jeb had to say about the situation when two vans drove in with handicap tags hanging from the rearview mirrors.

"Duty calls. Please let me know if we can help, promise?"

Amy nodded and walked with her to greet the newcomers.

CHAPTER 33

The new group of campers settled in easily, with only a few homesick the first nights. The special needs of these children for physical therapy kept Amy busy well into the late afternoons. Jeb stayed each night with Toby and thus, they saw little of each other. When they did, conversation was mostly about Toby and the latest from Izzy Winkler. Izzy had volunteered to take him home with her during the hiatus they were calling "Wedding Week," and she was also working overtime to terminate Cora Hooper's parental rights.

After lunch with his parents, Jeb began doubting himself. He loved Amy. Of that he was sure. Beyond that, he felt stuck. Friday morning before the last day of camp, Maggie found him sitting in the shade behind the barn with coffee and a half-eaten muffin.

"Not eating with Toby this morning?"

"Hey, Boss," he said, looking up, giving her a tired smile. "Nope, he wanted to eat with his buddies."

"Tough night?"

He nodded. "It's like we're back to square one. He was up screamin' at least seven or eight times."

"Probably the transition. He loves Izzy, but he's been happy and safe with you."

"Prob'ly. Any word about the mom?"

"Not yet. How're things with you and Amy?"

"I've barely seen her."

"Oh?"

"Between Toby at night and how crazy busy we've been."

"Are you avoiding each other?"

"No. I mean, not on purpose."

"Her dad bought two parcels of land."

"Yeah, Ben told me. Says he's gonna get Sam started on the building plans next week."

"That'll be nice, won't it? For the Fosters to have a place here? Means we'll be seeing them more regularly."

He shrugged.

"Okay, partner, what's wrong?"

"I'm crazy about her, Maggie! That's what's wrong. Am I the stupidest person in the world?"

"Of course not!"

"She's leaving, Mags, and I don't see me moving to Portland anytime soon."

"You never know."

"It's a great city, but not for me."

"Even if she's there?"

Another shrug.

"Well, gotta get going. Listen, Jeb, it's none of my business, but I'd try to talk things through before she leaves."

"Maybe."

"And I know she could use a friend right now, what with that horrid boyfriend pestering her day and night."

Jeb's mouth dropped open and he stared at his boss. "What?"

"Oh, I thought she would have told you. He just won't leave her alone, I guess. My Ben threatened to take Harley and go to Portland to shake him up."

"How long's this been going on?"

"Couple of weeks, at least. I've probably said too much."

"Why didn't anyone tell me?"

"We assumed you knew, you two being so close and all. You should talk to Amy."

Jeb shrugged. "Okay, see you at camp, Boss."

*****

At the end of a chaotic pool time, Amy caught up with Jeb, who had just packed Toby off. They had all marveled at how quickly Toby made friends, and this group of bunkhouse mates had really clicked. The four other boys had been very kind to the younger camper and included him in everything.

"Hey, Jeb, wait up."

In bathing trunks and damp tee shirt, he turned, hand on hip. "What's up?"

Amy sensed a mood shift, but wasn't sure. Every time their paths had crossed during the busy day, he had hustled away with no more than a nod. Accustomed to his warm grins and easy manner, she was confused by his expression.

"I thought we might eat together? At Toby's table."

"Not sure what I'm doing."

"Oh? Is something wrong?"

"Not with me."

She sensed his anger, but touched his arm. "What is it? What's wrong?"

"I thought we were friends, Amy."

"Of course we are, much more than friends," she said, smiling coyly.

"Well, then, why do I have to hear about that jerk Ryan's calls from someone else?"

"What are you talking about?"

"Maggie told me, Amy, so don't act all innocent."

"I'm not. I'm just surprised that you care."

"Care? What the hell, Amy? After everything that's happened between us, how can you ask if I care?"

"I didn't tell you about Ryan's calls because he has nothing to do with us. As I've told my dad, Ryan is my problem. I'm dealing with it."

"Not very successfully, if he keeps calling."

"What do you want? Should I give you a blow-by-blow every time he calls?"

"Of course not."

"Good. It's hard enough without having to relive it."

"What about screening your calls?"

"Believe me, I do that, but sometimes I forget. Besides, if I don't answer, he leaves long messages."

"That you just have to listen to?"

"Look, I'm happy to talk about this, but now's probably not the best time."

"Whatever. Look, I gotta go. I'll see you later, okay?"

Jeb stalked off, feeling like a world-class jerk, but unable to stop himself. What he really wanted was to draw her into his arms and kiss her silly. He had missed her so much the past two weeks, but with Harley on the pack trip, he hadn't had a break from night duty with Toby, and the stables were hopping until long into the night. By the time he sat beside Toby's wheelchair at the evening's campfire, he had cooled down and resolved that he would apologize in the morning.

As the campers sang "Kumbaya," Amy caught his eye at one point and thought she spied a softness. She smiled at him, wondering, as she had many times, if their relationship had been a mistake.

"Hey, Amy," Ruthie said, squatting beside her. "Maggie wants a word when this ends, okay?"

"Of course. Thanks, Ruthie. Any word from the pack trip?"

"I don't concern myself with matters pertaining to Harley Langdon."

"Still?"

"It's a long story."

"Aren't they all?"

"They're due back in the morning, I think. It's just the three guests and Harley and Rip, so hopefully things went smoothly. Supposedly they were all experienced riders."

As the campers dispersed for the night, Amy found Maggie by the dining hall. "Ruthie said you wanted to speak with me?"

"Yes. As I just told Jeb, Izzy Winkler called. She'll be here at eight tomorrow morning to pick up Toby, and she'd like to talk with us. She asked specifically if you, Jeb, and Pam could be there. Unfortunately, Pam can't make it."

"What's it about?"

"She didn't say—just that she wanted to get the team together. I asked Ruthie to come as well since she's spent a good bit of time with him."

"Okay, see you at eight, then."

"You okay?"

"Yes, just tired. Maybe too much sun today?"

Maggie placed a hand on her arm. "Like the rest of these cowboys, he's a hothead, always ready to defend the little lady's honor. They take their job as our protectors seriously. He'll cool down."

"I know. It's just…it's so hard to know what to do sometimes."

"I hear you. Ben and I had some huge ups and downs in the beginning, and look at Ruthie and Harley. They're crazy about each other and yet they're barely speaking."

"What's up with that, anyway?"

"I haven't the faintest idea. Harley is a man of mystery. I suspect Ben knows but is keeping his secret, and I'm not prying. They've been friends a long time."

"Well, good night, then," Amy said, squeezing Maggie's hand.

"Night."

CHAPTER 34

When they were all seated in the office, Izzy began. "Thanks for coming. I've been hearing from Maggie that Toby's had a spectacular couple of weeks?"

"Been really happy," Jeb said. "Really clicked with his new bunk mates. Last couple of nights have been rough, but nightmares are mostly down to one a night."

"And he's been doing well in therapy with me, and I think with Pam," Amy said.

"Yes, I spoke with Pam last night." Izzy looked around the room, eyes grave. "Well, there's no sense delaying this any longer. I'm 'fraid I have some bad news, folks."

"Oh, Jesus," Jeb muttered, certain of the social worker's next words.

Izzy's eyes gazed from Jeb to the others. "I am so sorry to tell you that as of September first, a judge has awarded Cora Hooper probationary custody."

"No!" Amy said.

Ruthie leaped out of her seat and started pacing. "How could they?"

"Oh, dear," Maggie said. "This is terrible. I can't believe it."

"Neither can I," said Izzy. "There'll be home visits three times a week, and she's required to get him to his preschool and therapy sessions. If she misses one, the custody decision will be revisited."

"What about the rest of the time?" Jeb asked, head in hands, afraid he might burst into tears. "That woman's not capable of taking care of him for five minutes, and how can we be sure that lowlife scum won't come near him?"

"If he violates the restraining order, which is still in place, Toby will be taken away from her."

Stunned, Amy looked at Jeb, his face a mask of fury. Then she asked Izzy, "What did Pam say?"

"That it was a huge mistake."

"Why doesn't the judge take our perspectives and hers into account?"

"I'm going before him next Thursday. I would very much like statements from each of you and his counselors. Mr. Langdon, too. Clear, dispassionate statements that recount his progress this summer. Pam is drafting one now."

"What about us joining you?" Maggie said. "Especially Jeb and Amy, who spend so much time with him?"

"I'll call Monday when Toby and I get back from the mountains and see if that's possible." Izzy was taking him to her grandparents' home in Sedona for the weekend. "I just found out about this yesterday at four-thirty, so there wasn't an opportunity to make inquiries."

"Well, do keep us posted," Maggie said. "I know I speak for all of us in saying that we would do anything for that sweet boy. I'm sure he's waiting for you, and I've got to get out and help direct traffic as parents come for pickup."

"Will do. Again, I know this is a major setback, but I promise you, it's not over," Izzy said, hugging each of them before walking out with Maggie.

Ruthie followed, leaving Jeb and Amy alone.

"You okay?" she asked softly.

"I can't talk about this right now. I'm sure they need us out there."

With that, he hurried out.

*****

With the last campers gone, the cleaning crew spent the afternoon straightening and cleaning the dining hall, kitchen, bunkhouses, and other buildings. By five, when Amy completed all the paperwork on the departed campers, she grabbed the manila mailers and strolled out to find Maggie and Harley sitting on the dining hall steps, chatting.

"Hey, Amy, all set?" Maggie asked, waving.

"All set. Shall I drop these at the post office Monday?"

"No, I'll take 'em. Thanks so much. I'm already dreading the week after next when you and your dad leave."

"Me, too. I'll be sorry not to finish out the summer. Is Diana all set?" She referred to the other physical therapist from Tucson who had shadowed her two days during the past week.

"Yes, and thanks for showing her the ropes."

"My pleasure. She'll be great. Is Jeb around?"

Maggie glanced at her boss, and Harley said, "I think he headed into town for the night. Sleep in his own bed and all. The cabin mattresses are not the best."

"Why didn't you guys say something?" Maggie asked, hands on hips. "We can easily replace them. In fact, I'll get Ben to order new ones this week."

"Hold yer horses, Mags. We're cowboys, used to sleepin' on the ground," he said, grinning. "Some lumpy ole mattress isn't gonna kill us."

"That's not the point. And it's all summer for Jeb. Oh, for goodness' sake, men!" She rolled her eyes at Amy.

"Well, I'll head out, then. Have a great night," Amy said.

"What're you up to?" Maggie asked, noticing her mopey expression.

"I'm hoping nothing. Dad was making noises about driving into Tucson, but I'm praying he's forgotten about it. I'd love to curl up with a book."

Or Jeb Barnes, Maggie thought, watching her. "Well, have a good one. We'll be seeing lots of you this week. I'm sure Leonora's given you a list, like the rest of us."

Amy's face brightened. "Yes, and I'm looking forward to helping with the shower, so I'll expect a list from you, too!"

*****

Amy returned to the Lodge and found her dad on the terrace, drink in hand. "Hey, sweetie, how're ya doin'?"

She bent over, hugging him as she kissed the top of his head. "Okay."

She plunked down in a chair beside him.

"Don't sound okay."

"Just tired, I guess. How 'bout you? How was your day?"

"It was fine, just fine." Spark set down his drink and sat up, staring over at her. "Now, are you gonna tell me what's wrong, or do I have to get a crowbar and pry it outta you?"

"It's everything. My job, Ryan's irritating phone calls, leaving the camp in the lurch after the wedding, and to top everything off, Toby Hooper's social worker came to get him today and his mom's been awarded custody starting September first, unless a miracle happens or she screws up."

"Which she will, from what you've told me."

"Yes and in the process will put Toby at terrible risk. He's been through so much. To return him to that environment after all the progress he's made. It's criminal, Dad."

"Want me to call Lyman? He deals with this kind of stuff all the time." Spark referred to one of his oldest friends, Lyman Manning, a prominent Portland attorney.

"What can he do?"

"Lyman has contacts everywhere, honey. He may even know the judge in question."

"No, Daddy, no Lyman, at least not yet."

"He can also slap all kinds of restraining orders and do-not-contact orders on Houseman."

Amy threw up her hands in frustration. "No, Daddy, he cannot! As I told you last time we talked about this, Ryan is my problem, and I'm dealing with it!"

Spark watched his daughter unraveling in front of his eyes. He reached over and took her hand. "I notice Mr. Barnes was not on your list of woes."

"Well, he should have been. He's driving me crazy, too."

"Have you tried talkin' to him?"

Amy gave her father a sarcastic look. "What do you think?"

"Hmm…" he said, scratching his chin.

"Can we just put my pathetic life aside for a minute, please? What're you doing for dinner?"

"Well, Leonora's busy with some Cowbelles function, so Ben and I were gonna drive down to Tucson to his favorite ribs place."

Which neither of you should be eating. "That sounds like fun."

"Wanta come along?"

She eyed him again, this time with a smile playing at the corner of her mouth. "And spoil your boys' night out? Never. I'm happy to stay here with a sandwich and a good book."

"Hey, Fosters!"

Ben Morgan Senior stepped onto the terrace, tipping his hat to several guests before removing it. Amy watched his approach, marveling at what a handsome, robust man he was. There were rumors about his weakening heart, but the elder Morgan could still turn heads when he walked into a room. His salt-and-pepper hair was longish and perfectly groomed, his smile gorgeous, and his blue eyes always twinkling. Wasn't hard to see where the Morgan boys got their looks. Leonora was no slouch, either.

"Here's my partner in crime now," Spark said, rising to shake his friend's hand. "Been tryin' to convince my girl to come along with us old geezers, but she's turned me down flat."

"Be *my* pleasure, I can tell you that, sweetheart," Morgan said, smiling at her.

"Thanks, guys, but I'm happy here. You go on. No more cajoling."

They each gave her a hug, and Amy watched the two old friends saunter out, many pairs of eyes on them. "Not too much grease, now!" she called, and her father raised a hand, waving as they disappeared.

CHAPTER 35

Amy showered and dressed, intending to order a sandwich from the room service menu, but as she pulled on a tee shirt and jeans, the prospect of her room's four walls and eating alone seemed depressing. "Oh, what the hell," she said aloud, grabbing her bag, slipping into flip-flops, and scooping up the key to the white whale.

On a Saturday night, Gracie's was hopping, with hardly a seat available. She sat at the counter and said hello to Rosa Faria as she rushed by with a heavily laden tray. "Hi, Amy, be back in a sec."

She had been hoping to see Jeb, but as she scanned the room, Amy saw no one she knew. A young blonde who looked about twelve emerged from the kitchen and set plates down for diners on either side of her. "Hey, be right with you." She dropped a menu in front of Amy as well as silverware wrapped in a red napkin.

A few minutes later, she returned from filling water glasses. "What can I get you, miss?"

"It's Amy. Hi. You're new here?"

"Not really, but I only work weekends. I'm Emory. I'm friends with Rosa. I'm not old enough to serve alcohol, so Rosa will have to get your drink, if you want one."

Amy smiled. "Well, Emory, I'd love the white fish special and a house salad with Gracie's dressing. Water's fine. If I want a glass of wine, I'll let Rosa know."

Emory produced her salad in record time, then flew off to clear tables. Amy ordered a Pinot Grigio from Rosa and sat sipping it between courses, gazing around at the busy room, townspeople and tourists happily dining and talking in the warm, inviting space. As she watched a young family gathering their things to depart, Gracie herself emerged from the kitchen with her dinner.

"Ms. Foster, hello. You dining solo tonight?"

"Yes, hi, and it's Amy, please."

"Your dad's a regular now."

Amy smiled at the tall, rail-thin owner, her hair askew, apron dotted with red sauce. "So I hear. I suspect your food's the main reason he's buying property in the Valley. He's going to have withdrawal when we return to Portland."

Gracie laughed. "I very much doubt that. Portland's a foodie Mecca."

"We do have some great restaurants."

"Well, better get back to the kitchen. Enjoy." Gracie nodded and disappeared, leaving Amy to enjoy the delicate fish, perfectly cooked in a light tomato-and-garlic sauce. It was nested on a bed of bitter greens, with baby carrots and asparagus fanned out underneath. It came with a side dish of polenta, light, fluffy, and savory. Despite her glum mood, Amy enjoyed every bite.

When Emory cleared her plate, only a few diners remained. Amy asked for her check, and Emory disappeared just as her boss reappeared. "Got room for dessert?"

Amy laughed. "'Fraid not. That was incredible, Gracie."

"Glad you liked it. Same dinner a certain obstinate cowboy wolfed down earlier this evening."

"You mean Jeb."

She nodded. "Saw you lookin' around. Ya just missed each other."

"That obvious, huh?"

"He's a good man, just a bit of horse's ass."

"I can't disagree with you there."

"It'll blow over."

"Maybe. Anyway, we'll be going home soon."

"He's crazy about you, you know."

"Does that make you sad, knowing Stacy as you did?"

Hands on hips, Gracie gave her a long, hard look. "Do I look sad?"

"Not really."

"Listen, hon. I don't know what the heck you two have goin' on, but the Stacy Winchester I knew would have wanted him to be happy, not mooning around like a lovesick coyote."

"That's what his dad said."

"And he's right. Jeb's stubborn, but he's no fool. He'll come around, if he's got any sense in that cowboy brain of his. Have a good night, hon."

With a wink, Gracie disappeared. After paying her check, she headed toward the white whale, then stopped in the middle of Main Street. Even though she had never been to the apartment Jeb had shared with Stacy, she knew the building, which was only two blocks away. Without stopping to think, she strode off in that direction.

*****

Jeb's apartment was above a hardware store, which had been in operation for over a hundred years. The storefront faced west, and the second and third floor apartments had balconies with unobstructed views of the valley. As she approached the building, Amy gazed up and spied Jeb on his second floor balcony, feet up on the rails, hat pulled low, watching the sunset, beer in hand. *The quintessential cowboy as always*, she thought, considering whether she should turn heel and run or proceed. The sound of her step must have caught his eye and Jeb looked her way, surprise registering on his face.

"Hey," she called, waving.

He stood and bent over the rail. "Hey, yourself. What're you doing in town?"

Amy shielded her eyes from the sun, looking up, trying to gauge his mood. "Can I come up?"

"Here? I mean, sure, hold on a sec. It's kind of a mess."

"I don't care, really. I promise not to look," she said, but he had already disappeared inside.

Shrugging, she tried the front door leading upstairs. It was open, so she climbed the stairs and waited on the landing. She could hear him rustling around inside, the sound of banging, clanging, and scraping making her smile. Finally, the door opened and he stood aside. "Come in. I tried, but it's pretty bad. What can I say? It's become a man cave since—well, since I've been here alone. Haven't spent much time here since camp opened, but enough to make a mess."

"You vanished before I said, 'I promise not to look.'" But she did look, and it was pretty awful despite his scurrying around and attempts to tidy up.

"Wanta beer?"

"Thanks, that'd be great."

He grabbed two beers from the fridge, opened them both, and handed one to her. "Come on out on the balcony. Sunset's a beauty tonight."

She stepped over piles of clothes, some of which appeared to be women's, and followed him out to sit in one of the two wooden rockers, painted bright red to match the building's trim. Amy wondered if this was one of his rituals with Stacy, beers on the balcony, watching the sunset.

As if reading her mind, he said, "Stace and I would do this once and a while, when she wasn't working. I try to get out here most nights. It's a great reward at the end of the day."

"It's beautiful."

"Best view in the Valley, except for those on Morgan's Run. They're pretty spectacular, especially from your fancy quarters."

"I think Maggie and Ben's house has the Lodge beat."

"Yeah, that's a pretty spot." He leaned back, gazing straight ahead. "Why're you here, Amy?"

"I just thought we should talk."

"About?"

"Well, for starters, about Toby, but also us? I'm really uncomfortable about what happened, and think we should discuss it."

"Look, Amy, I get it. I'm nothing to you but a vacation diversion. No need to explain why you don't tell me things goin' on, like that lowlife boyfriend's calls."

"It's been a little busy lately, and as I told you, Ryan's my problem. I'm dealing with it."

"Yeah, right." His voice had a hard, unfamiliar edge.

Amy felt as if he'd slapped her. "I'm sorry I didn't tell you about Ryan," she said quietly, sitting back, sipping her beer, allowing silence to stretch between them.

After several minutes, he sat up and looked at her. "I can be a bit of a horse's ass. Sorry."

She smiled at him, reaching over to take his hand. "Friends?"

"Always." Jeb longed to take her in his arms, but no way was he starting something that could end up in Stacy's bed. Instead, he squeezed her hand. "Stacy's dad's comin' up, Tuesday night, I think. I wanted to tell you so you wouldn't hear from someone else."

"Oh?"

"He's bringing her ashes and collecting her stuff that's still here. That's one of the reasons the apartment looks like a wreck. I'm also considering moving out."

"Oh, to where?"

"Morgans have offered me the cabin permanently. It's more home than this place now that Stace is gone. I'll miss the view, but the cabin's view is pretty damn great too."

She nodded but didn't know what to say. After several minutes, she said, "It's been quite a month, hasn't it?"

"Yup."

"You doin' okay about Toby?"

"What'd you think?"

"Jeb, Izzy's working overtime on this. She'll find a way. My dad has contacts, too."

"Well, someone better find a way, 'cause if they don't, come September he and I are outta here."

"Don't be ridiculous. You can't possibly consider—"

Eyes blazing, he turned to her. "That miserable excuse for a mother and her sleazy boyfriend will never spend another second with Toby! Ever."

"This is insanity."

"Not nearly as insane as giving him back to that trash."

She grabbed hold of his arm. "You can't be serious?"

He shrugged out of her grasp and stood up. "Never more so. That's one of the reasons I'm giving up this place, in case we have to run."

"I can't be hearing this. This is crazy. How would you take care of him? You'd be arrested and most likely jailed. Then what?"

"They won't find us."

"Yes, they will."

"And, Amy, if you're my friend, you will say nothing to anyone about this."

"I'm not sure I can do that. Not for your sake or Toby's."

"Then I was wrong to trust you. Are we done here?"

Amy's chest ached. She set down her beer and stood up, staring at him. "Good night, Jeb."

She walked out of the apartment and down to the street, the light of sunset bathing the pavement in rosy hues. As she neared the white whale, the tears came. and she hurried on blindly, hopping in and shutting the door before sobs wracked her slender frame. At that moment, her cell phone rang. She pulled it from her purse and spied Ryan's name on caller ID.

Rather than ignoring the call or hanging up as she usually did, she clicked on the phone on. "Ryan, go to hell. If you ever call me again, my dad and I are taking legal action."

Click.

Somehow, despite the heartache over Jeb, her rebuke of Ryan made her feel better, and she collected herself and drove back to the ranch.

CHAPTER 36

When Spark and Amy stepped from the white whale Monday morning, they were greeted by Ruthie Morgan, face flushed, eyes flashing fire The youngest Morgan stomped out of the barn and slammed into her truck. Only after she started the engine did she spy Amy.

"Hey, Ruthie, are you okay?"

"Yes. No. I'm fine. Gotta get to work. See you." With one glare at the open barn door, she backed out and disappeared in a cloud of dust.

"What's gotten into that little gal?" her father asked as they stared at the cloud of dust.

"Not sure, but if I had to bet, I'd wager it has something to do with Harley Langdon."

"Sweet on him, is she?"

"Big time, and he is on her. I'm convinced of it."

"So what's the problem?"

"I haven't a clue, and I've got too many worries of my own to ponder it. There's the villain now," she whispered as Harley appeared at the door.

Grinning, he tipped his hat. "Mornin', Fosters. Perfect day for a ride."

Wolf, Amy thought as they followed him into the barn.

Harley had already saddled Raine and Tara. The horses waited in the shade behind the barn, nickering softly. "Sure you're okay on your own, folks? Jeb'll be in shortly. He's cleaning up for his houseguest, Hank Winchester who's coming up from Yuma for the night. If you want to sit in the shade and have a coffee, I can call and check on his ETA, or I can take you once he arrives."

"Absolutely not!" she said a little too vehemently. She took a deep breath and said, "We'll be fine, thanks, Harley. Come on, Dad, let's get cracking. I told Maggie we'd be there at nine."

Harley watched Amy Foster practically fly into the saddle. *What's lit the fire under her beautiful bottom?* he wondered, knowing the answer-- *Jeb Barnes.*

"Well, if you're sure?" Harley said, helping Spark Foster to mount the gentle sorrel morgan. He exchanged a knowing smile with the man and gave Raine a pat. "Have a great ride. Beautiful day for it."

When they reached the Bear Creek trail and lost sight of the stables, Amy let out the breath she had been half holding since Harley had mentioned Jeb. *Maybe it is time to go home. Maybe we really aren't good for each other.* Her heart ached as the thoughts crossed her mind, and she wondered again how she would ever leave Jeb behind.

*****

"Got everything shipshape?" Harley asked, observing his assistant stowing his lunch in the office fridge.

"Yup."

"When's Hank get in?"

"'Bout five. Where's Ben?"

"Home."

"So it's just you and me?"

"Ben'll be here later, has guests right now. You okay, buddy?"

"Yup, fine."

"You don't look fine."

Jeb's face reddened. "Okay, I'll get started." Not waiting for Harley's response or instructions, Jeb headed for the stalls. Almost immediately, he reappeared. "Where are Raine and Tara? We've got lessons starting at ten."

"We can use one of the others—Cocoa, Misty, Annie, even Royal."

"But they're used to riding Raine and Tara. Where are they?"

"Fosters took 'em out."

"For how long?"

Harley shrugged, watching the color rise in Jeb's face. "Don't know. Could be all day."

"All day! Well, that's pretty damned inconsiderate, considering we—"

"Whoa, boy. Let's cool down. All's well, I promise. Cocoa and Misty are gentle as lambs, and if they want a more spirited mount, Royal's got plenty."

"That's not the point!" Jeb paced back and forth in the small office, knowing full well he was acting like a crazy person, but unable to stop himself.

"Okay, buddy. Sit down and tell me what *is* the point."

Jeb flopped in a chair, bending over, head in hands. "Hell if I know."

"I think I can take a guess. You're in love with Amy Foster, and you two have had a tiff."

Jeb looked up at his boss, a grin on his face. "Tiff?"

"I can use fancy talk when needed. Got a smile outta you, anyway."

"It's all my fault."

"That's a great start, buddy. Remember, it's always the man's fault. So, say you're sorry and get on with it."

"It's not that simple. Stacy's dad arrives today, and we're scattering her ashes. It's only six weeks since she died, for Christ's sake. What would he think if I told him about Amy?"

"Probably the same thing we all think. Go for it. You know Stacy would have wanted you to."

"Then there's Portland. It's a great place and all, but I don't want to live there. Too many people."

"And she does?"

"Well, yeah. I mean, her work's there, her dad, her friends, everything she cares about."

"'Cept you."

"Well, she won't care about me for long if I refuse to move."

"Who says she wouldn't move? Have you asked her?"

"We're not anywhere near that kind of talk, Harl. Now, can I get back to work?"

"Knock yourself out. If you've got the first lesson covered, I'll take the two stayin' at the Lodge."

Jeb hopped up and headed for Misty's stable. His lesson was with a woman from town, Lottie Pearson. An intermediate rider, Lottie adored Tara. She had offered to buy the gentle morgan several times, but the answer was always no, so she had started putting out feelers to buy her own horse. *There'll be hell to pay when Lottie sees Misty*, he thought, heading into the tack room.

CHAPTER 37

"Welcome Fosters," Ben Morgan said, waving from the back porch of his home as Amy and Spark dismounted and tied up their horses. "Emma will get them some water and oats, won't you, sweetheart?" His daughter stood beside him, nodding, a huge grin on her face. "They okay there, or would you like her to put 'em in the corral?"

Spark tipped his hat. "You're the expert, son. You know these horses."

"Em, go ahead and put 'em in the corral, then, okay?"

As Emma led them off, her limp almost imperceptible, Maggie appeared on the porch, baby Ben on her hip. "Come in. What can we get you? Coffee? Lemonade? Iced tea? Water?"

Amy hugged Maggie, then Ben. "Lemonade would be lovely, if it's not too much trouble."

"Spark?" Maggie asked, hugging Amy's tall, handsome father.

"Lemonade sounds terrific. Thanks, darlin'."

Glasses in hand, Ben and Spark began their tour, leaving Amy, Maggie, and the baby in the kitchen. "Thanks for having us, Maggie. He's been so excited about this. Planning a new house has really energized him. In fact, he loves it here. I wouldn't be at all surprised if he starts making noises about selling the Portland house and moving here permanently when we get home."

"I hear it's a gorgeous place."

"Yes, but every room, every stick of furniture reminds him of Mom. He loves it, but it's a sad place with her gone."

"How 'bout you? Would you or your brother ever live there?"

Amy laughed. "In the Magic Kingdom? Never. Buck and I dubbed it that years ago. I mean, it's gorgeous, but way too big."

"How are things?"

"If you mean with Jeb, horrible."

"Oh, no, what happened?"

"We quarreled. I went to see him the other night, to talk. Only made things worse. He's angry that I didn't tell him about Ryan's calls. Says he's gonna kidnap Toby rather than let Cora Hooper take him."

Maggie regarded her, eyes full of concern. "He's attached to him. We all are.""What will we do? We can't let him go back."

Maggie reached over and took her hand. "We'll find a way. Ben's looking into it, and his dad is, too. My father-in-law has a lot of clout in this state and many connections. Knows most of the state reps and senators as well as the governor. Judges, attorneys, you name it. He'll find a way."

"I hope so," Amy said, squeezing her hand. She gazed over at the beautiful boy in her host's lap, his brown curls and chestnut eyes so like his sister's. "He has the Morgan eyes, doesn't he?"

Maggie smiled, nodding.

"Can I hold him?"

"Of course," she said, settling her son in Amy's lap. "But don't be distressed if he starts to fuss. He's turned into a momma's boy the past few weeks."

The baby felt so good in her arms, and Amy gazed down at him, smiling. "Hey, cutie."

Baby Ben rewarded her with a huge smile as he reached up to pull her hair.

"He likes you," Maggie said. "Not many people can hold him right now."

Amy smiled. "So, let's talk shower. Anything else I can do to help?"

"You've got all the paper goods, right?"

Amy nodded.

"Thanks. That's such a huge help."

"I thought I'd come over around noon tomorrow to help you set up, unless you want me earlier?"

"Noon's great. I'm going to try to have Emma and the baby nap in the morning. Ben says he's taking the baby to work."

"Really?"

Maggie laughed. "That'll last about ten minutes, but they have a crib at the big house. They'll end up over there for sure."

Beth Morgan's bridal shower was from three to five, but Maggie had arranged food if the guests wanted to stay for an informal dinner.

"I'm looking forward to it," Amy said.

"Emma and I are, too. Only one dreading it is the bride."

"Oh?"

"Beth hates to be the center of attention."

"I know how she feels."

"Aren't you two headed over to their house next?"

"Yes. Lang's offered to show us around."

"Have you been there yet?"

Amy shook her head.

"Just wait—it's gorgeous. Sam and Lang outdid themselves, and the location is spectacular."

"When do they move in?"

"They're hoping after the honeymoon. I understand they've got furniture ordered, and Leonora and Martha Dillon are overseeing its installation while they're gone."

"They're lucky to have moms like that."

Maggie smiled. "It's a mixed blessing, but they're both terrific. Their instructions are clear—no unpacking boxes, just oversee furniture placement—and Lang and Beth have the rooms marked where furniture goes. I believe they agreed that Carmela could make up a bed for them, and that's it."

Spark stepped into the room and cleared his throat. "Well, darlin,' I believe I've found my architect. If Lang and Beth's house is half as spectacular as this place, Sam Morgan is hired."

Amy winked at Maggie. "As if that was ever in doubt. You ready to ride?"

"Yup." Spark took the last sips of his tea and set the glass in the large slate sink. "Back in the saddle for this tenderfoot."

Emma and Ben walked them to the trailhead and gave directions to the Dillon property. As Amy and Spark rode off, Emma called, "Remember to look for Turtle Rock! That's where you turn to go to Beth and Lang's."

"Thanks, Emma," Amy said, waving as they headed south, the sun now blazing hot.

*****

All new construction, Beth and Lang's house was a dramatic contrast to her brother's place but enjoyed equally spectacular views of the Valley and winery. Lang greeted them and proudly showed them around the house, which appeared to be completed except for a few doorknobs and light fixtures. Several workmen were busy in the bathrooms and kitchen. They nodded as the group passed through.

"It's kind of a luxury having these guys doing all this," Lang said as he showed them around the four large, inviting bedrooms, each with its own bath, custom windows, window seats, built-in bookcases, and beautiful woodwork. "I could do the work, but with my business and the wedding, I decided to throw up my hands and surrender."

"This is truly breathtaking, son. Reminds me of the houses on the islands near us."

"I imagine it does. It's not as Southwestern as it could be, but I've always loved the shingled cottages in New England. We've used siding that can take the Arizona heat, not shake shingles. Came out nice."

"Sure did," Spark said.

"I told Beth that any style she wanted was fine with me, but once we started throwing ideas around with Sam, this was the winner."

"It's beautiful, Lang," Amy said. "Perfect, in fact."

"We think so. Thanks." He smiled from one to the other.

Amy marveled at the handsome man. *He may not be a cowboy, but he holds his own with this crowd.* "And you're moving in after your trip, right?"

"That's the plan. The mothers are overseeing furniture installation, but we'll have a lot of unpacking to do. I'd guess with the camp and summer farm work, we'll be living surrounded by boxes till Christmas. Sorry I can't offer you anything to drink. I do have a few bottles of water in a cooler in my truck."

"No, thank you," she said. "We should be on our way. I'm sure you've got lots to do."

"My daughter's right. We brought our canteens, so we're all set. We'll get out of your hair. Longest I've ridden in years. Hope I make it back alive."

"I can take you in the truck and come back for the horses later?"

"Thanks, son, but if I'm gonna build a house out here, I've gotta get back in the saddle. We appreciate your showing us around."

"My pleasure."

"Sam Morgan's a gifted architect," Spark said.

"That he is," Lang said. "He'll be here tomorrow, right? I expect you're anxious to sit down with him."

"Already got an appointment," Spark said. "While the ladies' shower is goin' on." He winked at Amy.

"So glad you'll both be here for the wedding events. It means a lot to us and all the Morgans."

"We're honored to be a part of it, son."

"Yes, we are," Amy said.

"Only hope Beth survives it all," he said, grinning.

"I'm sure she'll get into the swing," Spark said. "Even the shy gals do!"

As Amy and her dad headed back, she thought about the two beautiful homes and the couples who had built them, so much in love, so happy together. *Will I ever find that kind of happiness?*

CHAPTER 38

"You're lookin' well, Jeb," Hank Winchester said, relaxing in a back booth at Gracie's. "And Gracie's food is better than ever."

"Thanks, Hank. And thanks for coming."

"It's what my little girl wanted. Since her momma died, I've never been able to deny her anything."

"How do you know this is what she wanted? She never said anything to me."

"Nor me, about the ashes, at least. Who thinks about dying when they're nineteen? But she sure loved you, and I know she'd want some part of her here with you. Couldn't get outta Yuma fast enough." Hank gazed over at him, and Jeb saw Stacy in the twinkle of his pale hazel eyes, his wide, genuine smile.

"Sunup was her favorite time of day."

"Always, since she was a baby."

"I picked a nice spot where we used to walk."

"That'll be it, then."

"Hey, cowboys, saved room for dessert?" Greasy apron, hair askew, Gracie appeared beside the booth.

"Not me, Gracie," Jeb said, stuffed after a huge platter of fish and chips.

"Me, neither, honey. We don't have food like this in Yuma. How much do I owe you?"

"Fat chance of that! Long as I'm cookin', your money's no good here, Winchester."

When Jeb gazed up at the tall owner, he spied tears rimming her kind eyes.

Hank's eyes filled up, too, and he smiled. "What we have here are the three people who loved my baby best."

"She was a very special young woman," Gracie said, patting his shoulder. "We won't ever forget her."

Both men rose and gave Gracie a hug, then headed out, Hank tipping his hat to every woman in the place. Jeb smiled, watching the women's response, remembering Stacy's words. *My dad's gotta be the biggest flirt in the state!*

*****

The two men rose in the dark and were standing on the rise at the Saguaro north trailhead as the sun rose in the east. While the sun was hidden by town buildings, its light bathed the sky in a soft peach.

Hank reached in his pocket for the small earthenware jar. "What'dya think? Is this the spot?"

Jeb nodded, remembering holding her hand as she chattered away with plans for the day ahead. "One of her favorites."

"To the west, over the valley?"

"Probably the most peaceful."

"Okay, then." As Hank reached in for a small handful of ashes, his eyes filled. He bent his head and recited the twenty-third Psalm: "'The Lord is my shepherd, I shall not want...' Good-bye, baby. I love you."

Jeb took the jar and shook out the remaining ashes into his hand. "Bye, Stacy. We love you, sweetheart." As he lifted his hand, opening it, a sudden breeze took the ashes up in a swirl of red and orange light. Both men stared until all dust and ash settled over the brush and open field, then turned and silently walked back into town.

Neither felt like breakfast, but they stopped for coffees at the bakery and took them to sit on a bench at the edge of the town green. Hank had already stowed his duffle in his truck as he had to get back to work by noon. They sat quietly for several minutes before the elder man spoke. "Well, that's it, then."

Jeb nodded.

"Don't be a stranger, son. I know Yuma's a step down from here, but I'd love to have you visit."

"Yes, sir."

"And none of this 'sir' business, either."

"Thanks, Hank. I hope you know you're always welcome here, too. The Morgans are really generous, and they'd love to put you up if the cabin's too small."

Winchester chuckled. "For this ole cowboy? Just give me a space long enough for the bed roll and I'm set."

"They were sorry not to see you. They wanted us to come to dinner last night, but I said we had to catch up."

"They're nice folks."

"Hank, does it bother you that I'm giving up our apartment and moving back to the ranch?"

"Hell no, son. Why would you think that?"

Jeb shrugged. "Somehow it feels like a betrayal of Stace."

"Well, it ain't, and it's what she would want. Just like she'd want you to get on with your life and be happy with your new lady friend, if she's what you want."

"You know about Amy? How?"

Winchester grinned. "You forget, I stopped for coffee with Gracie before I saw you yesterday."

"God, Hank, you must think me a world-class bastard for not telling you about Amy."

"Okay. Jeb Barnes, I'm gonna say this once, and then I never want to have this conversation again. My girl was the sweetest person in the whole wide world, with a heart as big as this valley. Do you think she'd want the people she loved to be unhappy? Hell no, she wouldn't. If there's an up there, she lookin' down cheering you and Ms. Foster on. I can tell you that for certain."

"But I—"

"No friggin' buts, do you hear me? If Ms. Foster's the one, grab hold of her and hang on, son. If she's not, find someone who is, *comprende*?"

"Thanks, Hank."

"Now this ole cowboy's gotta hit the road. Thanks for puttin' me up, and keep it touch."

The two men walked to Hank's truck, hugging before Hank slipped into the cab. With a tip of his hat and a warm grin, he said, "Keep me posted. I wanta hear any good news."

Jeb slapped the hood. Stepping back, he returned the grin. "Will do. Safe trip."

*****

Jeb was late for work, but as he drove through the ranch gates, he drove past the stables and headed up to the Lodge. He did not have a clear plan, but he knew he had to see Amy. As he headed through the lobby, intending to ask the desk clerk to phone her room, Spark and his daughter stepped in from the terrace.

"Hey, look who's here," the older man said. "Good morning, son. Too bad we just finished breakfast, or you could've joined us."

Rooted to the spot, Jeb realized how ridiculous he must look. "I…well, I, um, I wanted to speak to—"

Spark smiled, gazing from the red-faced cowboy to his daughter, whose face matched Jeb's. "Okay, youngins, this old man knows when he's a third wheel." He kissed Amy's cheek. "See you in a bit, darlin'."

"Be up soon," she said, finding her voice at last.

They watched Spark disappear up the stairs, then she turned to him. "Jeb, is everything alright?"

"Fine. I just wanted to talk to you."

Amy spied the sadness in his eyes, as well as something else. "I have a few minutes, but the shower is today, and I have a bunch of errands to run for Maggie."

"Of course. Sorry. I'll see you later."

She reached out and touched his arm, feeling his warmth. *How I've missed your touch, Jeb Barnes.* "No, Jeb, wait. Let's step outside." She led him out the front door, and they walked a short distance to the far side of his truck, a secluded spot with only the Valley in front of them.

Jeb realized he had no idea what he wanted to say, but he took her hand and gently caressed her silky skin.

"How did it go with Stacy's dad?"

"Fine, good. Hank's a terrific guy."

"You okay?"

"Yes. No. I don't know. I just knew I had to see you to say I'm sorry for being such a jerk."

"You're not a jerk. You're grieving."

"Maybe, but you've been nothing but great to me, and you didn't deserve all that crap the other night."

She squeezed his hand. "Friends again?"

Jeb turned to face her, taking her other hand in his. "Always."

Before either knew it, their lips had found each other, a gentle kiss that deepened as they drew closer, arms circling each other. "God, Amy, I've missed you," he whispered, voice husky.

"Me, too," she said, hand reaching up to caress his strong jaw.

"Sorry, forgot to shave this morning."

"Does it look like I mind?"

"I love you, Amy. That's what I came to tell you."

"I love you, too."

"Can we start again, maybe?"

"I'd like that." She kissed him softly. "I'm sorry, but I've got to go. See you later?"

"I'll call."

"Good."

Jeb smiled, a warm smile that lit up his entire body, a smile Amy had never seen before. *I'm looking at happiness, happiness and peace*, she thought, hoping her expression mirrored his own.

CHAPTER 39

"Hey, Amy, look what we've done!" Emma Morgan cried as Amy came into the kitchen laden with bags and boxes.

She followed the child to the back terrace, now festooned with streamers, balloons, and flowers. Pure white geese and ducks waddled around the perimeter, where a delicate, almost invisible chute of fencing surrounded them.

"Wow, Em, it looks beautiful! Like something out of a fairy tale!"

"I know. Daddy helped me. Carmela, too! Mommy's been busy with the baby most of the time." She frowned slightly, then brightened when Maggie appeared behind them, baby on hip.

"The decorators outdid themselves, didn't they? Ben's just run down to the stables to chat with Harley, but when he returns and takes my little friend, I'll launch into full party mode. This rascal did let me get dressed, so let's pray he doesn't spit up. As I told you the other day, he's in a real momma stage and doesn't like to be put down."

"Can you blame him with a momma like that?" Ben Morgan asked, stepping out the kitchen door, strong, tanned arms circling mother and child.

"Hey, Daddy. Amy thinks it looks like a fairy land."

"Told you, Peanut. Now let me take your brother so you ladies are free to party till you drop. Think Ruthie'll succeed in dragging our sister over here? This is her worst nightmare, I'm afraid."

"Never mind that, and no teasing," Maggie said, handing him the baby. "Ben's bag is all packed by the front door."

"Saw it. Can't get rid of us fast enough, can you?"

"Much as I adore you, husband of mine, yes. Now scoot." Maggie leaned forward and kissed father and child.

Wistful, Amy watched the interplay of the pair. The camp staff had dubbed them "the beautiful couple," and they were beautiful on the outside, but on the inside as well, never more so than when their deep love for each other shone for all to see.

"Hey, Peanut, knock 'em dead. Remember, I want a blow-by-blow tonight."

"You betcha!" Emma said, grinning from ear to ear. That expression, recently acquired, was a favorite of the father and daughter. "See ya later, alligator."

"Afternoon, baboon!"

"Go," Maggie said, swatting him playfully.

"Okay, okay. Have fun, ladies. By the way, Amy, what'd you do to young Barnes?"

Instantly reddening, Amy saw all eyes trained on her. Were there no secrets in this place? "Excuse me?"

"Just saw him, and he had a big shit-eater on his face."

"Ben!" Maggie said.

"Oops, sorry. Ignore that, Peanut. What I meant was—haven't seen the lad so happy in a long time. I mean, who shovels a stall grinning like a hyena? Manure could've been a mile high and he'd still have been smiling."

Maggie gazed over at Amy, whose cheeks were now crimson. "Okay, guys, enough. We get the picture. Now shoo!"

Emma followed her father to wave from the front porch, and the women retreated to the kitchen. "My obnoxious, nosy husband aside, I hope this is good news?"

"Yes. Maybe. We'll see. It's a start, anyway. Now let's get this shower organized, shall we?"

CHAPTER 40

"Are you sure you wouldn't like Jeb or me to come with you guys?" Harley asked, as he and his assistant looked up at Ben Senior and Spark. The two old friends sat proudly on their mounts, Ben Senior on his own horse, Royal, and Spark on Tara.

Clearly eager to be off, the Morgan patriarch waved his hand. "We're not dead yet. I think we can handle a short ride. I'll call when we get to the Lodge, and one of you can pick up the horses."

At that moment, his son and grandson appeared. "Dad? What'dya think you're doing?"

"Not you too! I'm taking a ride with my oldest friend, and we gotta get goin'. Your brother's meeting Spark at the Lodge in an hour."

"But, Dad—"

His father raised his hand. "Not another word, you hear? Now take my grandson in and find something fun to do. If he gets tired, bring him up to the house."

Ben opened his mouth to speak, but the warning he saw in his father's eyes silenced him. "Have a good ride, then. You got cell phones?"

Harley poked him in the ribs.

"The other nervous Nellie already asked," his father said, patting his front pocket. "Now move aside and let these old cowboys pass."

The three men stood in the shade and watched until the riders disappeared around the bend in the trail. Then Ben turned to his friend. "How the hell did this happen?"

Harley threw up his hands. "They came down and told us to saddle up the horses. Your dad's the boss, buddy. We underlings do what the boss says."

"He's got a bad heart! For Christ's sake, Harley, you can stand up to him!"

"Yeah, like you just did? Leave it be. Jeb's got a lesson in fifteen minutes, and I've got work to do. What are you and my little buddy gonna do?"

"Clean up the office. I've got a lot of paperwork."

"Good luck with that. Come on, lover boy, back to work," Harley said, grinning at Jeb, who had wisely hung back once they had helped Ben and Spark into the saddles. If Harley and Ben couldn't stand up to the big boss man, he certainly wasn't going to try.

*****

"Doesn't Beth look lovely?" Leonora Morgan said to Amy as the guest of honor opened a gift. Emma sat on one side of her with the important job of constructing the ribbon bouquet. Ruthie on the other noted the gifts and names of the givers in a pretty wedding journal furnished by their mother.

Amy nodded. "Yes, she does."

"I was afraid we wouldn't get her in the door, but Ruthie saved the day."

"All this, while amazing, is a lot for an introvert."

Leonora stared at her for an instant, unsure of whether to be offended at Amy's bluntness. "Yes, I suppose our eldest daughter is a bit of an introvert."

"So am I," Amy said softly. "Probably why I recognize it in others. Doesn't mean we don't like people. We love them, but in small doses."

"Lang compliments her. We're so pleased they found each other."

"They seem very happy. Dad and I rode over to their house yesterday. It's gorgeous."

"Yes, the three of them—Beth, Lang, and our son Sam—did a beautiful job with the plans."

"Dad's off to meet with Sam this afternoon about his house."

"I hope he builds it quickly. Ben is so pleased about having his dearest friend living nearby."

Amy knew the time comment was partially in reference to the elder Morgan's heart condition, but also because the two men obviously so enjoyed each other's company. Her dad was going to be bored to tears when they returned to Portland next week. "Better watch out what you wish for. Dad's really taken to the Valley. I wouldn't be at all surprised if he decided to make a permanent move after the house is finished."

"My dear, I'm sure you know how delighted that would make us. Uh-oh, that's the fourth salad bowl, isn't it?" she whispered, watching as Beth held up an enormous glass dish. "This is why I told her to use a registry, but when have my daughters—or sons, for that matter—ever listened to me?"

The shower guests were mostly friends of Martha Dillon and Leonora, with a few of Beth's high school friends, Rose Dillon, Lang's sister, Carmela, and several women from town, including Gabriela, a dress shop owner with whom Beth had become close friends. The dress Beth was wearing had come from her shop. There was one young woman, Hope Seymour, who had come up from Tucson, a friend of Beth's from the university, and one of the only people she had invited from her old life. Hope looked vaguely uncomfortable despite Maggie's best efforts to engage her.

After the gifts, they loaded plates with sandwiches, vegetables, and salads and sat in chairs, on the terrace walls, and on blankets spread on the lawn beyond the terrace.

"Finally, a moment to breathe," Maggie said, coming to sit beside Amy on the wall.

"You and Emma have outdone yourselves. It's a lovely party, Maggie."

"Yes, and she's had a ball. How're you doing?"

"Lovely. I'm enjoying watching everything and am so grateful to be included."

"Of course! I'm glad things are better with Jeb."

"Me too."

"Maybe someday we'll be hosting a shower for you on a beautiful Valley day?"

Amy blanched, then broke into a smile. "Time will tell. I'mjust glad we're talking again."

"He loves you, Amy, I'm sure of it."

"I know," she said quietly.

*****

"So, how'd it go with Sam Morgan?" Amy asked, gazing over at her dad. They were in the white whale headed for dinner in Tucson with an old friend of Spark's, a retired hospital administrator who had many clinical connections in the area. She knew this was his way of opening up the idea of a move to Arizona. She'd agreed to go along just in case she decided that's what she wanted to do.

"Super. Next thing is for us to walk the property tomorrow. He's got some ideas, and I told him what I was thinking."

"And that is?"

"Southwest all the way. Adobe, red tile roof, lots of windows takin' in those spectacular views, all one floor, bedrooms for you and Buck and a couple more for guests. You know your daddy likes room to move."

"No Victorian flourishes?" The moment the words were uttered, Amy regretted them as she watched her father's face fall, sadness replacing the excitement of a minute earlier. "Oh, Daddy, I'm sorry. I didn't mean to make you sad."

"No, worries, baby. We both miss your momma, but it's time to move on."

She reached over and squeezed his hand. *Yes, time to move on.*

*****

The dinner with Coleman Myers was lively and fun. Amy had no doubt that should she want a job, he would have several interviews lined up in the blink of an eye. After kissing her dad good night, she returned to her room and found three missed calls from Jeb.

He picked up on the first ring. "Hey, I was calling to see if you wanted to grab dinner, but I couldn't reach you."

"Sorry, I left my phone in the room. My dad and I met an old friend of his for dinner in Tucson." She decided not to tell him about Myers's connections or her father's obvious attempts to feel him out about employment for her.

"Guess the next few days are gonna be super busy."

"Sure are. You looking forward to the bachelor party?"

"Not especially. I'd rather be with you. All the Morgans together are pretty wild. I guess Lang's got a bunch of friends coming from Boston, too. Are you hens doin' something?"

"Hens?"

"Sorry, are you ladies doin' something?"

"Gracie's for dinner. Much tamer than your gathering, I'd guess."

"I'd really like to see you, Amy."

"There's Thursday and Friday nights?"

"Yeah, along with the rest of the world."

She laughed. "I was teasing. I know what you mean. Any chance we could go for a ride tomorrow morning before you start work?"

"We're kind of swamped, but if we met at six, I could probably go out for an hour or so."

"Perfect. See you then?"

"Can't wait."

"Night, Jeb."

"Night, Amy."

Chapter 41

"Another amazing Valley day," Amy sighed, gazing out at the green fields and mountains as the sun rose behind them. "Not sure how I'll readjust to rainy Portland. If we get three sunny days in a week, it's cause for a celebration."

Then stay, Jeb thought, looking over at her beautiful profile. She was riding Misty, and he marveled, as he always did, at how comfortable and steady she was astride a horse. He had no doubt she could easily handle Rowdy or Pepper, Harley's Appaloosa. "Yeah, we're pretty spoiled. Except for the two rainy seasons, this is pretty much the story all year round."

"So, now we've seen the sunrise and sunset together," she said, smiling over at him. "Where to now, cowboy?"

"How 'bout we ride to the top of Eastland Pass? That's the ranch's eastern-most boundary. We can stop and enjoy the view—it's pretty incredible—then head back. Our morning's pretty crammed. Harley has kids working over the next three days to clean the stalls and exercise the horses, but not today. We've got back-to-back lessons till late afternoon."

"Then lead the way," she said, nudging Misty to bring her to a gallop.

Jeb nudged Royal and the horse took off, catching his stable mate easily. When the males took the lead. Amy laughed. The pure joy of watching rider and horse always stunned her, *especially this rider*. Jeb led them across a vast meadow, slowing down as they began to climb the well-worn earthen trail. Amy followed at a safe distance, guiding Misty across the switchbacks as they emerged from the trees and scrub grasses to the wide open hillside dotted with saguaro and a variety of other cactus.

As they reached the top, she was amazed at the dramatic change in terrain. Gone were the green fields and lush undergrowth. They were in high desert now. As she gazed ahead, over the crest of the mountain, dry desert stretched as far as the eye could see.

"Wow, the Valley really is an amazing thing, isn't it?"

"Yup. Not many places like it in this part of the country, maybe anywhere."

"I keep meaning to look up the orographic effect on my computer, but never seem to have a minute."

"Want get down?" His smile told her everything she needed to know.

"Sure, if you can spare the time?"

Jeb jumped down and came over to catch her as she slid off the huge white stallion. Amy's feet never hit the ground as he drew her close, wrapping her legs round his waist. As he kissed her long and deep, his tongue teased and tickled hers. His hand traveled down to lift her tee shirt, cupping her breast.

She moaned, "Oh, Jeb, I've missed you so much."

Those were the last coherent words she spoke as clothes flew off and Jeb leaned back against a smooth boulder. A condom magically slipped into place, and he thrust into her warm wetness. Amy cried out and reared above him, begging him with each thrust to go deeper. Just before a roaring climax overtook them, Jeb whispered, "I love you, Amy, so much it scares me."

As their passion subsided, a calmness and peace enveloped them. Jeb held her against him, heedless of the hard stone beneath him. He trailed soft kisses down her neck to her breasts as Amy smoothed damp locks of hair from his brow and kissed his forehead.

"That was amazing, and by the way, Jeb Barnes, I love you, too. Let's be scared together till we're not anymore, okay?"

"Fine with me." He held her back slightly, smiling as he gazed into her beautiful eyes, noticing tiny flecks of gold in their hazel depths. "I'm sorry, my love, but I've gotta get back."

"I know," she sighed, her lips finding his for one more long, deep kiss.

As he set her down and they dressed, the sound of horse's footfalls came from below. They had just buttoned and snapped themselves into place when Ruthie Morgan appeared, hair flying, red-faced and dusty. She sat astride Jadie, her sturdy black, brown, and white pinto, bulging saddle bags on either side of her.

"Uh-oh," she said, face turning redder than it already was. "I've interrupted something, haven't I?"

"Hey, Ruthie, we're just heading back. Stopped for a minute to enjoy the view." Jeb said, grinning.

"Yeah, sure, and I'm riding a pink elephant."

Amy laughed. "It's true, Ruthie. Jeb has to get back to work, and I've got a list a mile long of wedding prep tasks, as I'm sure you do."

She shook her head, then slid down to stand beside them. "Not me. Just left my list with a note to my parents on the front hall table. I can't go through another wedding with Harley. Beth'll understand."

"But you're the maid of honor," Amy said.

"And your mom'll have a heart attack," Jeb said, worrying more about Ben Senior than his strong, resilient wife.

Ruthie shrugged. "She'll get over it."

Amy stared at the angry redhead for a few minutes, then decided that stern words were in order. "Ruthie Morgan, you get right back up in that saddle and head home. Maybe you can intercept the note before your parents see it."

"Will not! I am not going to give Harley Langdon the satisfaction! He's bringing a date to the wedding. Did you know that?"

Jeb stepped back, petting the horses, deciding that this conversation was way over his pay grade.

"No," Amy said, "I didn't know about the date, but it might be a relative, for all you know. Did you get a name?"

"Willow something. What kind of name is that, anyway?"

"Haven't you been dating these past few years? Harley's met your boyfriends, hasn't he?"

"This is different, and I would *never* bring one of them to a family wedding!"

"But he is, and you're going to have to deal with it, no matter who she is."

"No, I'm not. I'm heading into the mountains. Be back in time for camp opening."

"Oh, no you're not! Who's gonna help Maggie and me with the bachelorette party? Not to mention your incredibly important role as maid of honor. Beth'll be lost without you."

"She'll understand."

"That's not the point and you know it! Beth is your only sister, and she depends on you. I've seen how she's leaned on you dozens of times this summer. She will be devastated. Now, not another word. You get back on that horse and ride back with us. This is your sister's day and you're not going to spoil it!"

Jeb watched in awe of Amy's tirade. It wasn't long before Ruthie's face crumpled, and the tears snaked down her rosy cheeks. *Oh, boy, you're definitely outta your depth, cowboy,* he thought, turning back to the horses.

"When is ever gonna be my day?" Ruthie wailed, flailing her arms, stomping back and forth.

"Oh, sweetie," Amy said, moving to put her arms around Ruthie. "It'll be your day soon. You've got lots of time. If it isn't Harley, you'll find the one." *Although I've seen the way he looks at you. Not sure what this wedding date's all about, but that cowboy is head over heels in love.*

Jeb pulled his bandana out and handed it to Ruthie. "Come on, Ruthie. Let's get you home, okay?"

All the fight gone, Ruthie nodded, wiped her eyes, and blew her nose. "I'll wash this for you. Thanks, Jeb."

"You ready?" Amy asked, smiling at her.

"Bring on the lists!" Ruthie said, swinging up into the saddle.

"That's the spirit, partner," Amy said as she shared a wink and a smile with Jeb.

CHAPTER 42

The Bulldog closed for the night, allowing the Morgans and guests to take over the saloon for Lang's bachelor party. All the Morgan brothers had arrived, and by eight that night, they were in full party mode. Ben Senior and Spark sat at a corner table, enjoying the show in front of them.

"You have a fine-lookin' bunch," Spark said, eying the brothers. Ben, Sam, and Kyle were dark-haired and resembled each other, almost as if they were triplets, except that Sam, the runner, was thinner and leaner than the others. Sandy-haired Robbie took after his mother, his bright green eyes the mirror of hers.

Ben Senior beamed. "I expect we'll hold on to them."

"These guys could all be on the cowboy calendar. Dillon's no slouch, either, and his Boston buddies are nice lookin' fellas. Where Lang's daddy tonight?"

"They called and said he'd skip this so he can be at the other events. He hasn't been too well, and a hard drinkin' night isn't the best idea for Jaybo right now."

"Not the best idea for any of us ole cowboys, I expect," Spark said, clinking his beer glass against the one held by his friend.

"Yeah, but we've got my Nora watchin' out for us. If I'm not home by ten, she'll call out the cavalry."

Spark smiled. "You're a lucky man, Ben Morgan."

"Don't I know it."

"Hey, Dad," Robbie called. "You and Spark want anything?"

"We're good, son, thanks. If you want a breather, come talk to two old men. We wanta hear the latest from Sedona."

Robbie grabbed a beer and came to sit with them, regaling them with hilarious stories of his recent trips with the touristas. Robbie led wilderness treks out of Sedona. His parents had been angling for him to come home and run them from the ranch, but he always replied, "different terrain, wanta make my own way," or words to that effect.

Jeb watched the rowdy bunch playing pool and darts, many shots and beer chasers punctuating each round. He was always in awe of the Morgan brothers, and tonight was no exception. Finally, he allowed himself to be drawn into a game of pool, which he won, since he was the most sober one in the bunch. The penalty for winning was, of course, two shots and a beer chaser, so he knew his sobriety would be short-lived.

*****

Across town, Gracie's, too, had closed for Beth's bachelorette party, now in full swing. Much to the shock of her daughters, Leonora Morgan had hired a male stripper and after several glasses of wine was now stuffing twenty-dollar bills into his G-string. Gabriela Huff, Beth's friend and a town shopkeeper, was beside her, stuffing bills on his other side.

"Mother!" Beth cried. "Get away from there! Somebody do something about her!"

"I'm taking pictures, lots of 'em," Ruthie said, snapping away. "Then if she's ever givin' Dad a hard time, I can whip 'em out as blackmail."

Maggie laughed. "I expect they would give your dad a huge chuckle."

"Maybe I'll order poster size!" Ruthie said, sipping her beer, smiling over at Amy. She mouthed the words *thank you* before returning to her picture taking.At that moment, Gracie appeared with a huge bowl of paella, Rosa following with salad and a basket of breads. "Dinner, ladies," Gracie called. "And for heaven's sakes, leave that poor man alone!"

CHAPTER 43

Thursday dawned bright and clear. The stables were closed for two days, but the work of caring for the horses went on. Harley, Jeb, and two of the part-timers brought the animals out to the corrals, mucked stalls, and put in fresh hay, food, and water. As Jeb worked at the routine tasks, his head pounded. Beer was one thing, but shots of whiskey and tequila were quite another. He grinned, recalling the raucous evening, which featured Robbie and Kyle Morgan dancing on the bar as several of Lang Dillon's Boston friends sang bawdy songs written especially for the groom.

As the men worked in adjacent stalls, familiar voices called from the barn's entrance. "Hey, cowboys! You in there?"

Jeb paused, leaning on a pitchfork as Derek Callen, one of Lang's Cambridge friends, poked his head around the corner. "There's one of our main men! How're doin'? Lookin' a little green around the gills."

"I've been better."

"Where's your buddy, Langdon?"

"Mornin'," Harley said, stepping out of the adjacent stall. "What brings you guys over here so early?"

"Dillon sent us to see if you wanted to go to breakfast in town."

"We ate several hours ago, and we've got a few hours' work here."

Callen grinned. "Not if we all pitch in, right, guys?"

Harley nudged his hat back and scratched his forehead. "You're kidding, right?"

"Absolutely not. We came to Saguaro for the whole experience, so point us to tools and give us our orders. With eight of us workin', we should make short work of this. After that, the least you can do is have coffee with us. We already roused the Morgan boys. They're meeting us at ten."

"Okay. Jeb, go grab a few more pitchforks. These guys can finish the stalls, and you and I can bring in the hay and oats. Rip and Skip can bring the horses in later."

Jeb laughed and headed to the tool shed. "Sure thing, boss."

*****

Spark smiled at his daughter across the table as they enjoyed the Lodge's breakfast buffet. "How you doin', darlin'?"

"If I keep eating like this, I'll have to buy a whole new wardrobe when we get home."

"Nonsense, you've never looked better. You've been thin as a stick for months and still are. A little meat on your bones wouldn't hurt after what Houseman put you through."

Hearing Ryan's name made Amy blanch. Her father noticed immediately and said, "Oh, darlin', I'm sorry for mentioning that good-for-nothing."

"It's okay."

"No, it's not. Is he still calling you?"

To her father's surprise, Amy broke out in a grin. "No, as a matter of fact, I put a stop to that."

"Excellent. Glad to hear it. I won't even ask how."

She laughed. "Please don't. When does Buck arrive?"

"Around noon. Time will tell. You know your brother."

"I'm glad he'll be here."

"Me, too." He reached over and patted her hand, praying that the sadness of the past few months would lift soon. *Maybe between young Mr. Barnes and her brother, we can keep my baby smiling.*

*****

After a wild breakfast at Gracie's with the Morgans and Lang's friends, Jeb walked back to his apartment. Boxes and bags were everywhere. Hank Winchester had taken a few boxes of Stacy's things, then helped him pack up what he wasn't taking for charity. *Next week, after the wedding, I'll take them to Goodwill*, he thought as he gazed around at what remained of Stacy.

He had kept the few photos and mementos from trips and activities they had shared. These he put in a small wooden box placed in a larger box marked "Ranch." He called Amy, but the phone went straight to voice mail. He wondered if she was still screening calls and whether the old boyfriend was still harassing her. He missed her so much it hurt. If only he could pull her into his arms and obliterate all thought.

His gaze fell on the velvet box he had set on the mantel after he returned from his parents' home in Flagstaff. After the accident, through his weeks of recovery and Stacy's funeral, he had not known where it had gone. Then, as he prepared to come back to work, his dad produced it. Once home, he set it on the mantel and had not gone near it since. *It's time*, he thought. He snatched the box and headed out. When he reached Walton's Jewelers, he hesitated, then took a deep breath and pushed open the door.

Isaac Walton, the owner, stood behind the counter. Jeb was his only customer. "Hey, there. I was wondering if I might see you." The tall, slender shopkeeper wore a long black apron over a crisp white dress shirt and red bow tie. His silver hair was longish, thick, and perfectly groomed. His pale blue eyes sparkling with warmth. "I'm so sorry about your girl. Stacy was a sweetheart, loved by everyone in town."

Jeb swallowed, suddenly afraid he might weep. He straightened up, cleared his throat, and placed the velvet box on the counter. "Thanks, Mr. Walton. I wondered about this and what I could do as far as a return?"

"Say no more. I'm happy to issue a full refund. No problem at all. Just let me step into the office and get the paperwork."

Jeb nodded and Walton disappeared. He wandered from case to case as he waited, gazing down at men's watches, then moving on to all manner of jewelry for young and old. When Walton returned, eyes grave, manila folder in hand, he was surprised to see Jeb smiling.

"You know, Mr. Walton, I've been thinking. I've decided that rather than a refund, I'd like to see about an exchange."

CHAPTER 44

Buck Foster arrived a little before noon and had all the women at Reception swooning until Jim Thompson, the manager, took over and showed him to his room. *Can't blame them*, Jim thought, watching the broad-shouldered man work the room, sandy hair falling over his blue-green eyes as they rested on every female. *He's a looker and he knows it.*

A short time later, Adonis returned, strolling through the lobby with his father and sister on the way to lunch in town. "I see you've made quite an impression," Amy said drolly, following him out the front door.

Buck laughed, that deep infectious laugh that she loved, winking at a middle-aged guest who stood in the entryway.

Once settled in a back booth at Gracie's, lunch orders in, the three leaned back, pleased to be together. This was only the third time they had been together since Patsy Foster, beloved wife and mother had died.

"Sorry about Ally," Amy said. "But selfishly, I'm glad we have you all to ourselves, or here at all." Her brother's girlfriend managed The Whipple, a small, prestigious gallery in Los Angeles. Their collection of contemporary art was known around the world. Most of the original holdings had come from Andrew Whipple's private collection, but they now hung some of the most sought-after new artists in the world.

"Yeah, well, Ally and I had a good run, but it was time. Good to be with you guys, just us. Ally always sucked the air out of any room she walked into."

"I'm still sorry, Buck."

"Don't be. You're looking great, by the way. Better than I expected after that bastard Houseman's behavior."

"He's been calling her all summer, tryin' to patch things up," Spark said, shaking his head.

"What? You want me to set him straight?"

"No, I do not! Ryan is no longer a problem. Dead issue."

"Would that he were," Spark mumbled.

"Dad!"

"Just kiddin', sweetie, but we did have a whole posse of cowboys ready to string him up, if needed." He winked at his son.

"Dad!"

"Okay, okay. You know, these taco things aren't half bad," Spark said, waving one of the fish tacos she had persuaded him to try.

"Told you." She turned to her brother. "I've been tryin' to keep him eating healthy, but it's a challenge in beef country."

"Can't wait," Buck said, grinning at Rosa as she refilled their iced teas. "Wonder what's on the menu tonight. I'm ready for some grass-fed, farm-raised beef."

"You're in for a treat, son. I guarantee it."

"So, sister dear, back to how great you look. You doin' okay?"

"Yes, it's been a good change. You know I fought Dad tooth and nail about coming here for five weeks, but it's been nice to get out of Portland. I'll be glad to get home, but I've enjoyed it—the country, the camp work, all of it."

"And a certain Mr. Barnes hasn't hurt either," Spark said, winking at Buck. Amy turned bright red. "As I was saying, it's an amazing place, this green, verdant valley with the rest of Arizona like an oven and brown most of the year. The Valley stays cool and has perfect weather all year."

"Sort of like LA without the smog, huh?" Buck said. "Now, what about this Mr. Barnes?"

"He works at the ranch. You'll meet him tonight."

"And?"

"And we've been seeing a bit of each other."

"Great."

"We've had some bumps and rolls."

"Who doesn't?"

"His almost-fiancée—who worked here, by the way—died in an accident two months ago, and then there's me and the fallout from Ryan. Not exactly romance material, but Jeb's great guy and we've grown closer, especially with working at the camp. There's this sweet child, a four-year-old, Toby Hooper, whom we've both been supporting."

"So, what happens in September?"

"I'll be back in Portland, Jeb'll be here doing what he does, and we're praying that Toby's social worker finds a way to terminate his horror show of a mother's parental rights."

"Is that likely?"

"I don't know. The whole situation is very stressful."

Buck watched his sibling, certain there was more to the Mr. Barnes story, but decided not to press her. *I can't wait to meet the man who's brought the light back into my baby sister's eyes.* "So, Dad, what about this house you're planning?"

CHAPTER 45

A perfect evening with clear skies and a gentle breeze provided the backdrop for the rehearsal dinner at the Dillons' winery. The Morgans arrived in three vehicles, tumbling out in a flurry of laughter. Beth immediately excused herself and hurried off to find Lang. The past week had been overwhelming for the shy Morgan daughter, and she desperately needed her fiancé's strong arms around her. He did not disappoint.

"Hey, sweetheart, you okay? You look beautiful, as always, but you're white as a sheet."

"I'm fine now," she said, giving him a wan smile. "It's been bedlam at the big house, with my maid of honor threatening to defect so she doesn't have to see Harley and his girlfriend."

Lang chuckled. "Well, then, she's gonna be in for a big surprise."

Beth gazed up at him. "You know something! Tell!"

"That brought some color into those lovely cheeks."

"Lang, what is it?"

"You're about to see for yourself, my darling bride. Harley's already here." He pointed in the direction of the winery barn, its entrance festooned with flowers, ribbons, and balloons. Harley was just stepping out, his arm around a tall young woman, her straight flaxen hair falling over slender shoulders. She wore an off-white sleeveless shift that hung on her, simple white sandals on her feet. Pale green eyes scanned the crowd. She looked terrified. Jeb followed them, eyes downcast, unable to hide a grin.

Leonora and Ben Senior had already disappeared in search of their dear friends and hosts, Martha and Jaybo Dillon, Lang's parents, Emma with them. Rose Dillon, Lang's sister, had come out to greet the Morgan siblings. All stood together, every eye trained on the barn door.

"Well, there she is," Ruthie said, tears stinging her eyes, jaw set. "What a nerve." She crossed her arms in front of her and turned away.

"Kinda cute, but doesn't look like Harley's type," Sam Morgan said, squinting in the evening light.

"Looks about twelve," Kyle said.

"That's because she is or there abouts," Ben Morgan said, chuckling as his arm circled his wife's shoulders.

Maggie gazed up at him. "You know something, Ben Morgan. Now out with it!"

"Hey, buddy." Ben stepped forward to greet his friend. "And, this must be Willow? Finally, I get to meet the love of Harley's life." Surprised, she let the tall, gorgeous cowboy hug her, then stepped back, closer to her companion.

"Hey, everyone," Harley said, grinning from ear to ear with pride. "I'd like you to meet my daughter, Willow."

"Daughter?" Ruthie spun around, mouth agape.

Harley grinned and winked at Ben. "Yup. Willow, this is Ruthie."

"Hello," she said softly, reaching out to shake Ruthie's hand.

"Oh, yes, hi…great to meet you. I see the resemblance," Ruthie said.

"Everyone always says I look like my mom," Willow said, "But that I have my daddy's eyes."

Father and daughter made their way from person to person, saying hello. Stunned, Ruthie followed their progress, as the Fosters drove in. After meeting Willow, Spark excused himself. "Better go find the oldsters. Nice to meet you, sweetheart." Willow rewarded him with a beautiful smile.

Jeb watched as Amy said hello to each Morgan and introduced Buck. He could see the interest in Robbie's and Kyle's eyes. Who wouldn't be interested? She looked lovely in a saffron cocktail dress that hugged every curve, a delicate, lacy shawl draped over her shoulders. Her hair was swept up, and she wore simple, but elegant pearl earrings. When she finally broke away and spied him, she gave him the smile he liked to think was his alone. "Hey, Jeb."

"Hey, Amy. You look amazing," he whispered, giving her a quick hug.

"You don't look so bad yourself, cowboy." *That's the understatement of the century.* In khaki pants, a dark navy jacket, and a blue dress shirt that matched his eyes, he looked good enough to eat! "This is my brother, Buck."

"Pleased to meet you," Jeb said, shaking the other's hand.

"Likewise," Buck said, smiling warmly.

As they all headed in, Ruthie pulled her oldest brother aside. "You knew about this and didn't tell me?"

"Not my secret to tell, baby sister."

"That's just it! I'm your sister!"

"And he's my best friend."

"Well, now I want to know everything, so spill."

Ben had one arm around Maggie, who held baby Ben, and put the other around his sister. "I know it's hard, baby, but it's Harley's story. I'm sure he'll tell you if you ask."

"As if!" She headed off to intercept Buck Foster. *Two can play at this game!*

The caterers and the Dillons' chef, Jon Wilson, prepared and served a sumptuous meal, each of six courses perfectly complimented with wines from their vineyard. The small assemblage thoroughly enjoyed themselves on the warm, perfect evening.

In addition to the two families, Harley, and Jeb, the gathering included Lang's friends from back east. Scott Jackson, his college roommate and best man, gave a raucous toast, then led "the eastern contingent" in a bawdy, heartfelt song, entitled "Sweet Home in the Valley" to the tune of Lynyrd Skynyrd's "Sweet Home Alabama."

Then Ben Senior rose, squeezing his wife's hand. "Well, folks, what a pleasure it is to celebrate the marriage of our second child and eldest daughter. Her mother and I could not be prouder of Beth. She is the most courageous, strong person we know, and we know a few, don't we, Nora?" As he spoke, he gazed over at his daughter-in-law, Maggie, and winked.

"We are grateful for every day of our Bethie's life and thank God she and Lang found each other. Lang Dillon, I hope you know what a lucky man you are. And we can't get much luckier than havin' one of our beloved kids marry the offspring of such good friends. Jay, Martha, Nora, and I are pleased as punch about that, and I'm so grateful to see this day and have my oldest friend, Spark Morgan, here with me. So, to Beth and Lang!" With that, he raised his glass, and the group followed suit.

A tremendous cheer followed. Then Lang stood and toasted his parents, future in-laws, and his bride. As coffee and desserts were served, the toasts seemed to have petered out when, to everyone's surprise, Beth stood up and clinked her glass with a spoon. Lang's jaw dropped open, and he stared up at her.

Beth smiled shyly and swallowed. "I know, I know, no one expected this. I might not get through it, but I'd like to try. Lang is the best thing that's ever happened to me, and I am the luckiest woman alive." She bent down and kissed him, then stood up, back straight. "I love my fiancé more than life itself, but this toast is also about my family. You're loud, nosy, exasperating, and exhausting, but I love you all so much. My mom and dad gave me life and my livelihood and they, along with my siblings and Lang, literally saved my life this past year. No one could ask for a more amazing sister, or brothers who care so much. I...I..."

As Beth voice faltered, tears sprang to her eyes, and Lang started to rise. Ben Morgan patted his shoulder and came to his sister's side. "I got this one, buddy." He put his arm around her. "Okay, sweetie. We'll do this together, okay?" She nodded. "Was there something else you wanted to say?"

"He's my twin, in every way but birth date. Can you help with this, big brother?"

Ben grinned broadly. "Happy to. Our parents have given us so much here at Morgan's Run, the most idyllic place in the world in which to grow up.No one could ask for better. Most importantly, they taught us how to love. Their relationship has always been the model to which all of us have aspired, and believe me, theirs is a tough act to follow. Our dad was right. Beth is the strongest woman in the world. She also has a soft, tender heart big enough to hold us all. My siblings and I could not have made it this far without out this woman's steady presence. I hope you guys are as happy as Maggie and me, and Mom and Dad. Lang Dillon, you're a Morgan brother now, so don't screw it up."

Beth laughed and poked him. "Ignore him, Lang! Thanks especially to Martha and Jay for this perfect evening. And thank you to everyone for making tonight so very special. I love you all." With that she dissolved into tears and collapsed into her brother's arms. As everyone applauded, Ben gently settled her back beside her fiancé.

Tears in her eyes as she watched the siblings and the deep love they had for one another, Amy's eyes scanned the group until she found Jeb across the table and smiled. As he returned her smile, the love in his eyes felt like a warm embrace. *Will we ever know this kind of happiness?* she thought, holding his gaze for several seconds before turning back to the others.

Later, in the rush of good nights, Jeb found her. "Hey, Amy, good night. Sorry we didn't get much time together."

"There's always tomorrow. Save me a dance?"

"I'm not a very good dancer, but you can have them all."

"I'm going to hold you to that." She spied Buck and her dad waiting by the white whale and reached over to squeeze his hand. "I've gotta go."

Jeb released her hand, already missing the warmth of her touch. "Buck seems like a great guy."

"He is, and he likes you!" she called, running off to join her family.

Yeah, right, Jeb thought as he watched her go. Once she disappeared into the SUV, he turned away to find Harley and Willow.

"Hey, buddy," Harley said. "You ready?"

Jeb considered walking the three miles back to the cabin, but decided not to chance meeting a rattler or pack of coyotes. "Ready when you are, Harl."

CHAPTER 46

Friday morning, Harley and Jeb worked alongside their part-timers to clean out the stalls and feed and take care of the horses. Several of the women who boarded their horses also came to help out. They always seized any opportunity to assist tall, handsome Harley with whom they were all in love. Willow came along and proved a huge help. Jeb watched, amazed. She possessed the same languid movements as the father she never saw the first twelve years of her life. Only in the past two years, as her mother became sicker, had they begun to spend time together.

Harley poked his head around the stall door. "Okay, honey, time to go. You got this, buddy?"

"Sure thing, Boss. The guys and I'll finish up. You heading back home?"

"Soon, but gotta make a few stops. Maggie's invited Willow for lunch, and I'm off to chat with a certain redhead. Don't want to have fireworks on the dance floor this evening."

Jeb laughed. "Good luck! See you later, Willow. Save me a dance?"

She smiled her father's kilowatt smile, then nodded. "Yup, see you later." She was already in love.

*****

Harley dropped Willow with Maggie, and he and Ben drove over to the big house. They found the three Morgan brothers on the front porch, feet up on the rails, enjoying coffee. "Hey, guys, come join us," Kyle called.

"I will, brother, but Harley's got some business to take care of with our little sister."

"Uh-oh," Robbie said, shaking his head. "Good luck with that one. She's still mad as a hornet."

"And she's not here," Sam Morgan said, setting his mug on the table and rising to shake Harley's hand. "Barely saw you last night, Harl. Your girl's adorable."

"Yeah, she's pretty amazing."

"Where is she?" Kyle asked, gazing toward the truck.

"Eating lunch with Mags and the kids," Ben said. "Stayin' out of the line of fire."

"She doesn't know about Ruthie, does she?"

"First off, there's nothing to tell about Ruthie. She's like a little sister to me," Harley said, gazing from brother to brother. "But I know she's been angry and confused these past few months, and that's not fair. I want her to hear the story from me."

"What is the story?" Robbie said, sitting back down.

"I'll let your brother tell you. He knows the whole thing. Now, where is my favorite redhead?"

"At the farm. Both she and Beth are there, if you can believe it. Raoul told them he could handle things, but you know our sisters."

"Okay, then, I'll be off. See you guys later." He looked over at Ben. "Want me to pick you up on my way back to get Willow?"

"Thanks, buddy. I'll be here."

As Harley's truck rumbled off in a cloud of dust, all eyes turned to their oldest brother. Ben poured a mug of coffee and sat down on the railing facing them.

"So, tell, or do we have to push you off the porch?" Kyle asked.

"I can't believe you kept Harley's secret, even from Maggie."

"My oldest friend asked me not to say anything, so I didn't," Ben said. "Maggie gets it, we're cool. Talia Goldstein was Harley's girlfriend their freshmen year at the U of Northern Arizona. I met her a couple of times. She was a sweet girl, too sweet for Langdon in his wild years. Anyway, she left school after that year and Harley never heard another thing. He never knew she was pregnant when she left and knew nothing about Willow until two years ago.

"She and her mom live with her grandparents Si and Lydia Goldstein. Si's a psychology professor at Northern Arizona."

"So she never left home—Willow's mom, I mean?" Sam asked.

"Talia's dying. Breast cancer. She had it five or six years ago and they thought she'd licked it, but it's come back like gangbusters and it's spread everywhere."

"That sucks," Kyle said.

"Big time," Ben said. "Talia is, or was, a gifted silversmith, but when she got sick again, she couldn't afford to live on her own, and she knew it wasn't fair to Willow so she moved in with her folks. Almost two years ago, she called Harley and asked to see him. He's been going back and forth ever since. The elder Goldsteins are not in the best of health, and Talia was afraid raising a teenager would be too much for them."

"So she wants Harley to take her, if something happens to her?"

"Not necessarily. Willow's very attached to the grandparents, especially Talia's mom. And they're crazy about her. It's been a balancing act, but Harley's been handling it well. Doesn't push, just shows up and goes with the flow, watches to see where he can help. He offered to pay for an apartment if Talia wanted to be on her own, but she's pretty weak and prefers to stay put. He pays for caregivers during the day to spell the grandparents."

"So is there hope—for the mom, I mean?" Sam asked.

"At this point, not much," Ben said. "Couple of times they were all set to call in hospice, but then she rallied."

"Poor kid. That's rough," Robbie said.

Kyle nodded. "At least her big, strong dad's back in her life. She clearly adores him."

The four brothers sat catching up until Harley's truck appeared about a half hour later. "So?" they all asked in unison.

"So, fine. I told her, she listened, end of story," Harley said, visibly shaken. Ben watched his friend and knew that while a burden might have been lifted, relating the story and remembering all the lost years with his beloved child had cost him. Ben had missed the first four years of his Emma's life, and the sorrow of that loss still hurt at times.

"Okay, guys," Ben said. "We'll be off. Where's Mom, anyway? Not like her to miss a gathering of her boys."

"She and Martha went into town for breakfast. Said she had to get away for an hour," Robbie said. "In fact, speak of the devil."

They turned and spied Leonora Morgan's car heading up the drive.

"That's our cue," Ben said, heading down to Harley's truck, waving to his mother as she parked.

The others went down to meet her, helping bring in boxes and bags from the bakery and cheese shops.

CHAPTER 47

Spark, Amy, Buck, and the elder Morgans stood on the back terrace, gazing out at the enormous wedding tent. Flaps up, the tent's poles framed a magnificent view of the valley and mountains. Chairs had been set up on the terrace for the ceremony, and a broad arbor fashioned from twisting branches of mesquite stood at the west end, adorned with desert flowers. Grace Bering, a local pastor, was performing the service. At the moment, the diminutive minister, dressed in white robe, sat in the shadow of the arbor, reading a book.

"This is the kind of night we prayed for," Ben Senior said, patting his old friend's shoulder. "So glad you three could be here."

"Thanks for including me," Buck said.

Amy gazed at her brother, who looked especially handsome in a beige linen suit. *Watch out, ladies. Here he comes!*

"We're delighted, son. Now that your dad's building here, we hope to see a lot more of you." He winked at Buck, then turned to Amy. "And my dear, I don't think I've ever seen you look lovelier."

She blushed. "Thank you, Ben." Amy adored her dress. The color of the sky, its bodice hugged every curve, and the flared skirt swished when she walked, making her feel wanton and sexy. It had come from Gabriela's, and the shopkeeper had insisted she buy strappy silver sandals with two-inch heels to complete the ensemble. These Amy planned to ditch as soon as they got to their table.

"I'm not much on the fashion front—that's my Nora's province—but I know gorgeous when I see it."

"You can thank Beth's friend Gabriela. She wouldn't let me leave her shop without buying it."

"Well, she was right. Made my Beth's wedding dress, too, I understand." He leaned closer, voice low. "Even got my Nora into the shop. For years my bride's traipsed all over the Southwest shopping, but lately she's come back from town with quite a few purchases."

"She sure looks beautiful today," Amy said as they spied Leonora Morgan cross the terrace to give instructions to the caterers. She wore a pale pink brushed linen suit, the top adorned with elaborate jeweled designs, the silvery glass beads twinkling in the sunlight. Her blond hair was swept up and silver jewelry sparkled at her neck and ears.

"My Nora grows prettier every day."

Amy watched her father's friend, his adoring eyes fixed on his wife, and wondered if love like that was still possible. As if on cue, she spied Jeb as he came in with Harley and Willow. He looked especially gorgeous in a dark suit that hung perfectly on his strong, wiry frame.

"Ah, there's your Mr. Barnes and the Langdon fellow. His daughter's a cutie, isn't she?"

Buck nodded, watching his sister. *She's in deep*, he thought. He liked Jeb Barnes but decided if he broke his sister's heart, he might have to kill them both him and Ryan.

"Well, folks, gotta excuse myself and collect the bride. I expect she's about ready to run for the hills unless I catch her first. See you after."

As Ben Senior stepped away, Jeb spied Amy and gasped. She literally took his breath away. Surprised at the sound coming from his assistant, Harley followed his gaze. "Someone looks mighty fine tonight, doesn't she, buddy?"

"*Fine* doesn't begin to cover it. 'Scuse me, Harl, Willow." Drawn like a moth to a flame, he started across the terrace, only to be intercepted by the Morgan boys and then Lang's Yankee contingent. He barely had time to wave before Amy, her brother, and Spark were swept up by the group and ushered to their seats.

As the music changed, all eyes turned as Emma, the flower girl, slowly came forward, strewing desert rose petals along the aisle. All bridesmaids and flower girls wore dresses in a luminous shade of teal, each styled differently. Maggie's fit her like a glove, its simple lines broken only by a wide collar and plunging necklace that revealed her glorious cleavage. She winked at Jeb, then Amy as she passed by. She was followed by Rose Dillon, her dress straight, simple, and elegant. Ruthie's dress flared out at the waist. Her curly hair was swept up, makeup expertly applied by the team her mother had hired. She looked radiant, ten years older than her twenty-four years. Every man on the terrace could not take his eyes off her.

Finally, the processional started, and Beth Morgan, in a strapless gown overlaid with Belgian lace, appeared at her father's side. As the gentle strains of "Here Comes the Sun" began, she walked straight and tall, eyes never leaving Lang's, her hand grasping her father's arm in a death grip. Like his sons, Ben Senior wore a morning coat, a desert rose at his lapel. He looked proud enough to bust the buttons of his jacket.

Amy turned from Beth to the groom under the arbor, standing beside his best man, Scott Jackson. Lang's blue eyes were riveted on his bride. As she watched Lang follow Beth's every step, tears filled her eyes. *What a moment to share in two people's lives. Such an honor.*

CHAPTER 48

"It was a lovely ceremony, wasn't it?" Gabriela said, standing with Amy and her brother.

"Sure was," Amy said, eyes scanning the crowd for Jeb.

Beth and Lang had insisted on a small ceremony, but there were over a hundred people invited to the reception. Jeb's parents had come for the ceremony but were already departing, on their way to her college roommate's wedding in Sonoita.

"Sarah's waited forty years for this," Lily told her son. "I have to be there."

"It's okay, Ma, really."

Jake Barnes patted his son's shoulder. "We'll stop by and take you to lunch tomorrow, if you're free?"

"Thanks, Dad. Just give me a call when you're getting close. It's the opening day of camp, but I can probably spring free for an hour."

"We'd love to have Amy join us," Lily said, hugging him.

"Thanks, Mom. Have fun and tell Sarah I say congrats."

As Jake and Lily headed out, thanking the elder Morgans on their way, ranchers, townspeople, and friends from near and far trickled in. Kyle Morgan had brought Maggie Morgan's dear friend, Dara, whom he had been seeing on and off. Sam and Robbie Morgan were unattached, but it was clear to Amy that something was cooking between Sam and Rose Dillon. While Robbie had danced with several women, Amy could see his eyes were fixed on Hope Seymour, Beth's Tucson friend. After hearing about Ruthie and Harley's history, Buck had backed off and was now dancing with a curvaceous ash blonde.

"Your brother's found a sweetheart," Kyle said, coming to stand beside her, his arm around Dara.

Amy laughed. "Always."

"Cute together, aren't they?"

"Who is she?" Amy asked.

"That's Beth's chiropractor, Carrie Hale. She lives in town. My sister's a workaholic, so the only friends she has are service-related."

"Not true," Maggie said, approaching from behind and poking her brother-in-law. "Hey, Dara."

The longtime friends hugged.

As Kyle dragged Dara back to the dance floor, Amy turned to Maggie. "The ceremony was lovely. You all looked so beautiful, and what a great job Emma did."

"She was pretty incredible, wasn't she?" Maggie said, smiling. "Have you seen Jeb?"

"No, every time I try to find him, one of Lang's Boston crew yanks me back to the dance floor. I passed him dancing with Willow. So sweet of him."

Maggie patted her arm. "The sweetest. Those Boston boys are formidable, aren't they?"

"That's why I'm hiding out here behind this floral arrangement.""They've certainly kept Ruthie busy. I actually think Harley's getting a little jealous."

They both laughed, spying Harley across the tent, a scowl on his face.

"Maybe a little jealousy will be motivating?" Amy said, smiling as she gazed around. Lights twinkled everywhere. Their surroundings were like a magical palace in the clouds, far removed from day-to-day life. "Leonora outdid herself, didn't she?"

"Yes, she's amazing," Maggie sighed.

"Everything's perfect," Amy said. *Except I'm not with Jeb.*

"Did you eat?"

"Stuffed myself, and I fear we'll have to wheel Dad out. He cannot pass a table or station without filling his plate again."

At either end of the tent there were three stations, each with a different set of offerings. The seafood station tables groaned with platters of shrimp, fish, crab, lobster, and clams flown in from back east. There was also a pasta station, Southwestern bars at either end, a farm-raised bar with succulent tenderloins, roast pork, and barbecued chicken, and a stir-fry station with vegetarian offerings.

Maggie chuckled. "I have no idea what Leonora's plans are for all this food. Even your dad and these cowboys can't make a dent in it. They'll be taking truckloads into Tucson tomorrow."

"I love Beth's alternative to cake," Amy said as they watched wait staff pass platters of cookies and cups of flan and other puddings and custards.

"She hates cake. Lang too. And she absolutely refused to make a spectacle of herself cutting anything!"

"I'm with her. Give me ice cream or pudding any day!"

"There's plenty of both, all night, I expect," Maggie said as something caught her eye. "Uh-oh, I see the sitter. Must be time for a feeding. Don't want to start leaking through my dress. Would you excuse me, Amy?"

"Of course." Amy smiled, but her eyes betrayed sadness for an instant.

Maggie reached over and squeezed her hand. "He'll find you. These cowboys are pretty resourceful. Be back soon. And, by the way, I love your brother."

Amy smiled. "He has that effect on many women." She watched Maggie wend her way through the crowd, then turned her attention to the throng on the dance floor. Buck held the chiropractor close as they moved in perfect synch to "Crazy Love." Nearby, Sam and Rose danced more sedately but clearly were enjoying each other's company. Robbie Morgan had yielded the lovely Hope to one of the Boston crew and was now twirling Emma in the middle of the room. Ruthie was dancing with Scott Jackson and Willow, her dad. *But where was Jeb?* Try as she might, Amy could not see him anywhere.

In answer, his voice startled her, and she turned. "Hey, didn't mean to scare you."

"Oh, Jeb, yes…hi, I was…I've been—"

"Busy, I saw. Those Yankees have taken over, haven't they?" Gray blue eyes studied her. "You look amazing, Amy. I've been trying to get to you all night, but every time I try, one of the Yanks grabs you."

"Why do you think I'm hiding here behind these flowers?"

"Wanta dance?"

She held out her hand. "I thought you'd never ask."

CHAPTER 49

As the band started playing "The Way You Look Tonight," he smiled and took her hand. "They couldn't have picked a better song. You look incredible, Amy."

Jeb drew her close and Amy sighed, relaxing into his arms, realizing how much her body had been craving his touch and how lost she'd been without him. "Oh, Jeb," she whispered.

"I know, sweetheart. Me, too."

He kissed her neck, sending shivers through her. Amy circled her arms round his neck, drinking in his musky scent. *Home,* she thought, closing her eyes and letting the music and his strong arms carry her away.

Suddenly, Jeb's arm yanked back, and Amy found herself staring at a slightly inebriated Chris Paxton, one of Lang's Boston crew. "Hey, cowboy, no fair hogging all the gorgeous ladies. I'm cutting in." Before either of them had time to protest, Paxton had whisked her away. Jeb watched, slack-jawed, then retreated to the edge of the dance floor. He felt as if his heart had been torn from his chest. *It's only a dance,* he told himself as he came to stand next to Harley, who was grinning like the Cheshire Cat.

"Hey, buddy, tough break. How're you doing?"

"I'd like to have decked him, but I'm fine. How 'bout you?"

"Willow's havin' fun, Ruthie still isn't speaking to me, and she looks as though she might elope with one of the Boston crew, but I'm doing great."

"Why don't I believe you?"

Harley smiled. "What?"

"You've kinda blown your 'she's like a little sister' cover, Boss."

"Don't have a clue what you're talking about. Have you had too much to drink?"

"Fine, play dumb. Where's Willow?"

"She's over with Emma. Despite the age difference, they've bonded."

Jeb followed his gaze and spied the two girls sitting at a table with the elder Morgans, talking and laughing. "She's a cutie, your Willow."

"Yup. You know, you could've told that Yank to bugger off."

"Yeah, right, and caused World War Three in the middle of the reception? No thanks."

The song ended, and the band began Seger's "Old Time Rock and Roll." Paxton looked ready to keep dancing, but Amy excused herself and stepped away, retreating to her father's table, at the same time her eyes scanned the room.

"She's lookin' for you, buddy," Harley said.

"Maybe."

"Never took you for a world-class idiot, Barnes. Go get her before another one of those bozos grabs her."

Jeb hesitated for a minute. Then, taking a deep breath, he headed off into the crowd.

"That's the spirit!" Harley called, his own eyes riveted on Ruthie Morgan as Scott Jackson spun her around and caught her in his arms. He shook his head but could not take his eyes off her. *She isn't a little girl anymore, cowboy. What the hell are you waiting for?*

"Hey, Dad," Amy said, patting Spark's shoulder as she sat beside him. "What're you doing all alone?"

"I'm happy, honey. I'm about to join Ben and Nora at their table, but got distracted watching you and your brother twirlin' around out there. He seems quite smitten with the chiropractor."

"Have you ever known Buck not to be smitten with every pretty woman in a room? It was Ruthie Morgan yesterday, the chiropractor today. No telling who tomorrow will bring."

Spark chuckled. "That's our Buck. And you've certainly been the belle of the ball tonight, honey. Every time you go by, you're in the arms of another handsome fella. This ole man's head is spinning."

She shook her head. "Tell me about it! The East Coasters are driving me crazy. How often do you have a situation like this with so many more men than women?"

"We're in the Old West, honey. Where do you think mail-order brides originated?"

Amy laughed.

"Uh-oh, here comes your Mr. Barnes. *He* may have something to say about all your cavorting."

"Dad!"

Spark rose and gave her a hug. "That's my cue. I'm off to join my buddies. Have fun, darlin'."

"Hey," Jeb said, suddenly shy as he reached her. She looked up. Their eyes met, and he couldn't breathe.

"Are you okay?" she asked softly.

He nodded as strains of Etta James's "At Last" reached them. He held out his hand. "Want to try again?"

"Love to."

"And this time, no one is cutting in."

"Won't get an argument out of me," she said, taking his hand, knowing with certainty that she would follow this man anywhere.

As he drew her close, she felt his erection and gazed up with surprise.

His lips grazed her ear, and he whispered, "Tonight is literally killing me. That dress is amazing, but what I wouldn't give to rip it off you."

"Whoa, cowboy. That can be arranged, but how are we going to get you off the dance floor?"

He laughed. "I'll think of something, or we'll just have to stay glued to each other till everyone else leaves."

"Fine by me."

*****

The dance ended and Jeb led her out the side door of the tent, down the hillside, and over the wide lawn. When they reached one of the benches at the edge of the lawn, they sat, Jeb's arm circling her shoulders. Amy rested her head on his shoulder and sighed. "This is where I've wanted to be all day."

"Me, too. I needed us to be alone cause I have something to say."

Amy cringed as he withdrew his arm and pulled back. Fearful that he would make yet another pronouncement about his plan to kidnap Toby, her jaw dropped as he knelt in front of her, his eyes gazing up, full of love, in his hand a tiny ceramic box.

"I love you, Amy Foster, more than life itself. I've come to the place where I cannot imagine life without you. I love it here, but will move anywhere as long as I'm with you. I know I'm not educated and may never be, but I swear I will do whatever it takes for the rest of our lives to make you happy. I know I don't have the right to ask, but will you marry me?" He opened the box to reveal a delicate ring, a sapphire surrounded by tiny diamonds, lying on a blue velvet cushion.

Her eyes filled with tears as she nodded, then whispered, "Yes."

"Yes? You mean it?"

"What do you think, cowboy?"

"You…we can take this back and get something you like better."

"I love it, and I love you. I can't imagine life without you either. I don't care where we go, where we live, as long as I'm with you. We'll figure it out together."

"You said yes?"

She laughed, looking down at his amazed expression. "Yes, I did. Now kiss me, cowboy, or I might take it back."

Jeb stood and swooped her up in his arms, kissing her deeply as they spun around. "Thank you, my love, thank you!"

EPILOGUE

As campers streamed in for the start of the third session, Amy rushed around, meeting children and their caregivers, arranging therapy schedules and wondering how she would ever be able to turn everything over to her replacement in three short days. She had said good-bye to her brother that morning, and Spark was packing and meeting with contractors, setting up building schedules before their departure. Despite the busyness, she had a smile on her face. Congratulations from everyone at camp continued as the news of the engagement spread. Spark and Buck had been delighted, as had all the Morgans and their friends, which made their happiness all the more sweet. Jeb called his parents that morning. Both were thrilled and planned to stop at camp briefly to celebrate over lunch.

Amy spied Maggie and Harley and waved. "Hey, good morning!"

Maggie rushed forward and gave her a hug as Harley followed, a huge grin on his wolfish face. "Ben and I couldn't be happier for you and Jeb," she said.

"Thanks, Maggie. Where is he, anyway?"

"Oh, you mean the cowboy who's been walkin' around the stables all morning in a daze, with a big shit-eater on his face?"

Maggie jabbed her boss in the ribs. "Stop it, Harley!"

"Man keeps repeating 'she said yes,' like a mantra."

Both women laughed, then turned as two more carloads of campers drove in. "Excuse me," Maggie said, and she hurried off to greet the newcomers.

"Here's the man now," Harley said, looking toward the bunkhouses. "I'll leave you to it. And, Amy," he said, gently taking hold of her arm. "Don't mind my teasing. I'm real happy for you."

"Thanks, Harley. Coming from you, that means a lot," she said, then turned to watch her fiancé's approach. "Good morning."

"Hey, good morning. We still on for dinner tonight?"

"Absolutely. Looking forward to it."

"Wish it could be all night, but gotta get back for my buddy. Speak of the devil. Isn't that Izzy's car?"

They turned and waved as Izzy Winkler drove up. In seconds, Jeb had Toby out of his car seat, swinging him around, throwing him in the air. "Hey, buddy, we missed you!"

Expression grave, Izzy pulled his bags out and handed them to Jeb. "Have you two got a minute?"

"Of course," Amy said.

"Hey, buddy, let's go find Andy and Greg. They've been waiting all morning to see you."

At that moment, Greg Smith appeared on the path leading to the bunkhouses and waved. Jeb helped Toby into his wheelchair. "Okay, buddy, you over to your bunkhouse and I'll meet you at lunch."

They watched as Greg wheeled Toby off. Then Izzy said, "Is Maggie around?"

"Sure, I think I saw her heading for the office. Let's talk there," Amy said, leading the way into the building.

They found Maggie on the phone, but she waved them in and soon finished her call. "Hi, Izzy, how are you? Did you and Toby have a good week?"

"The best, thanks. I have some news, and I wanted to share it with you three because I need your help."

Jeb closed the office door. Fearing the worst, they stared at Izzy.

"Cora Hooper died two days ago."

Aghast, Amy said, "How?"

"A batch of bad heroin, or so they think."

"Does he know?" Jeb asked.

"No, I decided not to tell him until I can arrange a placement for him. I'm working on it now. My first choice is to locate an adoptive family, but if not, I'm aiming for the most supportive, loving foster family I can find."

"Is that easy?" Maggie asked.

"No, but I won't rest till I do it. What I need from you is to give him the same kind of care and support you have been giving him, and when the time's right, I'll come out and tell him."

They talked for a while longer. Then Izzy departed. The rest of the day went by in a blur. Jeb's parents came and went, expressing genuine heartfelt happiness to both of them. When the dinner bell sounded, Jeb found Toby and promised he'd be back at eight to take him over to the cabin. After that, he went in search of Amy.

She was in the office, a stack of folders beside her as she completed notes on the new arrivals.

He tapped on the open door.

"You ready?"

She gazed up and gave him a weary smile. "Yup. Where're we going?"

"You'll see. Come on."

"Do I need to change?"

"Nope." He reached out and took her hand. "You're perfect just the way you are."

They hopped into his truck and he drove off, turning in at the stables. "I thought we'd take a ride, if you're not too tired?"

"I'd love that."

"I had Johnny make us a picnic," he said, pulling a backpack out of the truck.

Tara and Royal were saddled and waiting at the side of the barn. When she looked at him with surprise, he grinned. "Had the guys get 'em ready before they left."

For a while they rode in silence, Jeb leading the way. When they reached open meadow, he said, "There's a really nice spot 'bout a half a mile down, okay?"

"Let's go."

She nudged Tara, and the horse took off at a gallop. Jeb followed, drawing alongside her as they reached the middle of the field. "Head for that tall willow," he called, marveling, as he always did, at her ease in the saddle.

When they reached the clearing beside the massive desert willow, he jumped down and came to her, reaching up as she slid down into his arms. Horses left to their own devices, the lovers embraced, Jeb's lips everywhere, his hands moving from her slender neck down to cup her firm breasts, finding her nipples hard and erect as he teased and caressed. "Oh, my God, I've missed you, Amy," he groaned as she returned his kisses, wrapping her legs around his waist, hands running through his hair, damp with sweat and desire.

"Sorry, sweetheart, I'm pretty gamey after today," he said as he pulled her tee shirt over her head, unclasping her bra, his mouth capturing her smooth, round breast.

"So am I. Now hush and get your clothes off! I want you inside me in ten seconds flat, cowboy."

He laughed. "Amy Foster, you are a wanton woman!" He unzipped her jeans, then his own and ripped off a condom wrapper with his teeth.

Amy dropped her lacy panties and took the condom from his hand, slipping it on, stroking and caressing, as he groaned under her touch.

"You wanta kill me before the wedding, woman?" He leaned back against the willow's smooth trunk and lifted her, thrusting deeply. In tandem, they crashed deeper with each thrust until they reached a blinding climax that left them spent and breathless.

"My legs are gonna give out, sweetheart. I have to set us down or I might drop you." As Jeb spoke, he whistled for Royal. The horse drew near enough for him to grab a blanket, which he flung out in front of them.

Miraculously, they made it to the ground still together, Jeb still deep inside her. They lay in each other's arms, sated and content. Finally, as the light began to fade, he nuzzled her neck. "You hungry?"

"Only for you."

"Hmm, I'll see what I can do about that." He kissed her deeply, and she felt him grow hard.

"Think the condom's safe."

"It better be, cause I'm makin' love to my fiancée now."

This time they took it slow, with every thrust bringing sweet shivers of pleasure. In the growing twilight, their eyes met and stayed locked through an agonizingly beautiful climax.

With tears in her eyes, Amy whispered, "Oh, Jeb, I love you so."

"I love you, too, sweetheart, and while I'd happily stay like this forever, I've got the little guy waiting on me."

"Of course, we've got to get moving." She kissed his nose, then drew back, sighing with the agony of separation before searching the ground for her clothes. As they sat eating Johnny's delicious chicken and mushroom baguettes, she looked over at him, eyes suddenly serious. "Jeb, I have something I want to ask you. I've been thinking about Toby all day, and I wonder if—"

"We should try to adopt him?"

She stared at him. "You too?"

"From the moment Izzy gave us the news."

"Do you think we'd have a chance?" she asked, eyes wide in amazement.

"The best chance of anyone I know."

"Should we call Izzy?"

"First thing in the morning."

"I love you, Jeb Barnes."

"I love you, too, Amy Foster, and I'm gonna love you even more as a mom."

"We'll be a family."

"The first real family that little guy's ever had."

Please read on for chapters from ***Hestor's Way!***

ABOUT THE AUTHOR

M. Lee Prescott is the author of dozens of works of fiction for adults, young adults, and children, among them **Prepped to Kill, Gadfly, Lost in Spindle City (Ricky Steele Mysteries), A Friend of Silence, In the Name of Silence and The Silence of Memory (Roger and Bess Mysteries), Jigsaw, Song of the Spirit**, and her newest contemporary romance series, **Morgan's Run,** of which **Jeb's Promise** is the third! Three of her nonfiction titles have been published by Heinemann, and she has published numerous articles in the field of literacy education. Lee is a professor of education at a small New England liberal arts college, where she teaches reading and writing pedagogy. Her current research focuses on mindfulness and connections to reading and writing. She regularly teaches abroad, most recently in Singapore.

Lee has lived in southern California (loved those Laguna nights!), Chapel Hill, North Carolina, and various spots in Massachusetts and Rhode Island. Currently she resides in Massachusetts on a beautiful river, where she canoes, swims, and watches an incredible variety of wildlife pass by. She is the mother of two grown sons and spends lots of time with them, their beautiful wives, and her amazing grandchildren. When not teaching or writing, Lee's passions revolve around family, yoga (Kripalu is a second home), swimming, sharing mindfulness with children and adults, and walking.

Lee loves to hear from readers. Email her anytime at mleeprescott@gmail.com, and visit her website to hear the latest and sign up for her newsletters!

AUTHOR WEBPAGE AND NEWSLETTER SIGN UP

A Note from the Author

I am thrilled to bring you Amy and Jeb's story, the third of *many* **Morgan's Run** books still to come! Thank you so much for reading. These beloved characters will be around as the series continues to grow. The Morgan's Run books are set in the gorgeous American Southwest, an area of the country that is dear to my heart because it is home to my youngest son and family, but also because its beauty is so extraordinary and so startlingly different from that of my New England home. What a backdrop for romance and adventure!

If you like ***Jeb's Promise*** and would be willing to write an Amazon review, I would very much appreciate it! In fact, I will be happy to send my first two reviewers a free copy **of another of my titles!** If you submit a review, just email me at mleeprescott@gmail.com with your name and address and I will see that you receive your free copy of whichever title you choose!

If you would like to sign up for future book releases and occasional notices about my books, please visit my Author Website and sign up for my newsletter. I promise I will not share your address, nor will I flood you with emails. Do visit my site to read more about my books and to hear what's next.

Finally, this book has been revised, proofed, and edited many, many times, but my intrepid assistants and I are human, so if you spot a typo, please email me at mleeprescott@gmail.com and I will fix it. If you'd like to know more about my other books, please scroll ahead to the next section, which is followed by sample chapters of *Hestor's Way,* a sexy romance in my **Well-Loved Series.**

Warm wishes,
M. Lee Prescott

Contemporary romances and mysteries by M. Lee Prescott include:

The Ricky Steele Mysteries
Book 1: Prepped to Kill
Book 2: Gadfly
Book 3: Lost in Spindle City

Also featuring Ricky Steele:
Jigsaw

Roger and Bess Mysteries
Book 1: A Friend of Silence
Book 2: In the Name of Silence
Book 3: The Silence of Memory

Contemporary Romances

Well-Loved Romances
Widow's Island
Hestor's Way
Glass Walls (coming soon!)

Morgan's Run Romances
Book 1: Emma's Dream
Book 2: Lang's Return
Book 3: Jeb's Promise

Young Adult Historical Romance
Song of the Spirit

Hestor's Way

Love is the last thing on gifted artist Beth Hadley's mind as she prepares for a one-woman show while enjoying a bittersweet summer before her son, Kit, leaves for college. Then, out of the blue, an unexpected, secret love blossoms with Jack Talbot, Kit's best friend. The two begin a passionate affair that could destroy her world, tear her family apart, and shatter the peace of her close-knit community. As Beth struggles with guilt and remorse over the relationship with Jack, an old love returns and with him, a chance for deep, abiding eternal love. Is it too late for her?

SAMPLE CHAPTERS OF HESTOR'S WAY
CHAPTER 1

The studio's screen door banged behind her, and Beth headed through the gardens toward the house. Passing through the grape arbor at the path's end, she spied her son, Kit, as he raced across the terrace.

"Hi Mom! Gotta go. See you this afternoon?"

Her eighteen-year-old jumped over the terrace wall and waved as he headed for the driveway and his beat-up Volvo. His father's gift of safe, reliable transportation for the summer.

She marveled at the change in her only son. Where was the round-faced, chubby boy? He had disappeared, and now there stood a six-foot-tall man in his place! Of her three children, Kit looked the least like his sandy-haired father. Dark curls framed his slender face—"the young Shelley," Beth's friend Clarice called him. Although tall, he was slight, almost delicate on first glance until one noticed the powerful legs from years spent on the soccer field. Kit would be playing soccer at Bowdoin in the fall.

"Kit, remember to ask your boss about tomorrow night. It's Nanny's birthday," she said, referring to her youngest.

"Mom, don't worry. We're only workin' a half day, then coming back here to work in the barn. We'll probably head to the beach after that, but I'll be home in plenty of time to get the grill going."

"Kit," she called as the Volvo's door creaked open. "I forgot to tell you, Dad's coming. He…well, he asked and I said fine. You know how he is about the grill."

"Well, tough shit. It isn't his house or his grill anymore."

She came to stand beside him, eyes soft and pleading. "Kit, please, it's a little thing, and it's Nanny's night."

"It's not a little thing to me. Who does he think he is? We've been doin' fine without him. Now he thinks he can waltz back in whenever he wants and take over. God, and you just let him, every single time!"

"Honey, I know it's hard, but it's only one night. I'd never have made it through the last three years without you. We can do this. Have a birthday party for Nanny and be together. You're right about the grill, though. I'll have a word with Dad. You should do the cooking. But, Kit, do try to be civil, okay?" She rubbed his shoulder.

Shrugging from her touch, he dropped into the car seat, muttering.

Beth's heart ached, watching him and remembering the shy, introverted fifteen-year-old who'd so desperately tried to take his father's place three years earlier.

"It's okay, Mom. I'll be home around five, but don't expect me to be jolly. Is she coming?"

"No Chloe." She closed the car door. "You'll be civil, for Nanny's sake?"

She noticed a glimmer of a smile as he pulled away. "Stinker!" she called as the Volvo tires crunched down the drive.

Turning toward the house, she glanced down at her watch. Nearly nine. Kit was late for work again.

When she entered the kitchen, Kat, her oldest, stood at the kitchen counter, barefoot, in the long tee shirt she used as a nightshirt. Kit, short for Kittredge, and Kat, short for Katherine, had been Alan's ideas.

"Hi Mom." She turned and gave her a sleepy smile as a dollop of strawberry jam dropped from her knife to the floor. Tall and slender like her mother, Kat also had long, straight hair, lighter than Beth's chestnut color. Auburn tendrils framed her sleepy face, as she smiled sheepishly, stooping to wipe up the jam. "Oops."

Beth flicked on the burner under the teapot. "Late night, huh?"

"Kinda. You didn't wait up, did you?"

"I heard you come in, if that's what you mean, but I was only semiconscious. So?"

"So, Rob took me to Newport and we went clubbing."

"Clubbing? Kat, you're only nineteen."

"Mom, it's not that kind of clubbing. We didn't drink, not even Rob."

Rob had just turned twenty-one, and the difference in their ages worried Beth. He and Kat had been dating since her freshman year at Dartmouth. Rob would be a senior this fall, Kat a sophomore. His parents lived in New Jersey, but Rob had found a job painting houses with a local contractor in Windy Harbor for the summer. He shared a house with four other guys who had already thrown several raucous parties.

"Kat, you know I trust you, but I'd rather you stayed closer to home."

"There's nothing to do here. If the Harbor wasn't so dead, we'd stay home, but it is. You worry too much. Anyway, we'll be taking a break next week when Rob goes to training."

A nationally ranked collegiate soccer player, Rob had hopes of a professional career, and it looked as though he might have a shot at it.

"Kat," she began, her voice tentative as she embarked on a touchy subject. "I know we've discussed this before, but I wanted to check that you and Rob are taking precautions."

"Mom!"

"I'm serious. I'm not implying that you're sexually active, and I don't mean to pry."

"We are, on both counts," Kat replied. "Mom, we've been sleeping together for over a year, but it's okay. Rob uses condoms every time. Want to know what brand?"

"Very funny."

"Don't worry. We're careful." Kat put her arms round Beth's shoulders and hugged her.

She returned the embrace, then turned away, not letting her daughter see the tears in her eyes. "Fine, that's all I need to know."

"Mom, we had this conversation six months ago."

Beth blushed. "Did we? I'm sorry." Relieved and embarrassed, she rushed to add, "Maybe you and I can snatch some time together in the next few days? I feel like I've barely seen you since you got home." Beth played with a lock of her daughter's hair. Even in a ripped tee shirt, with sleep-drenched eyes and tousled hair, what a beautiful woman her eldest had grown into.

"Sure, love it. Let's plan something for my day off. Shopping, a movie?"

"Or a canoe trip up the river or a day at the beach?"

"Yeah, sure, sounds good. This jam you made is great. A little runny, but I love it. Can you save a couple of jars for me to take back to school?"

"Of course. Your brother's already put three aside."

"The pig, he doesn't even like your jams."

"Now, now, stop it and don't be greedy. You'll have to leave a jar or two for Nanny and me. We like it too, you know."

"Speaking of Nan," Kat whispered, sitting down next to her mother at the long wooden table. "I haven't gotten her anything yet. What's she want for her birthday? I thought I'd ride up to the Mill shops after work today and get her something."

Beth laughed. "You know Nanny; she likes almost anything, especially coming from her older sister. Just surprise her. You always do."

"Dad's coming, isn't he?"

"How'd you know?"

"Nanny told me, plus we ran into him last night and he mentioned it."

"Ran into him where?"

"Thames Street, can you believe it? We go down to Newport to get away from Windy Harbor for a few hours and who's the first person I see after Rob parks the car, but Dad? Chloe was draggin' him around to every shop on Thames. He looked real happy, as you can imagine. You know how much he loves to shop."

Beth laughed, almost pitying her ex-husband. "Chloe must have strong arms."

"What an airhead. What he sees in her is beyond me."

Youth, Beth thought, but added charitably, "Chloe is far from an airhead. She's a gifted artist, and you know how much that means to Dad."

"Yeah, if you like nihilistic heavy metal."

Her daughter was referring to Chloe's massive metal sculptures, welded together with a blowtorch. She smiled, brushing a lock of hair from Kat's forehead. "Now, now. Anyway, your father's coming tomorrow around six, and I thought we'd eat and then have presents. Supper around seven? What do you think? That way we'll be finished in time for the fireworks."

"Rob is taking me."

"Why don't you have Rob and the kids come to the house to watch them? We can all sit out on the porch and..."

"Thanks, Mom, but we really like to be up close and personal, right underneath 'em."

"Uh-huh."

"We're meeting a bunch of kids in the Commons at nine," Kat continued. "Kit's friends will be there too."

"Suit yourself, but remember fourth of July or not, Nanny comes first. Just family till eight-thirty."

"Course, Mom. What do you think?"

Her children treasured the rituals and traditions that accompanied birthday celebrations. The previous September, Kat had been despondent when Dartmouth's preseason field hockey schedule had taken her away on her birthday. To make it up to her, Beth and Alan, on one of the rare occasions when she'd agreed to go anywhere with him, had packed the other two into the car, along with a birthday cake, dinner, and presents, and traveled to New Hampshire. They found a campground nearby where they could grill shrimp -- Kat's favorite meal -- and have cake and presents on the cool September afternoon, sharing a few precious moments together. When they walked onto the practice field, Kat's face had made every minute of the three-hour drive with Alan worth it.

CHAPTER 2

The light was perfect, or nearly so. A faint mist in the air sprayed the canvas, running the colors slightly, but Beth didn't mind. Not with early morning light like this, clean, soft, and pure, filtering through the trees at the edge of the pond, bathing every inch of the grassy woods with warmth. The trees mirrored in the pond's glassy surface stretched their branches from sky to the middle of Echo Lake, their reflections an impressionistic extension of reality.

She was working on a commissioned piece for the Wanamakers, who owned the stone cottage at the far edge of the pond. Together they had scouted every inch of the far bank on which she now sat until they fixed on the very spot where her easel rested, a spot Herb Wanamaker had marked with a white stake. After a week of mornings spent in the shady spot, Beth had nearly completed the picture of the turn-of-the-century cottage dwarfed by the towering elms and firs that surrounded it. Some last-minute touches and the painting could go to the framer.

Beth enjoyed working outdoors but had had little time for it the past six months. Her agent was pressing her to show, and she needed at least thirty paintings for a one-woman exhibit. A prestigious local art gallery granted three solo shows a year and chose its artists carefully. Every exhibit at the Lynch Gallery attracted national attention, drawing critics from New York, Boston, and California. Rick Gould, Beth's agent, had been negotiating with Margot Lynch for six months on his client's behalf, but so far the gallery owner showed no signs of capitulating.

Beth had tried, unsuccessfully, to tell herself that it didn't matter. Fueled by the influx of summer people, the local market for her work remained strong. She usually sold fifteen or twenty paintings a year, and several gift shops carried her prints, postcards, and notepaper depicting local scenes, all consistent sellers.

It wasn't that she needed the money. Alan had been very generous in the divorce and had cheerfully divided his considerable assets in half, signing the house completely over to her. "Guilt money," Beth's attorney called it. It wasn't money she needed from her work, but something else, less tangible and much more important. Maybe it was recognition, or perhaps the opportunity finally to emerge from Alan's formidable shadow.

Satisfied with the painting, she packed up her things and called to Jasper. Jasper had been Alan's dog, an old springer spaniel, left behind when his adored master had walked out. Chloe was allergic to dogs. Jasper usually went to work with Kit, but his morning he had trailed along with her instead.

The route home took her through the village, where she stopped for tea and muffins at Begley's. Upon leaving the café, she spied Ed Talbot and waved. Ed was a lobsterman and father of her son's close friend Jack. Windy Harbor was just as its name implied, a town built around a harbor. Main Street ran north to south, the southern end running smack dab into the water, its long piers stretching for almost a quarter mile into the bay. In keeping with an old whaling village, the narrow streets were lined with all manner of Cape Cod architecture. A few larger homes were sandwiched in between capes and colonials, some with porches trimmed with lacy gingerbread. Widow walks crowned a number of the larger homes' mansard roofs.

Beth and her family did not live in the village proper, but in an outlying area known to the locals as Hen and Chicks. So named because of its peculiar topography, a large knoll, the Hen, surrounded by many smaller hills, the Chicks, the area had originally been part of a three-hundred-acre estate. When the original landowner sold off the rolling woods and fields, he had divided the properties into five- and ten-acre lots. Most of those original boundaries remained today.

Soon after their son's marriage, Alan's parents had purchased a five-acre lot for the young couple, and the newlyweds built their home together. Both Rhode Island School of Design graduates, they had definite ideas about the house's design. Their collaboration had produced a comfortable, light-filled home, a sort of "adapted saltbox" with a few extra interesting angles.

As the family expanded from two to five, they added on several times, but each addition succeeded in retaining the shingled charm of the original structure. No longer boxy, the house now crawled out both east and west, hugging the landscape that surrounded it. Like the brambles and beach roses growing in wild profusion around the property, the additions appeared to have sprouted from the sandy soil, fed by the passage of time and pruned by the winds.

To the north, a freestanding barn served as a two-car garage and woodshop. Alan's summer project their third year in the house, the barn had been build entirely of salvaged wood taken from several city demolition sites. Alan's one request in the divorce settlement had been to have access to the woodshop. While his furniture workshop was attached to his new home, he still kept machinery and an enormous collection of tools in the barn.

The rear of the house faced south toward open fields dotted with fruit trees. Beyond the fields, woods stretched for miles. It was common land held jointly by all owners of Hens and Chicks property. The common land would always remain a wilderness populated by deer, foxes, coyotes, and smaller mammals as well as countless species of birds. Situated along the Atlantic Flyway, Windy Harbor played host to thousands of migrating birds with the changing of the seasons. The small pond at the back of their property had afforded them hours of bird watching over the years.

Beyond the pond, in the southeast corner of the property, Beth's studio stood alone, surrounded by fields of Queen Anne's lace and goldenrod. Built by Alan as a present on their tenth wedding anniversary, its exterior was weathered shingles like the house. The large, airy one-room studio welcomed light through floor-to-ceiling windows on all four sides; its north wall was one huge expanse of glass. Whitewashed barn boards covered the interior walls. There were a small bathroom, a refrigerator, a hot plate, and a black slate sink for washing up, but few other amenities.

A dilapidated couch and chairs were arranged around an enormous, threadbare oriental rug that had belonged to Beth's grandmother. Dominated by shades of burgundy and dark blues and yellows, the carpet ran to the very edges of the wide pine floors. The only other furnishings were two bookcases and a massive white Hoosier cupboard housing her paints and supplies. Two easels supported works in progress at opposite ends of the room. Warm in the winter and breezy in the summer, the studio was Beth's spiritual home. It was here where her soul resided, at peace, while she worked.

A driveway stretched around to the back of the studio so she could bring in supplies by car, but generally she walked from home to the studio along the gravel path through her gardens. A profusion of perennials lined the path—hollyhocks, delphinium, asters, baby's breath, statice, yarrow, coreopsis, foxgloves, and many varieties of flowering bushes. Every year she added a few new plantings, and her labors rewarded her with riotous color from early spring to late fall.

As she pulled the car to a stop alongside the house, she heard laughter and shouting coming from the barn. "Fuck you, too, Hadley!" he called, emerging from the side door covered in sawdust.

"Jack? Is that you under all those shavings?"

"Mrs. H., hi," he said, grinning sheepishly as he spotted her. "Sorry about that—the yelling, I mean. We're almost through in there, and we were foolin' around. We'll clean everything up."

"Where are you Talbot? You chicken shit!" Kit called, crashing through the door. "Uh-oh, Mom, hey."

"Hey yourself. Taking a little break, are you?"

"Sort of…well. Really, we're finished, aren't we, Jack?"

"Yup." The other smiled a beautiful open smile that Beth returned.

Jack Talbot was Kit's best friend. Both were on the same construction crew, and they spent nearly every waking moment together.

It was an unusual friendship. Jack was fifteen years older, one of the harbor boys who had never grown up. On off-moments Jack and Kit worked for Beth. Their current project involved cleaning out the barn loft, hauling junk to the dump to clear storage space. In a year or two, she and her sister planned on selling their mother's cottage, Hestor's Way. At that time, she would need the room to store everything from the cottage. Lanie would have no use for it in her Boston apartment, but Beth was certain her sister would not allow Beth to dispose of or sell one stick of furniture, one piece of chipped crockery, one moldy, moth-eaten blanket, or one spineless, dog-eared Agatha Christie novel, at least not right away.

Jack had filled out the past few months. Looking at him, Beth experienced the same sensation as when she regarded her son. With his sandy hair covered with sawdust, broad shoulders straining the fabric of his faded blue work shirt, he was a handsome man indeed.

"How 'bout some lunch, you two?"

"Great, sure, Mom. Just let us clean up this mess and we'll be in."

They joined her several minutes later, still talking and laughing. Both had changed into tee shirts and swim trunks.

"We gonna head out after lunch, if it's okay. Go out on Pete's boat, fishing or diving."

"Lucky you. What can I fix you? I've got turkey, cheese, avocados, lettuce, tomatoes, tuna fish?"

"What about veggie burgers?" Kit asked, rummaging in the freezer.

Beth watched him, wondering what or who had turned him into a vegetarian overnight. "You might find a package in the downstairs freezer. Run down and check. That what you want, Jack?"

"I'd take a turkey sandwich, if you have enough," he said, coming to stand beside her. "I can make it, though."

"Okay, I've got pita bread here, and there's whole wheat in the freezer. White and Italian, too." Stepping aside, she continued to assemble ingredients for her own lunch, a pita pocket stuffed with slices of avocado, lettuce, tomatoes, and alfalfa sprouts. As she worked, she popped wedges of luscious, ripe tomato into her mouth. Kit finally appeared, proudly displaying a package of soy burgers in hand. "Anyone want a slice of tomato? These early ones are from Wilson's stand, and they're incredible."

Kit wrinkled his nose, making a face. "No thanks, Mom."

For reasons Beth could never fathom, all of her children disliked fresh tomatoes. Much as they loved Italian cooking and tomato-based sauces, none would willingly eat an uncooked, "raw tomatoes," as Nanny called them.

"I'll take one," Jack said, both hands occupied as he constructed a monstrous turkey club sandwich.

Laughing, Beth popped a thick tomato wedge into his mouth. "Here, I'll slice a few more for your sandwich."

"Thanks, Mrs. H.," he mumbled, tomato juice trickling from the corner of his mouth.

"Not too much of a slob, are you Talbot?" Kit elbowed him as he reached over to pop his soy burger into the microwave.

"People who do not appreciate the sensual pleasure of a fresh, ripe tomato should not call people slobs, dear son of mine."

"There you go again, always taking his side! You'd think *he* was the favorite son." Kit threw up his hands in mock dismay.

"No, but he is a guest."

Her lunch assembled, Beth poured three tall glasses of iced tea and retreated to the terrace. To her surprise, the boys joined her. Pleased at the unexpected company, she rose and made room for Jack at the end of the chaise longue.

"So, I just saw your dad in town. How's the rest of the Talbot family?"

"Great. Dick and Perry are away at camp for two weeks, in New Hampshire, and Caitlin's working at the marina, in the bait shop."

"How old is she now?"

"Nineteen."

"Amazing. It seems like only yesterday your mom was pushing her in the stroller."

"Mom, you're doing it again. You promised, no more living in the way-distant past."

"Oops, sorry, you're right."

She turned away, hiding unexpected tears. The summer had been a roller-coaster ride of ups and downs as she anticipated losing yet another of her children. He was right. She had been reminiscing about the past lately, with too many references to her babies, and she knew it was wearing thin with Kit. Despite his mother's protests, her son felt guilty abandoning his household obligations and worried constantly about who would take his place when he left in September.

Sensing the tension between mother and son, Jack intervened as he always did, lightening the mood. "So, what project do you have for us next, Mrs. H.?"

"The basement," she replied, turning back to her sandwich. "It needs the same going over as the barn. And there are a bunch of boxes you guys can take over to Mr. Hadley's. Old books, college notebooks, sketchbooks and things. I'll see what he says, but if I know Alan, he'll want them all."

"I doubt they'll fit with Chloe's décor," Kit muttered, taking a last bite of veggie burger.

It was on the tip of her tongue to ask how he knew so much about Chloe's décor when he had supposedly never set foot in his father's new home, but she stayed silent, not wishing to provoke an argument in front of Jack.

CHAPTER 3

"No, Rick," she said for the tenth time. "I'm taking Nanny and her friends to the beach. Period."

"Beth, be reasonable. If I can set something up with Margot this afternoon, it might be the break we need, *you* need. Sweetheart, I'm serious. She'll be making her decision about the gallery's fall schedule soon. They've gotta print programs, get the right people here."

"It's Nanny's birthday. We're having a beach picnic, then a family dinner and that's enough. It's a perfect beach day by the way. Wanta join us?"

"Just want I need, a bunch of teenage girls screaming in my ear. Thanks, but no thanks. I'll just sit here and weep over missed opportunities. Not to mention all the precious hours you're wasting away from your easel."

"Don't sound so despondent, dear agent of mine. You can always meet with Margot by yourself. You have the portfolio. I trust you. Besides, you'll do better without me. You always do."

"Bullshit. Margot likes to bond with her artists, not their underpaid, unappreciated agents."

Giving up, she sighed, the futility of further argument clear. "Rick's a bulldog," Alan had told her five years earlier when he had recommended that Beth hire him. Alan had been right. "Alright, you win, dearest. Go ahead and set something up with Margot for another day this week. Any day but Friday is fine with me."

"Hmm, I'll see what I can do. I am going into the city tomorrow. Maybe Margot and I can muddle through today alone."

"That's the spirit. And remember, we'd still love to have you stop at the beach for a piece of birthday cake."

"Gritty butter icing—now, isn't that tempting?"

"Bring Gary along. It'll be fun."

"Get real, girl. Gary, sand, water? No way. He's working and besides, he'd spoil the party with all his complaining. Been in a filthy mood lately. Impossible to live with."

The two men had moved in together a year after Beth and Alan's marriage, and the occasional separation notwithstanding, their relationship had endured.

"Good luck with Margot," she said, hanging up.

He really has gone crazy over this Lynch Gallery show, she decided as she keyed in her friend Clarice's number. It was not the end of the world if Margot Lynch turned her down. A disappointment, yes, but there would be other shows.

"Hey, Clary."

"Who the hell's been talking on your phone?"

Clarice never bothered with hellos.

"I've been calling for hours."

She was a shameless exaggerator.

"Sorry, Rick's been haranguing me about the Lynch show."

"Time for you to invest in call waiting, dearie, or keep your cell phone charged and on. With three teenagers, you need to be reachable at all times. What's the story with Miz Margot? You're a shoo-in for that show. The gallery would be lucky to get you, for Christ's sake. Besides, I have it on good authority that Miz Margot no longer makes the decisions."

"Oh?" Beth sat back, waiting for the gossip that was sure to follow. Clarice despised Margot Lynch. The two strong-minded women had served on too many committees together, usually taking opposing sides on whatever issue arose. There was no love lost between them.

Beth and Clarice had been roommates at the Rhode Island School of Design and had stayed in touch over the years. After years in the Midwest, Clarice and Ben had moved back east to Providence, Rhode Island, where Ben had grown up and where they'd both gone to college.

They had rented a small apartment in Providence, an hour's drive from Windy Harbor, but six months later they packed up again. Like Beth and Alan, they had wanted to start a family. Clarice, a very successful freelance silversmith, whose studio was at home, convinced Ben that a move to Windy Harbor "was best for the children," so Ben commuted to his graphic arts studio in a converted mill building in the south end of Providence.

"Yup," Clary continued. "Margot the Magnanimous has ceded all decision-making to the prodigal son, returned from the wilds of Chicago."

"You mean Graham?"

"None other. I'm surprised Rick didn't mention it. Surely he knows? Maybe not. I know cause we ran into him the other night. Better call Rick, hon, or he'll waste a lot of time sucking up to the wrong person."

She laughed. "I'll let him find out himself. At least he'll be off my back for a while. Graham, you say? I had no idea he was back. Why, it's been years since I've…"

"He's still gorgeous, by the way. We saw him at the Butlers' last night. Salt and pepper, but otherwise he looks the same. It's been how many years since he was back in the area?"

"Well, Nanny's fourteen so that's it—fourteen, at least as far as I know."

Several weeks after Nanny's birth, Graham Lynch had come to see Alan. Her body hidden under a shapeless muumuu, Beth had excused herself immediately and left the two men to catch up. Graham had been Alan's best man, but as the years passed, the two friends had drifted apart. That had been just fine with Beth because, from the moment she met the shy, slightly awkward friend of Alan's youth, she was inexplicably drawn to him. Despite the fact that she and Alan were wildly in love, the unreasonable, surprising attraction persisted, and she never completely trusted herself to be alone with Graham. Some years later she had greeted the news of his marriage to a high-powered Chicago attorney with a mixture of relief and jealousy, glad at least that they would be living halfway across the country.

"From all the reports, he's home for good," Clarice continued. "So you're a sure bet for the show no matter what Mommy Dearest says. You guys go back a long way, don't you?"

"I'm sure that will have no bearing on his decision. After all, the Lynch is not the Guild."

She referred to the Harbor Arts Guild founded by herself and eight other local artists. The group had pooled their resources and purchased a small garage in the village center, which they had converted into a small gallery where they could exhibit and sell their artwork. Alan was not a member of the Guild. His furniture, too pricey for Windy Harbor, went directly to a gallery in New York City. Even so, Alan had provided much of the capital and completed the lion's share of carpentry work for the building's restoration.

"That's right, it's not as cool or prestigious as the Guild!"

"Very funny. The Lynch has a national reputation. They can't be handing out favors to old friends."

"Beth, get real. Who are they gonna get who's more talented than you?"

"Thousands of people. Almost anyone. Let's drop this, okay? I've got a lot to do, and I'm calling about Carrie. Want us to swing by for her on our way to the beach?"

"That'd be great. I'm swamped here. Probably won't make it down to the beach after all. I'm sorry."

"That's okay," Beth said, secretly glad. Once the girls were fed, they would run off and leave her with her book for an hour or so. "I'll catch up on all your news tomorrow night. Hope it's good weather. We're all looking forward to our first beach cookout of the summer."

"Ben's dragging me over there tonight to watch the fireworks. Just the two of us, because the kids are going in four different directions."

"Mmm, romantic."

"Yeah, the two of us and several hundred horny teenagers."

Beth laughed. "You'll fit right in. If I know Ben, he'll find a secluded spot."

After thirty years of marriage, Ben and Clarice were still honeymooners.

"Ha. See you in a few minutes, then." The change in the voice she knew so well told Beth her friend was blushing.

Two hours later, Beth was serving chicken salad rolls and sodas to Nanny and four friends under the shade of an enormous blue-and-white-striped umbrella. She had brought china, a linen tablecloth, and napkins, and they were sipping soda from Beth's best crystal. Nanny had requested an "elegant beach picnic," and she was getting it.

"Thanks," Chrissie Moniz mumbled through a mouthful of chicken salad.

Dark-skinned, raven-haired, Chrissie's voluptuous body stretched her tiny lime-green bikini to its limits. Her dark eyes twinkled as she added, "This is the best, Mrs. Hadley. Nanny is so lucky."

"Mom's gonna be pissed she missed this," Carrie Rollins added, smiling at Beth.

She had her mother's enormous blue eyes, but otherwise Carrie was the image of her father. Her easy smile a mirror of his own, her complexion, while not the deep chocolate-brown of Ben's, was still a far cry from her fair-skinned mother's. She, too, wore a bikini, hers looser, less well defined, on her flat-chested, boyish frame. Her long, reddish hair cascaded in ringlets to her waist and was tied back in a loose ponytail with a twist tie she had borrowed from Beth.

"I'll catch up with her tomorrow night, but I don't think I'll bring these wine glasses across the way." Beth referred to the beach across the harbor's channel reachable only by boat where they went for summer cookouts.

After the sandwiches, a tiny marble cake appeared, which the girls devoured down to the last crumb. Then, hopping up, they declared themselves ready for a walk. As Carrie and Crissie headed off, Nanny lingered behind.

"Thanks, Mom. It was great!"

Beth smiled. "Having a good day so far?"

"The best!"

"There's more coming."

"I know. Thanks for having Dad. I know you'd rather not."

"Nonsense. I'll enjoy every minute of your party. Tonight's focus is on a certain fourteen-year-old, I believe, not on a couple of old divorcés."

"It still hurts, doesn't it?"

The question startled Beth, and she peered into the blue eyes, wondering at the reason for her daughter's question. Nanny had never wanted to talk about the divorce, and Beth and Alan hadn't pressed her. Three years ago, the two older children had had endless questions, demanding almost continual updates, but Nanny had said little, seeming to accept the divorce like she did everything, with an easygoing affability. An almost innate sense of security seemed to carry Nanny through the crisis; however, recently she had had her first boyfriend and subsequently her first heartbreak.

Beth brushed errant strands of sandy hair from her daughter's cheek. "Yes, it does sometimes, but not like three years ago. It's much smoother sailing now."

"You'd still rather not see him. I know that."

"Sweetheart, this is different," she replied, cupping the smooth, soft chin in her hand. "This is your birthday. Remember Kat's last fall? We had a great time, didn't we?"

"Yeah, except you looked like you were gonna throw up all the way up and back in the car."

Laughing at the idea of vomiting all over Alan, Beth said, "Don't worry. We're not traveling by car tonight, and I'm going to have a great time at your party. Honest. Dad, too."

"Not Kit."

"Of course he is. You know Kit. He's still angry with Dad."

"Hates him. He does, Mom, so don't even try to deny it. Chloe too, especially Chloe."

"Nanny, your brother doesn't hate Dad. He's just going through a rough time. He's about to leave for college, and he's worried about us and who'll take his place. He's tried so hard the last three years to fill Dad's shoes."

"I'll say. Thinks he can boss me around worse than Dad ever did."

Leaning over to hug her, Beth said, "Well, don't worry. He'll be fine tonight. He's just tired out from his job, and you know when Kit gets tired he gets a little testy."

"Plus he stays out till dawn with Jack and the guys."

"You'd better scoot off and catch up to the girls. Remember, this is your party. We'll have a great time tonight. Don't worry."

If Dad behaves, she thought, watching Nanny run down to the beach after the others, her compact, sturdy frame in sharp contrast to her taller companions. All except Nanny wore bikinis. Except for Carrie's, the others left little to the imagination, especially from the rear. Nanny, who declared bikinis to be uncomfortable and silly, wore a navy racing tank. She swam two miles every day of the summer.

Yes, Beth thought again, pulling out her book and leaning back in her beach chair. *If Dad behaves, we'll have a lovely time. Miracles can happen.*

And, Alan did behave, through most of the evening, at least.